Wisdom

to

Know

Elizabeth Maddrey

Kinsale Kisses: An Irish Romance

For the most recent listing of all my books, please visit my website.

For Mom,
Whose selfless determination to make a difference for life
was a living example of Christ's love that will stay with me always.

"You look like a prostitute."

Lydia frowned. "Brad likes my legs."

Kevin admired the long, shapely legs of his best friend from where he was sprawled on her living room couch. "Won't you be cold if you show so much of them?"

"It's September, not the middle of January. It's still warm out." Aggravation written across her face, she patted her hem. "Besides, the skirt reaches the end of my fingertips."

"Your elbows are bent."

"That rule shouldn't apply to me, I have long fingers."

Kevin cocked a brow. "You wouldn't wear that to church."

"We're not going to church." Lydia shot him an impish grin. "Besides, there are a couple of guys there who wouldn't usually give me the time of day...maybe if I wore this, I'd get their attention."

"More than likely." Kevin shook his head. "Where are you going? You never did say."

"Dinner downtown, then to a club, in Georgetown I think."

"Bridge club?" He asked hopefully.

Lydia snickered. "Dance. But then you knew that. And before you ask, no, I don't know which club. But," she lifted a red-tipped finger to forestall his comment, "since it's Brad, it'll be either swing or salsa."

Kevin frowned. "Everyone is going to see your underwear in that skirt."

Lydia rolled her eyes.

Kevin started to speak several times before rubbing his forehead. "I'm just trying to look out for you, kiddo."

"Thanks, Mom."

"Didn't you just finish complaining that Brad treats you like an object?"

She gave a grudging nod.

"You think it might have something to do with clothing choices?"

Lydia crossed her arms. "I should be able to wear anything I want and still be treated with respect."

"Sure, in a perfect world. But seriously, Lyd, that outfit…" He paused and considered the short skirt too-snug top and shook his head. "It doesn't scream 'Respect me'."

Pouting, she pushed his feet out of the way and flopped onto the couch beside him. "I appreciate your concern."

Kevin snorted.

"No, I really do." She smiled and patted his knee. "You're like the brother I never had."

He winced.

"Still, a date with your almost fiancé is surely a reason to dress up, right? Or did you want me to wear something like that?" Lydia gestured to a conservative black jacket draped on the arm of the sofa.

"What's wrong with it?"

"That's for work. This is a date. You don't wear work clothes on a date."

Kevin stood, glancing at his watch, "Whatever, Lydia. I drove into McLean to see if you were free tonight, not to be a stand-in for a girlfriend. Or a brother. You look great and you know it." A brief, wistful look flashed across his features. "I'm sure Brad will agree." His hand on the knob of her apartment door, he turned and added with a resigned sigh, "You know where to find me when you get home and need to complain about how he spent the evening undressing you with his eyes."

"That's not fair, Kevin."

"Tell me about it," he muttered, slamming the apartment door behind him.

Lydia plopped into the pew beside Kevin as the organist began the prelude. He glanced up from his perusal of the bulletin and arched his brow. "Late night?"

Groaning quietly she nodded and rested her head briefly on his shoulder, muffling a yawn. "Why is it that Sunday morning always comes so soon after Saturday night?"

Kevin patted her head and nudged her off his shoulder. "Ah, the price of the partier. I, you'll notice, am well rested and was here early enough to mingle and get coffee." He gave her a broad grin. "Are those dark circles under your eyes or were you in a fight?"

Lydia stuck out her tongue and rummaged through her purse, emerging with her compact. "Idiot," she hissed at Kevin as the pastor welcomed everyone.

Kevin chuckled quietly and raised a finger to his lips.

All through the worship music, Lydia tried surreptitiously to find Brad in the sanctuary. Periodically Kevin would elbow her and she'd attend to the music more, singing the actual words instead of mouthing "watermelon". As the final song drew to a close and the music minister began to pray, her phone buzzed quietly in her purse. Hoping to appear unobtrusive she peeked at the readout. A text from Brad. The corners of her mouth quirked upward. Probably letting her know he wouldn't be at the service. At least now she wouldn't have to wonder where Brad was sitting. Lydia looked forward, focusing on the pastor.

She flipped open her Bible to follow along as the pastor read aloud. After several verses she glanced at Kevin. He was absorbed in the reading—probably wouldn't notice if she checked her phone. Even if he did...who cares? Maybe Brad had asked her to meet up for lunch. She had to find out.

Babe, had a blast last night. 2 bad U wanted an early night—ran into Staci leaving UR bldg. We're hitting brunch now. Call U l8r—B

It figured that Staci was lying in wait. Probably had the hallway staked out just in case he didn't stay the whole night. Lydia considered several choice words to describe Staci's character. *Who are you to talk?* Where had that come from? After all, she hadn't stolen Brad from anyone and now he was basically her fiancé. He'd all but said a proposal was coming—he just wanted everything to be perfect. That had to mean snow and Christmas lights. She was nothing like Staci. She studied her left hand and pictured it with the one and a half carat oval diamond in a simple but elegant platinum band. She'd pointed out the ring casually one day when they'd been doing some window shopping. Two more months to go. Then she'd be one more step away from the "single and disappointing" label she suspected her parents and sisters always applied to her behind her back. Well, at least she'd be rid of the "single" part of it. And Staci would have to back off. Lydia bit back a sigh. She could last two more months.

Her phone buzzed again with another text message. Before she could read it, Kevin grabbed her phone with a scowl. Heat stole across her cheeks. Who did he think he was? She stiffened her spine and forced herself to attend to the last few minutes of the sermon.

When the organ postlude began, Lydia stuck out her hand. "Point made."

"Touchy." Kevin pulled the phone from his shirt pocket and handed it to her. "Must've been some date."

"You know, you could try to be happy for me. You've been my best friend for as long as I can remember and I'm basically engaged to Brad."

Kevin flinched. "You know why I can't be happy about that. But," he held up his hand to stop her interruption, "I did promise to stop mentioning that I love you." He managed a wry smile. "You might try and remember that best friends is not the ending I want for our relationship ... and consider the situation from my perspective sometime. See you in class?"

Lydia watched as he walked away without waiting for a response. Was he ever going to realize that she just couldn't see him that way? At a light touch on her shoulder she turned, smiled broadly, and dropped the phone into her pocket. "Hi, Daddy."

The pastor grinned and pulled Lydia into a tight hug. "Lyd. I didn't expect you to make it this morning when I didn't see you for coffee time."

"Daddy, I make better coffee at home, you know that. Why do you think I would subject myself to the stuff you make by the gallon here?"

"I don't know, ten minutes with your dad and mom?"

"So you can grill me about my Saturday night date? I don't think so. Have a little faith, Daddy, you raised me right." Her phone buzzed and she leaned up to kiss his cheek. "I should go and see if that's work related before heading to class."

"Will we see you for lunch?"

"Probably not today, but I'll let you know if that changes." Lydia squeezed past him and hurried from the sanctuary.

Pushing her way through the throngs gathering in the foyer for coffee, Lydia offered falsely bright smiles to those who called her name and mimed that she'd be right back. She finally made it to the restrooms and locked herself in one of the stalls. Closing the toilet lid, she perched on it and scrolled to the latest new text.

Whose number was that? Frowning, Lydia opened the message and her screen filled with a picture of Staci and Brad in a lip lock. Her insides plummeted. How could he? A new message buzzed, this one from Brad.

Not what it looks like. Call U l8r.

She snorted and snapped her phone shut. That was probably only the beginning of what it looked like. Hands shaking and mind reeling, she stood, flushed the toilet for appearance's sake, and made her way to the sink to wash her hands. Despite vigorous scrubbing, she couldn't get the illusion of a diamond ring off her left hand. Staci had been after Brad since they met, but he'd chosen her, hadn't he?

"Engaged to be engaged," she muttered.

She paused to chat briefly with several clumps of people as she made her way to the large room where the singles met for fellowship and enough Bible study to get by. At the door to the classroom, Lydia paused and fixed a smile on her face. She wasn't going to dwell on it. Not right now. Maintaining the image was more important.

ଔଞ୍ଚ

Lydia's phone rang as she exited through the church's front doors.

"How's my timing?" Brad's voice was relaxed and cheerful.

Lydia's heart sped up at the sound of his voice even as her stomach twisted. "Not bad at all. I'm heading to my car. Where should I meet you?"

There was a long enough pause that Lydia glanced at the screen of her phone to make sure the call was still connected.

"I'm, uh, kind of beat today actually."

Lydia frowned and leaned against the door of her car. "Are you coming down with something? I could bring you some soup."

"Don't trouble yourself, babe. I think I need to rest." There was a muffled giggle in the background. Brad hissed.

Though she hadn't caught the words, Lydia couldn't miss the meaning. Her voice dripped icicles, "I see. Well. I'll just leave you to *recover*."

She ended the call, heat rushing through her. Who did he think he was? Who did he think he was dealing with? Her gut twisted, the flames fading. He'd cheated on her before—multiple times--usually with another girl in the single's group who couldn't wait to rub her nose in it, so this was certainly consistent with his pattern. Except things had changed, hadn't they? She'd given him what he wanted and they were on their way toward being engaged. Lydia closed her eyes and lowered her forehead to the roof of her car. She'd been played. Again. She struggled to swallow the lump in her throat. Now what?

"Honey, are you all right?" Lydia's mother gently patted her arm and peered at her with concern. "I figured you'd be off on a date by now...Your father mentioned that you wouldn't be making it for lunch, was he wrong?"

Lydia opened her eyes to look at her mother. She was a clear vision of the future: blond hair gone ashy, sparkling blue eyes now peeking from behind small wire framed lenses, the same peaches and cream complexion that glowed in her own mirror every morning and an extra twenty pounds that somehow managed to look comforting. If only Lydia could capture the sense of calm that radiated from her mother, too.

Lydia shook her head, forcing a bright smile. "I'll be fine. But you're right, I am running late. Sorry about lunch. Maybe next week."

Her mother's shoulders sagged minutely before she leaned forward to brush a light kiss on her daughter's cheek. "All right then. Maybe next week."

Lydia watched her mother cross the parking lot to the car where her father waited. Everything in her deflated, her energy draining out her toes. Thoughts whirling, she slid behind the wheel and headed home.

"Hey, Kevin. Got a minute?" Lydia held the phone to her ear with her shoulder as she scrambled eggs for her Sunday lunch.

"Sure, what's up?"

"He did it again." She transferred the eggs to a plate and carried them to the kitchen table as she waited for a response. "Still there?"

"I'm here…I'm just not sure what you're expecting me to say."

Lydia pushed the food around her plate. "Am I stupid?"

"No. But you deserve better."

"I don't want another lecuture, Kevin. Not right now."

"I can't help you with this, Lydia. Besides, you don't really want me to…maybe you're not the only one who deserves better."

"Kev…"

"No. If Brad called you because he was having trouble with his current girlfriend, how would you feel?"

"It's not the same thing."

"It is to me. I've gotta go. I'll see you around."

Lydia set the phone down by her plate and stared at it. *Did I just manage to lose my boyfriend because I gave him what he wanted and my best friend because I couldn't?* She rubbed her temples and forked up a bite of eggs, scarcely tasting them.

❦

Lydia checked her phone again. She was past hoping that Brad's number would show up in her missed call list, but she had to check. It had been two weeks to the day and he hadn't even tried to explain. She'd heard his voice in the hallway of her apartment building a few days after their last date and had spent several frantic minutes straightening up, practicing her icy speech and eventual forgiveness. But the knock never came. Instead, she'd watched through the peep hole as he and Staci had headed out. She gritted her teeth against the clawing pain in her stomach. Had she meant that little to him?

Kevin hadn't called since that day, either. In many ways, she missed him more. Especially now that it was clear that she and Brad were through. None of her girlfriends were the type she could commiserate with. They'd be too busy gloating and smirking behind her back. If the situation was reversed she would have done the same to them. She sighed. Maybe this was what she deserved. Kevin had even started avoiding her at church. Every time they made eye contact, he'd veer off in the opposite direction, leaving a piercing pain in her heart.

She sighed and closed the door, glad to be home. She kicked off the heels she'd worn to church as her stomach gurgled. Lydia glanced down at the casual khaki slacks and green top…she could change later. Maybe her appetite would cooperate today. It'd be nice not to spend another day nauseated at the mention of food. Why couldn't people just stay home from work when they had the stomach flu?

Wrinkling her nose at the mostly empty refrigerator, she grabbed an apple and bottle of water as well as the magnetic notepad from the fridge door. She plopped down at the kitchen table and pulled a pen from the catch-all basket next to the salt and pepper. Might as well put together a shopping list—she was going to have to hit the store eventually. Since the first bite of apple seemed like it was going to stay down, she took a few cautious sips of water.

Her cell phone rang and her pulse jumped. Maybe Brad had finally come to his senses. She glanced at the caller ID, her heart sinking. Maybe she should just let it go to voicemail? That was too childish, even for her.

"Hi, Mom." She leaned back in the chair, propping her feet on the seat of the chair across from her.

"Lydia, I thought maybe I was going to get your voicemail."

Lydia flinched. "Sorry."

"I tried to catch you at church but you zipped off before I could get away from the Hendersons. You know how they can be." Mary's voice was warm. She might complain, but the Hendersons were one of the highlights of her mother's Sunday morning pastor wife duties. At eighty-five, with something like sixty-six years of marriage behind them, you couldn't help but like them.

"They're great, aren't they?" Lydia smiled, bringing up the image of her surrogate grandparents. "What's up?"

"Your father and I were hoping you could make it for lunch." There was a long pause. "Could we put something on the calendar? If you want to go get your planner, I'll wait."

"Sure, hang on a second." Lydia scooted away from the table. She'd get something penciled in and figure out how to cancel later. It'd get them off her back for a little while at least. But what she really didn't need right now was another pity lunch where her parents, and whichever of her perfect sisters happened to be in town, pointed out all the ways she was ruining her life. Planner in hand, she settled back into her chair at the kitchen table and flipped to the month of September. Her eyes skimmed absently over the dates. Her mother's voice buzzed in her ear as she quickly flipped pages and recounted six weeks. "Not possible."

"Ok, well what date is possible, Lydia?" Her mother huffed out an irritated breath.

She cleared her throat. "I'm going to have to get back to you, Mom."

"Lydia…"

"Mom, I have to go…I'm going to be sick." She hung up the phone on her mother's protests and dropped her head to the table. Mouth dry, she tried to swallow. This couldn't be happening.

Tearing the grocery list off the pad, she slipped the phone in her pocket and headed for the store.

வு&லு

The plus sign taunted her. Lydia stared at the pregnancy test on her bathroom counter. How was this possible? A primal scream echoed in her head. She sank to the floor and leaned against the tub. Now what was she supposed to do?

She didn't have an answer. Staring at the ceiling, she tried to picture telling her mom and dad that she was pregnant. There would be yelling. And tears. And, worst of all, more disappointed looks. Bad enough that she hadn't found and married a nice Christian man in college, then started popping out grandchildren like her two older sisters. Or that she wasn't bound for the mission field like her younger sister. And with Brad completely out of the picture, there was no hope of salvaging her plan to marry someone bound for great things politically. Lydia frowned. There were other men she knew with political aspirations, but none had the charisma of Brad…nor had they made the strides toward fulfilling those aspirations like Brad. They would likely end up being also rans. Being the wife of a loser was not the kind of success she needed to prove to her family that she was just as good as the rest of them.

Dropping her head to her knees she gave up fighting the tears. There was no point. She'd just proven that she was exactly the failure they thought she was. And Kevin? Lydia hiccupped as the tears turned to wrenching sobs. She doubted his so-called love for her extended to the baby of another man.

What if she didn't tell them? Her heart quailed at the thought. But...it was one solution. Could she do it? Brad, and the status she'd have as his wife, was still out of the picture...but the rest? If she could cover this up, maybe she'd still have a chance to prove that she wasn't a disappointment after all.

Lydia turned off the alarm and glanced at the clock. Again. At least now she could justify getting up, even if it was only 5:00. She went through her morning routine on automatic, taking only enough care with her outfit to make sure it was clean and not what she'd worn to work on Friday. She was out the door by a quarter to six and winding her way through the back streets of Arlington into downtown D.C. This was the right thing to do. The responsible thing. The sane thing. No one had to know and, when it was done, she could just move on. She wouldn't let herself think about it. She couldn't.

She found a parking spot about a block from the clinic at 6:15. Should she sit in the car for the next hour or go in search of coffee? There was an open coffee shop two blocks back. Maybe doing something close to normal would help settle the whirlwind of butterflies in her stomach. Double checking that her doors were locked and that the meter had enough time on it, she headed down the street, her breath hitching as she strode past the clinic's discreet sign.

The coffee shop was busy. She spent her time in line pretending to be absorbed in the menu. Was it obvious why she was in the area? Cautious glances out of the side of her eye eased some of the tension in her shoulders. She blended in well enough. Just another worker bee getting a caffeine fix. Lydia had chosen this location to minimize the possibility of running into anyone who might recognize her. She didn't know anyone who lived or worked in this area and, more importantly, neither did her parents. Rather than press her luck, she got her coffee and a scone to-go and made her way back to her car.

Settling into the seat she inhaled the scent of the coffee and spread the scone out on a napkin on her lap. She wasn't supposed to eat or drink before the procedure, but just having the normal morning smells around soothed her. She set the coffee in her cup holder and carefully began to pull all the blueberries out of the pastry, making neat little rows of the blue fruit along the edge of her napkin to pass the time.

At 7:15, after a quick glance around, she pushed through the clinic doors and signed in, stomach churning. They called her back almost immediately and she left the crowded waiting room. The sick feeling increased as she walked past exam rooms with closed doors. The nurse chattered cheerfully as she directed Lydia to sit asking various medical questions, as if she was there for a manicure or haircut. Her head spun. They marched her through the process so smoothly—like it was no big deal—nothing more than a hiccup in her day. At one point she froze, ice flooding her veins. Was this really the only way? Before she could work up the nerve to voice her concerns, she was on the table and the chance of turning back was long gone. By 9:00, Lydia was back in her car, sobbing hysterically as she tried to merge into the end of rush hour traffic.

She managed to pull herself together on the drive to her office. What had she done? The right thing. It had to have been the right thing. Right? She spent a few minutes trying to repair her makeup in the parking garage before giving up. It wasn't going to get any better. There was clearly something was wrong. Maybe she could pass it off as tired. Even if they didn't believe her, the response would keep everyone at arm's length. She swallowed two more aspirin with the last of her now-cold coffee before heading to the elevator and a full day of public relations.

By lunch, the "mild cramping" she'd been warned about had escalated to pain worse than anything Lydia could remember. She rested her head against the cool tile wall of the restroom and considered taking the rest of the day off.

The door swung open and one of the administrative assistants hurried in. Noting Lydia's posture, she grimaced sympathetically. "Bad cramps?"

Lydia nodded, straightening, and pumped soap into her hands.

Pursing her lips, Ashley rummaged around in her bag, eventually emerging with a small prescription bottle.

"Here, take these. I finally managed to convince my doctor that mine were bad enough to need the occasional prescription pain killer."

Lydia rinsed her hands and reached for a paper towel. "Don't you need them?"

Ashley shook her head. "Nah. I don't take them all the time, so I always have an extra stash at home. But I get every refill I'm allowed just in case, you know?"

Lydia hesitated before reaching for the bottle. "Thanks."

"Don't mention it." Ashley glanced around. "Seriously. Don't mention it. We'd both be in a heap of trouble. If this happens a lot, give my doctor a call. She'll make you chart your pain levels for six months before she'll write the scrip, but it's worth it. And," she paused and lowered her voice, "if you need more before that time is up, let me know. I'll give you another friend's number."

Lydia blinked. She glanced down at the pills. She should give them back—this had to be illegal. A stab of pain had her clutching the bottle in her fist. She cleared her throat. "I'll keep that in mind."

Back at her desk, Lydia read the label. At least it was something she'd heard of. Should she look up the side effects? Fingers on the keyboard, she paused— probably not the best thing to have in her corporate search history. After a covert glance into the cubicles around her, she swallowed one of the pills. Less than half an hour later she was feeling like she'd be able to make it through the day. Even with the ebbing pain, weight settled across her shoulders. She shouldn't have taken someone else's prescription. These drugs were controlled for a reason. But after what she'd done that morning, did it really matter? Surely now she was beyond redemption.

CRED

Lydia dropped her laptop and purse inside the door to her apartment and looked around. She leaned against the door before turning to lock it. Nothing had changed, but everything was different. She shook her head to try and clear the voices that whispered condemnation in her head and made her way on autopilot to her bedroom. She barely noticed the deep browns and teals on the walls and bed coverings that just yesterday had stood as the calming center of her world. Kicking her shoes in the direction of her closet, she stripped off her work clothes on the way to the shower. Once steam poured over the top of the stall she stepped in, wincing as the blistering water struck her skin. She made no move to adjust the temperature but instead grabbed her loofah and scrubbed herself raw.

When the water ran cold, she turned off the tap and wrapped herself in her bathrobe. Sliding into her slippers, she padded into the kitchen, bypassing her usual after-shower rituals of body lotion, manicure maintenance, and hair care. Lydia stared into the refrigerator for several minutes before closing the door. She thought a moment, opened the door again and pulled out a bottle of water, carrying it into the living room. Tucking her feet under her, she curled into the corner of the couch and flipped on the television.

Her eyes landed on the phone. It'd be nice to hear Kevin's voice—and he always made her feel better. But what would she tell him? He'd keep her secret if she asked, but he'd hate her. Even more than he already did. She couldn't take that.

She'd thought she was out of tears, but a fresh flood spilled down her cheeks. Sleep. She needed to sleep. She took another of Ashley's pills and waited for the warm sense of disconnection to overtake her.

Lydia woke, choking back a scream. The television showed a man shouting to an audience of trim, toned women about the benefits of his new sit up machine. Rubbing her eyes she fumbled for the remote and clicked it off. The blue glow from her DVD player told her it was 3:12 a.m. She stretched, working the kinks out of her neck and knees, and sipped from her tepid water to clear the taste of terror from her throat. With a sigh, she reached up and turned off the table lamp. Stretching out on the couch she tugged a decorative throw over her legs. Pictures of prenatal development from long ago biology classes tormented her, barring her from further sleep. She spent the rest of the night watching the digital readout under her TV tick slowly toward morning. She should pray...but there couldn't possibly be a point. Surely God was done with her now.

At six, she gave up and made coffee. Maybe the painkillers had contributed to the nightmares, but they'd at least let her get some sleep…and half of a pill was enough to silence the voices in her head. She downed the pill with her first mug of coffee, pushing herself through the motions of her morning routine until the comfortable haze kicked in. The supply in the pill bottle was already dwindling. She'd have to get the number of Ashley's friend.

Kevin frowned at the phone and tapped his fingers thoughtfully on his knee. He'd been watching Lydia for the past month at church…and at work. Heat stole across his cheeks. He'd gotten into the habit of driving by her office around the time she usually pulled into the parking garage. In the past it had given him a little lift to see her put together for a day of handling the big shots. Lately it had only added to his concern.

He frowned and muttered, "She made her position clear." He looked blankly at the screen saver photos on his computer before letting his gaze roam across his home office. He lingered on the photographs of distant places that had once been part of a calendar. He hadn't visited any of them…yet. His sleek L-shaped desk was currently covered with software design specifications and customer memos. The other two walls were mostly window, letting in lots of sunlight and giving him easy access to distraction when he needed it. He rolled across the floor to the window and looked across the back yards of his neighbors. Smiling slightly, he saw kids playing while their parents, just home from work, tugged leaf blowers and rakes out of sheds. It was probably time to take care of his own leaves. Thanksgiving was rapidly approaching and most of the trees were finally bare.

He'd bought this house nearly two years ago with the intention of marrying and raising his own family. At the time, it seemed like he was actually making progress in his quest to convince Lydia that he was not her best girl friend. He paused and pursed his lips, searching his memory. "Ryan." He nodded and rolled back to his computer. "And then Ryan happened. And, after that, Mark. Now Brad." Kevin puffed out his cheeks letting the air explode from his lips with a pop. He let out a mocking laugh as he saved the work on his machine. "And now I talk to myself, alone in the garret."

Kevin rubbed his neck and stared at the phone. With a quick shake of his head he pushed himself out of his chair and headed into the hallway. Passing the two other bedrooms and hall bath, he made his way to the stairwell and down to the main level. Making a bee line for the fridge, he grabbed a bottle of iced tea, unscrewed the top and took a long drink. Tapping one finger against the glass bottle, he reached for the phone hanging on the wall by the stove and dialed.

As it rang, Kevin boosted himself onto the counter and sipped his tea, smiling at the cheerful voice that greeted him.

"Hello?"

"Hi, Mrs. Brown, it's Kevin."

"Kevin. What a delightful surprise." Kevin listened as pots clanged in the background. "Haven't I told you to call me Mary?"

"Yes ma'am. Sorry. Am I interrupting dinner? I didn't pay attention to the time."

Lydia's mother laughed. It was like the delicate tinkle of crystal. Just like Lydia's laugh. "Not at all, I've just started banging around in here. Nothing will be ready for at least an hour. Now," she paused and he could hear pages in a book flipping, "tell me."

Kevin smiled slightly. The command was so much like his own mother when she sensed something was on his mind. "It's Lydia...I'm just concerned and wondered..."

There was a slight snort over the line. "If we knew what was wrong?" She sighed, "Kevin, Paul and I have been trying to decide if we should call *you* to find out, but we didn't want to put you in the position of having to decide whether or not to break her trust."

Kevin picked at the label on his tea bottle started peeling it away in small strips. "I was worried you'd say that." He sighed. "We haven't really spoken in almost two months. I got annoyed with the whole Brad thing and, well," he set the tea on the counter and paced across the small kitchen, "maybe I shouldn't have."

Mary's voice was full of sympathy. "Oh Kevin, you two have argued before, even about her boyfriends, and it's never been like this."

"I know. But…"

"No, no buts. I have nothing to go on other than a mother's intuition, but I really think there's more than that at play here. I've been praying that I'd know what to do but, well, so far all I've come up with is to keep praying."

He ran a hand through his light brown hair and straddled a kitchen chair. Resting his elbows on the wooden back he stared out the back door. "Should I call her?"

After a lengthy pause Mary cleared her throat. "I don't know. I'm probably not the best person to ask. You might have noticed that everything I do these days is exactly the wrong thing when it comes to Lydia."

Kevin could hear the wry smile in her voice and his heart ached for her.

"As her mother, I desperately want you to find out and then tell me. But I can't honestly say that's the best thing for either of you. I just don't know."

He nodded slowly and let out a long breath. "That's fair. Thanks, Mrs. B."

"Mary."

"Right. Mary… if I find something out and can fill you in, I will. Add some discernment for me into your prayers though, would you?"

"Absolutely. Take care, ok? And Kevin…thanks."

"Sure. Bye." He clicked the phone off and gazed out into the back yard.

Lydia had started staying in for lunch. Kevin had spent a full week haunting some of the regular places Lydia frequented for lunch, aiming for a casual meeting that he could stretch into a friendly invitation to dinner as he'd done so many times in the past. When he had no luck, he finally pieced it together. A brief conversation with the one coworker of Lydia's he recognized confirmed it. Which meant he was going to have to be direct.

Kevin practiced various smiles in the reflection of the condo building's elevator doors as he rode up to Lydia's floor. Amused at himself, he adjusted his grip on the bag of Chinese takeout and squared his shoulders before he muttered a quick prayer. "*All right Lord, this is all You.*"

The scent of spicy beef and vegetables wafted up from the containers, making his stomach rumble as he raised his hand to knock briskly on Lydia's door. A sitcom jabbered away on the TV inside. Kevin let out a breath he hadn't realized he was holding. She was home. Several minutes ticked by. He knocked again, louder. Scowling, Kevin considered the door when there was still no answer. He set the bag down at his feet, snapped the cell phone off his belt, and punched in Lydia's speed dial. He heard the ring echo inside the apartment. When the answering machine clicked on, he knocked loudly again and hit redial. The third time he repeated this, there was bad tempered shuffling on the other side of the door.

"Go away, Kevin."

"Lydia, come on. The food's getting cold and I'm hungry."

"So go home and eat. It's not like you were invited over."

"If I wanted to eat at home, I would be at home. I also would not have a bag full of food from your favorite Chinese place when the one close to my house does the delivery for me." He paused, "Come on, let me in."

Lydia opened the door a crack and poked her head into the hall, a frown etched across her features. "It's messy and I'm not apologizing. I will, however, reiterate that you weren't invited." She pushed the door open farther to make room for him to enter.

Kevin smirked and slid through the open door, barely making it through before she snapped it shut. His eyebrows lifted as he took in the disarray. Stacks of mail teetered precariously on the coffee table. Water bottles holding various levels of liquid were littered everywhere. Work clothes were draped over the backs of chairs, mismatched shoes poking out at odd angles underneath. The carpet looked as if it hadn't been vacuumed in months. Kevin sniffed gingerly. At least the air didn't match the clutter. He caught Lydia eyeing him. Saying nothing, he turned toward the kitchen, waving the bag at her as he passed.

He set the food on the kitchen table and strode to the cupboard that held her plates. The kitchen was a sparkling puddle of cleanliness in an otherwise filthy apartment. He glanced at Lydia as she glared at him from the doorway. Her hair and eyes lacked their usual shine and her clothes hung on her frame.

"Well, come on. You can't eat from over there." He set the plates and silverware out and unpacked the bag, naming the contents as he pulled out containers. "Dumplings, Hunan beef," he looked up and grinned, "no broccoli. Crabmeat wontons and," he produced the final dish with a flourish, "double cooked pork." Setting the empty bag on the floor, he sat and began piling food onto a plate. "No rice for you, since I know you feel it's an unnecessary participant in an otherwise delightful meal."

He slid the now heaping plate over to an empty spot at the table and began filling his own plate.

When Lydia made no move to join him at the table he leaned back in his chair and studied her. "I haven't taking up biting people, you know."

One corner of Lydia's mouth twitched up and she pushed off the door frame. She flopped into a chair and poked at the food on her plate. "Why are you here, Kevin?"

Kevin forked up a huge bite and talked around the mouthful. "Because I missed the charming way you have with words." He flashed a grin. "Actually, I figured if your coworkers ran into me at lunch one more time I was likely going to get brought up on stalking charges." He pushed away from the table and pulled open the fridge. "Got any Coke in here?"

There was nothing but water and condiments. And a container in the far corner that might be growing a new life form. Wincing, he grabbed two bottles of water and returned to the table. What was she living on with a fridge that bare?

Lydia nibbled on the corner of a wonton. "That doesn't answer the question, it just changes it, and since you know perfectly well what I mean, I'm going to ask again, why are you here, Kevin?"

He ate quietly for a minute before setting down his fork and meeting her gaze. "Because I'm sorry I was a jerk about Brad. Because we're friends, or used to be. I'd like to think we still are. And because even if we're not still friends, I know you well enough to know something's not right. Honestly," he threw his hands in the air, "at this point, people who don't know you at all know something's not right." He reached across the table and tugged open her balled fist, resting his fingertips on her palm. "And if that's not enough, I'll say what we both know, even though you hate when I say it. I love you. So talk to me."

Lydia pulled her hand away and shook her head furiously. "You don't love me, Kevin. It's not possible."

He began eating again. "It is. But it's also not the issue, so let's not change the subject." He glanced up, head cocked. "The food does more good if you actually eat it instead of pushing it around on the plate."

She took a bite. "Happy?"

"Delirious. Start talking."

Lydia shook her head.

Kevin leaned back in his chair, balancing on the two rear legs. "Well, that's progress at least. I expected to have to fight the 'I'm fine, there's nothing' battle with you."

He tented his fingers and tapped them together.

Lydia shifted in her seat as she continued to eat, keeping her eyes fixed on the rapidly clearing plate. When she finished, she pushed back from the table and carried her empty plate to the sink.

"Kevin…"

"You know you can tell me anything, Lydia. You're my best friend, and I thought I was yours." He stood and crossed the room to stand behind her at the sink. He leaned forward and rested his chin on her head.

Lydia cleared her throat and wiggled away. "You know I hate it when you do that. I'm not short and we're not in high school anymore."

Kevin laughed. "One of those statements is true at least, Shorty."

Lydia stuck out her tongue. "Abnormally tall person."

Her laugh died out and she clamped her hand over her mouth and ran from the room.

"Lydia?" Kevin hurried after her but stopped when the bathroom door slammed in his face. He knocked, "Lydia? Are you ok?"

The sound of retching was the only answer. Kevin stared at the door. What was he supposed to do now? He ran a hand through his hair and was about to knock again when the toilet flushed and Lydia, face pale, opened the door.

She rested her forehead against the door frame. "You should go, Kevin."

"Are you sick?" He paused and considered, his eyes narrowing. "When did you actually eat a real meal before just now?"

"Haven't been hungry."

"That's not really an answer, Lyddie."

She shrugged.

He frowned. It wouldn't do any good to lose his temper--kicking someone when they were down wasn't the best way to win trust. But honestly, what was she thinking? The silence stretched across several moments. Finally he took her hand and tugged her from the doorway.

"Come on, let's try this again the right way."

Lydia's eyes flew open and she stumbled after him. "What are you doing?" She shook her head vigorously as he pushed her into the chair at the kitchen table. "I'm not eating anything else." Temper lit in her eyes. "I don't actually enjoy being ill."

Kevin said nothing as he began a systematic search of her cupboards until he found the mugs, some chicken broth, and tea bags. He filled one mug with water and stuck it into the microwave while he looked for a can opener for the broth.

"Are you listening to me?" Lydia tapped her fingers on the table and scowled when the only answer was the beep of the microwave followed by a mug of steeping tea being set in front of her.

"Let that sit a minute or two, it's too hot right now anyway. Then you're going to drink it, all of it. After that, we can discuss what happens next."

"Who do you think you are?" Lydia pushed the tea across the table, the hot water slopping over the edge onto her hand. She shook it off and stuck the burned finger into her mouth. "I'm a grown up, Kevin. Besides which, you've made it perfectly clear what you think of me, so I'm not even sure why you care."

Kevin sat back down across from her. "I made it clear what I think of Brad, which has nothing to do with what I think of you. You sell yourself short entirely too often. But if you really want me to go, I'll go. Though you should know I'm not going to stop worrying about you, and neither are a lot of other people who care about you."

"Ah yes, the hordes of people who have been thronging to my door filled with concern." She rolled her eyes. "Including you. I'll say again, you made it clear how you feel about me two months ago, and you've done very little since then that would make me believe your explanation now. For all that, you're the only one who's been by, and I suppose I should be grateful. But I'm not an idiot," she dunked the tea bag up and down in the hot water, "I know how to feed myself."

Lydia took a huge gulp of the now over-brewed tea and grimaced.

Kevin pushed the sugar bowl closer to her and chuckled as she spooned heaps of sugar into the tea before sipping again.

"Want more?" He reached out for the mug. "Or do you want to wait a bit and see how that sits?"

"I'm fine. Look, Kevin, I appreciate you stopping by, ok? But I'm fine. You should go."

"If that's what you want. But Lydia?" He waited until she met his gaze. "I know you're not fine, even if you won't talk to me about it. Find someone to talk to, ok? Even if it's Brad."

"It won't be Brad, you're in luck there. We broke up a while ago."

"Is that what this is? Breakup mourning?" A grin split his face. "So call the girls and go do," he paused and wiggled his fingers, "whatever it is girls do for that. Trash Brad, obviously. Eat ice cream, get goop slopped on you at a spa, that kind of thing."

Lydia arched an eyebrow.

"I'm not a girl. I don't know what goes on in your secret rituals." Kevin stood, tucked in his chair, and reached out to ruffle her hair. "Don't mourn him too long, ok? He wasn't worth your time when you were dating. He's sure not worth your health now that you're not. I'll look forward to getting my Lydia back when you're feeling better."

Lydia nodded, blinking rapidly as her eyes filled with moisture. "Thanks for checking on me."

Kevin frowned as she shut the door so quickly it clipped the back of his shoes. The locks snicked into place and the TV came back on. With a sigh he headed toward the elevator, digging his cell phone out of his pocket. He punched in the Brown's number but hung up before the machine answered. He wasn't convinced that the break up blues were really the problem, but he also wasn't sure how hard he ought to push, or if he even deserved to try after deserting her for so long.

Lydia watched through the peep hole as Kevin headed for the elevator. Who was he calling? It wasn't necessarily about her but still. Turning, she surveyed her apartment with fresh eyes. It really was a mess. She swiveled, staring at her reflection in the mirror that hung over the catch all table to the left of her door. She was a mess, too.

Ok, no more wallowing. People are noticing. I know how to put up a front better than this. She squared her shoulders and glanced at the clock on her DVD player.

The last time she'd tried to vacuum, violent sickness followed. The sound had transported her back to the clinic, leaving her shaking and on the verge of hysteria. She was going to have to hire someone. Preferably someone who didn't mind her being out while they cleaned. Were cleaning services open on Saturdays? She flopped onto the couch and dragged her laptop onto her lap. *Let's find out.*

Lydia scanned several websites and used their online forms to set up appointments for estimates. With the vacuuming issue taken care of she snapped her computer closed and looked around again. How had she let it get this bad? She pushed off the couch and started tidying up the detritus of living that had collected with her neglect.

When things were reasonably put together, she sat on the padded stool at her vanity. Staring at her reflection she really saw herself for the first time in two months. It was no wonder he stopped by. Lydia stuck out her tongue. Well, at least it was still possible to look worse. Checking the time again she reached for the phone and dialed.

"Hi Laura, it's Lydia."

"Lydia?" The voice on the other end of the line sounded confused.

"Lydia Brown? From church and, well, forever?"

There was a minute of silence before Laura cleared her throat. "Ah. Lydia, it's been, well, what? At least three years?"

Heat stole across Lydia's cheeks. She tried to keep her voice upbeat, but misery crept in. "I know and I'm sorry...I...I shouldn't have called, I'll let you go."

"Wait. Lydia?"

"Yeah?"

"You called me, so...?"

She should just hang up. There were other options. She caught a flicker of her reflection. She needed help now. "Do you still do hair?"

ભ્ઠ

Almost an hour later, Lydia opened her front door and smiled tentatively. Laura stood with her arms crossed, one hip jutting out. She had on faded jeans and a baggy sweatshirt the bright orange of a cereal box. Her chestnut hair was pulled into a ponytail with ruler-straight bangs fluffed over her forehead. Warm brown eyes considered Lydia with speculation.

"You know, I almost called you twelve times on the way over here to have you make an appointment at the salon." Laura strode through the door, wheeling a laptop-sized bag behind her. "Now I get why you called. There's no way you would go out looking like that…Though for your hair to get to this point," she reached out and rubbed the ends of Lydia's hair between her fingers and pursed her lips, "you *have* been going out looking this rough." She threw her head back and laughed. "There's one on me…Lydia Brown out in public without her polished perfection. Clearly there have been ice storms down below."

Lydia shut the door and clicked the lock. Turning, she chewed on her lower lip and nodded once. "I guess I deserve that, and more, so you go ahead if it helps. Let's go in the kitchen. It'll be easier for me to clean up. And I'll just state for the record that I'm sorry. I know that doesn't make it better, but I also know there's nothing that can." She shrugged one shoulder, pulled a chair away from the kitchen table and sat. "On the other hand, I was trying to do you a favor, no matter that I went about it badly."

Laura lifted her case up onto the table, unzipping it and rummaging through the hair styling tools it held. "Clearly, dating my fiancé was a favor." She rolled her eyes and snapped a cape around Lydia's neck. "You let me know if that's too tight, ok?"

Lydia cleared her throat and gave a little tug to the strangling cape. "No, it's fine. Laura," she swiveled her neck so she could look up at Laura's face, "I wasn't the first or the only person Ryan was cheating with. I was just the only one who made sure you would find out about it." That sounded lame out loud. She squeezed her eyes shut. "Like I said, I know I did it the wrong way, but you needed to know before you went ahead and married him. I really am sorry."

Laura put a hand on either side of Lydia's face and turned her head to face forward. She dragged a comb through Lydia's hair, stopping to tug through several tangles, in silence. After several minutes, she stopped and rested her hands on Lydia's shoulders. "In the end it was for the best. I have a hard time believing you actually had any thought to *my* best interest, but that could be humiliation speaking. On the other hand, if I'd married Ryan, I would've missed out on Matthew. So in the end I guess I should say thank you."

"I'd be happy if you would just say you forgive me."

"Already done." Laura ran her fingers through Lydia's hair and shook her head. "What exactly are you expecting me to do with this mess?"

"Fix it?"

"I didn't bring my clippers, Lydia."

"Come on, it's not that bad...right?"

Laura raised her eyebrows. "It's not good. You're going to have to go short if you have any hope of getting back to healthy hair. And then we'll need to talk about how long you're spending with the blow dryer and why you appear to have abandoned conditioner."

"Short it is. Can we aim for professional short rather than man-hater short?"

Laura snickered. "Of course." She tugged on Lydia's hair. "Up. To the sink. The sooner I start, the more likely that I can make it home before Jennie needs to be fed."

"Jennie?"

"Our daughter, Matthew and me. You knew we got married, right?" She rinsed out Lydia's hair, wrapped it tightly in a hand towel, then nudged her back toward the chair.

Lydia sat and thought, wincing slightly as Laura's comb worked through tangles. "I think my mom might have mentioned it, but that was a while ago, right?"

Laura nodded and began pinning sections of Lydia's hair out of the way. "It's been two and a half years now. Our courtship was a bit of a whirlwind, though we've known each other since we got out of school—he was at the salon too."

"Oh, that Matthew."

"Yep."

"So are you both still at that salon? That must be nice."

"Actually, we're not. We both wanted to have our own salon someday and, well, we figured why not make someday today? We jumped in with both feet as soon as we got married and it's the best thing we could've done." She began snipping and shaping a short, cropped hairdo that mixed professional style with easy maintenance. "I've got the flexibility to be home with Jennie or bring her in to work if I need to. I can still take clients and Matthew's in heaven not having to do hair all day. He really thrives on the managerial aspects of the business, which is good because I get bored with the paperwork. I could do it, but it's nice not to have to."

Lydia watched her hair fall to the floor as Laura continued to ramble on about the salon and her husband and child. Laura's voice got quieter until it faded into a buzzing noise that floated around Lydia, drifting to the floor with the wisps of her hair. She closed her eyes and tried to focus on breathing in and out while Laura worked.

"There." Laura held up a mirror and waited. When she got no reaction, she nudged Lydia's shoulder. "Now is when you tell me how great it looks, though you'll probably want to open your eyes first."

Lydia jolted and forced her lips into a smile. She turned her head to both sides and nodded. "You said short…it's definitely short."

Concern flickered across Laura's face.

"I like it. It'll just take some getting used to…but I bet I have an extra twenty minutes in the morning now." She set the mirror in her lap and turned to face Laura. "More than that, I appreciate you coming over here when you had no reason to and about six hundred reasons not to."

Laura paused in the process of packing her tools. "Honestly, I wasn't going to. I figured that surely it being the Saturday before Thanksgiving would give me an out. But Matthew made me. And," she pulled the other chair from the table and swung it around so she could sit with her knees touching Lydia's, "I think he was right to."

Laura hesitated a minute then reached out and rested her fingers on the top of Lydia's hand. "We used to be friends…maybe we can be again." She tilted her head to one side and narrowed her eyes. Reaching into her bag, she grabbed a pair of shears and snipped an errant hair in Lydia's new bangs. Pursing her lips she nodded briskly. "We could start by you telling me what's going on."

Lydia hesitated a minute before shaking her head. "I don't think I can right now. I won't insult you by saying nothing's wrong, since no one believes me when I say that anyway but," she shrugged and ran fingers through her hair, "for now, can you let me be grateful for the haircut?"

Laura nodded slowly. "Fair enough. I accept Visa, Master Card, and agreements to come to dinner and meet my gorgeous daughter."

Lydia laughed and went to get her planner. After they'd agreed on a date, she insisted on paying for the haircut even though she had to forcefully slip the check into Laura's pocket. After tidying up the mess, she settled in front of the TV for another sleepless night.

The ringing of her phone woke her. Lydia sat up and rubbed her eyes. The clock on her DVD player said it was nearly 1:30. Judging from the sunlight streaming in her windows, she could only assume that meant afternoon. She stood and stretched the kinks out of her arms and legs, hobbling stiffly for the phone.

"Hello?"

"Hey, Lyd. It's Kevin."

Lydia scrubbed a hand over her face. "Hi Kevin."

"Did I wake you up?"

"Apparently. What's up?"

"I just wanted to make sure you weren't mad at me. You weren't at church and, well, I thought maybe it was because of last night."

A smile tugged at her lips. "Sorry to disappoint you, pal, but I overslept."

"Sleep is good…Busy this afternoon?"

"No, but I think I'm going to hang here. I've got some work that I should catch up on, that kind of thing."

"All right, well, I'll be home if you change your mind."

"'K. And Kev? Thanks." Lydia hung up the phone and sat for a few minutes. She really did have work she ought to try and attend to. "But first, a shower."

She stumbled down the hall to her bedroom.

Kevin looked at the disconnected phone as he hung up, "You're welcome." He leaned back in his chair and propped his feet on the edge of his desk. Though he wasn't working, he enjoyed just being in his home office. It was the one room of the house that he had decorated completely for himself, so he found it restful.

"That's what you get for buying a house on the theory that you're going to get married." He sighed. "Still, it's an investment. Which will come in handy when they throw you in the loony bin for having conversations with nobody."

Before he could come up with a stunning retort for himself, the doorbell rang. "Well and truly saved by the bell. Oh, Kevin," he shook his head and pushed himself out of his chair, "you probably need help, dude."

He chuckled all the way downstairs.

Still laughing, Kevin pulled open the door and saw Laura and Matthew on the porch, a squirming Jennie straddling Matthew's hip.

"What's the joke?" Laura grabbed Kevin and hugged him tightly.

"Me." He held out his arms to Jennie, "You gonna come see Uncle Kevin or do I have to beg?"

Jennie squealed and threw herself at Kevin. "Hey Matt." He inclined his head inside and stepped out of the way. "Come on in. I probably have some lemonade or iced tea in the fridge if you want some."

"I'll get it." Laura started toward the kitchen. "I know where everything is."

Settling on the sofa in the living room, Kevin shifted Jennie to his knees and began to bounce her. She giggled like mad. "So, not that I don't love it when you drop by, but what brings you over?"

Matt shrugged and gestured toward the kitchen. "You'll have to ask Laura, I'm just along for the ride." He eyed Kevin, speculation glinting in his eyes. "You could use a trim, you know that?"

"Man, are you going to get on me about that every time I see you? One day I'm going to show up and make you cut my hair. Then you'll be sorry."

"Not if your money's good I won't be." Matt laughed and settled deeper into the couch. "Laura's been on a tear about visiting you since she got back from Lydia's last night."

"Lydia? My Lydia?"

"Lyddie Lyddie Lyddie." Jennie began to chant.

Kevin tweaked her nose. "Imp." He gently put her down. "You know where the toys are, kiddo."

Grinning, Jennie stood, taking a moment to get her balance, then ran to the drawer under the giant TV across the room. Tugging it open, she lost herself in squeals, jabbering as she began to pull out the contents.

Laura came in carrying three glasses of lemonade. "I'm not sure I actually consider this lemonade, Kevin. It's yellow, but if an actual lemon was used in any part of the processing, I'll eat the wrapping that held the powder."

"Hey, it's sweet, yet tangy. That makes it lemonade."

Matt cast a sidewise look at Kevin. "I'm going to have to side with Kevin on this one, hon. Besides, did you know our friend here still carries a torch?"

"A torch?" Laura wrinkled her forehead.

"You know, a torch." Matt clasped his hand dramatically over his heart. "For Lydia. Or should I say, 'his' Lydia."

"This from the man who spent hours on that very couch bemoaning the fact that the girl he was in love with was engaged to another?" Kevin rolled his eyes.

"I didn't realize you were still focused in that direction." Laura scooted forward in her chair and rested her hand on his knee. "Don't you think it's time to let go, Kevin? Move on?"

Kevin patted her hand. "Matt was saying you went to see her last night? I thought you weren't acknowledging her existence after her ill-advised but fortunate-for-you fling with…what was his name?"

Laura made a strangled noise and Matt chuckled.

"You know his name quite well. And yes, I admit things worked out much better." She flashed a loving smile at Matt and let her gaze rest on Jennie as she played happily with a stuffed elephant. Steeling her gaze, she looked back at Kevin. "But that doesn't mean what she did was right. Still, I realized last night that I've forgiven her and can even be a bit grateful. And I told her that. So…maybe we can repair our friendship."

"That'd be good. She needs a friend right now." Kevin spun the glass of lemonade in fingers, making patterns in the condensation.

"Do you know what's going on there?" Laura's face showed concern.

"Just that she and Brad broke up. But I think there's more to it. She's been through break ups before and never had this kind of reaction." Kevin sighed and set the glass down by his foot. "She wouldn't tell me anything else though."

"Probably have the wrong equipment for that kind of confession, pal." Matt's joking tone was laced with sympathy.

"Yeah, probably." Kevin ran a hand through his hair. "I take it she wasn't any more forthcoming with you?"

Laura shook her head. "I was hoping maybe you'd know something that could steer me in the right direction. But still…if she won't talk to you, it'll be a while before we can rebuild our relationship to the point where she's going to turn to me." Laura frowned and drank deeply. "Honestly, even before the whole big…mess…"

Matt snorted out a laugh. "..Mess. There goes the prize for understatement of the year."

Laura stuck out her tongue and continued. "I considered her my friend much more than she did me. I wouldn't have been able to tell you that then, but looking back, well, it's all a bit clearer."

Kevin nodded and puffed out his cheeks.

Jennie looked up and grinned, racing across the room on her fourteen-month old legs. She reached up and pushed on his cheeks. Kevin made loud splurting noises as the air escaped, sending Jennie into gales of laughter.

"Maybe what we need to do is commit to pray for her. The three of us." Matt spoke thoughtfully. "I don't see anything more that we can do right now, but maybe with our help she'll let the Holy Spirit in again."

"Good idea, Honey."

Kevin looked up from playing with Jennie. "I already do, but having you join me in that would be really good. There's nothing anyone can do until she's ready." He pulled Jennie onto his lap and snuggled her against his chest. "I can't offer five star fare, but if you want to hang around for the rest of the afternoon, I could probably scare up something for dinner that won't kill you."

"Now that's an offer too good to refuse. I'm in if she is."

"Since I'm going to have to cook dinner either way," Laura fixed Kevin with a mock glare, "might as well include the starving bachelor."

"What channel is the game on?" Matt reached for the remote.

Kevin raised his eyebrows. "Did you forget whose house you're at? You're welcome to look, I'll even watch with you, but seriously, why would you think I'd know?"

Matt laughed and began flipping through the on-screen guide.

Laura snagged Jennie from Kevin and settled her on her hip. "I'm going to go see if there's anything edible in the kitchen while I still have time to run to the store. Come on, Jennie, let's go look for something to eat."

Kevin watched as Jennie and Laura headed to the kitchen. Sighing, he propped his feet on the coffee table as Matt found a football game on the TV. "Who's playing?"

"Does it matter? It's football."

"The hairdresser who loves football. That's rich."

Matt punched Kevin's arm. "Stylist, man, stylist. What can I say? I like the game. Anyway, I'm more of a salon manager these days; surely that puts me back on the masculine side of the spectrum?"

Kevin snickered then winced as the quarterback was sacked mercilessly. "That's gonna leave a mark."

"It's no good if it doesn't." Matt laughed and settled back, toeing off his shoes and propping his feet on the coffee table as well. "This is the life, man. This is the life."

"Part of it, at least."

"Touchdown!" Matt threw his arms in the air as one of the teams scored. As the replays began, he tossed a glance at Kevin. "What are you up to for Thanksgiving?"

"Actually, I have to go to England for the month of December for work."

Matt shot him a curious glance.

"Big install, the client wants the project lead in attendance, blah blah. But I figured hey, free trip to London for a month, so why not? Anyway, I'm heading out on Wednesday. Get there and get settled before everything kicks off next Monday."

"Sounds nice. That's gotta be costing them a mint though."

"Apparently the client's willing to pay it…and they have a corporate apartment they're setting me up in, so that'll be a bit nicer than a hotel. Probably cheaper for them, too. You three doing anything special?"

"Laura is going to try her hand at cooking for the masses." He glanced toward the kitchen. "My folks and hers are coming over, big family celebration. My mom is terrified. I tried to talk Laura out of doing the whole thing and I tried to convince my mom she's really a pretty fair cook, but," he made a helpless gesture with his hands, "it's going to be interesting." He paused to watch penalty replay and grunted at the call. "Got any extra room in your suitcase?"

"Suitcase?" Laura and Jennie came back in balancing the lemonade pitcher and a bowl of chips. "Where are you off to, Kev?"

"London, for work." He frowned at the bowl of chips. "Any idea how old these are?"

"Nope, the use-by date had worn off the bag, but they taste ok. By the way, you have no salsa, how is that even possible?"

Kevin shrugged.

She grinned and shook her finger at her husband. "And don't think I didn't just hear you trying to get out of our Thanksgiving. It's going to be fine, you'll see."

"Of course it will be."

"We're going to run to the store for a few things. Any requests?"

"You don't need to do that. I can order pizza or something."

"It's no problem. But hearing you're going out of town makes me feel better about the state of your refrigerator." She leaned over and kissed Matt on the cheek. "Back soon."

"You want to leave Jennie?" Matt asked without taking his eyes off the screen.

"I got her. You two have fun."

Lydia hadn't managed to wiggle out of Thanksgiving at her parent's house. She let her mind drift as she sat in her car staring from her spot at the curb at the simple two story brick Colonial she'd grown up in. Her gaze wandered over the lawns of the houses to either side, as familiar to her as her own yard. Her parents had made it a point to know the neighbors, no matter who they happened to be. She and her three sisters had all had good friends that lived next door at one time or another.

She jumped at the rap on her window and turned to meet laughing blue eyes.

"You coming in or are we providing car-side service?" Her oldest sister, Priscilla, had her nose pressed against the window, making smudges on the glass.

"All right, all right. Leave off on the window decorations already." Lydia took her key out of the ignition and grabbed her purse and a store-bought pumpkin pie from the passenger seat. Her sister stumbled backward as she shoved open the door. "Oops."

Priscilla laughed and slung an arm around Lydia's shoulders, eyeing the pie. "I see you slaved over dessert this year."

Lydia hunched her shoulders. "I've been busy."

"Hey, Dan, hear that?" Priscilla called over to her husband who was busy unloading a cooler from the back of the minivan they'd pulled into the driveway. Their six year old twins raced around making Indian noises and the three year old howled to be let out of his car seat.

"Hear what?" Dan looked up. "I don't hear a thing. There's nothing but peace and blissful silence in my world." He grinned, and winked at Lydia. "Hey, Lyd."

Lydia jammed an elbow in her sister's ribs. "Hi, Dan. Prissy here was maligning my pie."

He craned his neck and noticed the box. "Ah, well, she'll still probably eat half of it if we don't watch her. Pregnancy does that to her."

Lydia felt all of the blood drain from her face as she fought to force a smile. "That's great."

"I know, I know. I said I was done at three." She shrugged. "But, well, four is good too, right?" She grinned and unclipped the youngest from his seat. "Come on, big guy, let's go find Gramma. Lyd, you could help Dan with the food, since you've only got the pie box."

Priscilla trotted up the steps to the house calling for the twins to get out of the garden and come inside.

Lydia leaned against the back of the van and watched Dan craft a delicately balanced pile of food on top of a cooler. "Need a hand?"

"Nah, I've got it. You get that pie inside before it gets cold."

"Ha ha. You're as mean as she is. Just for that, I'm not helping." She pushed off the van and headed inside.

To the outside eye it would probably look like unsupervised chaos. Lydia paused in the doorway and shook her head as she saw the twins, loaded down with plates, racing one another to set the table while the littlest scrambled around poking at all the outlets. Probably looking for one that wasn't covered.

Lydia scooped him up and smacked a noisy kiss on his cheek. "Heya, Drew."

Drew grinned and opened his mouth wide so Lydia could see the half-chewed ball of something chocolate that he was working on.

"Oooh, yummy. Who gave you that?"

"Gampa." He squirmed in her arms. "Down pwease?"

"Maybe he'll get me one, too." She set Drew back on the floor and poked her head in the den where her dad sat in a recliner ostensibly watching football, though Lydia saw he had a book in his lap as well.

"Reading or watching, Dad?"

"Lydia." He slipped a bookmark between the pages of his book and set it aside so he could stand and give her a hug. "I wasn't sure you were coming."

Color stained her cheeks as she returned the hug. "I know I've been hard to get a hold of. Work's been busy."

"Isn't it always?" He smiled and Lydia noticed the wrinkles at the corners of his eyes for the first time. He settled back into his chair. "To answer your first question, reading." He grinned guiltily. "But I have the TV on so that when Dan gets inside he won't have to comment on his father-in-law's complete lack of interest in sports."

"Which I'm going to do now anyway." Dan laughed as he flopped onto the sofa, peering around Lydia to see the game. "And I would have known…you've got the wrong game on. But I'll give you points for trying."

Paul tossed the remote to Dan. "I guess this is a good development, it's hard to read when you're trying to camouflage a book. I may actually have to give in to bifocals the next time the optometrist brings them up."

He sighed and opened his book.

"Are Martha and Naomi coming?" Lydia looked from her dad to Dan.

Dan shrugged, motioning for her to move.

Lydia perched on the arm of her dad's chair. He looked up and patted her knee. "Martha and Jeremy are at Jeremy's folks in New York. I think they're planning on being here for Christmas though, but you'd need to confirm that with your mother. They've changed their minds so many times that I've gotten lost." He shrugged. "Naomi decided not to come home because her young man invited her to meet his parents. Doesn't seem possible that the baby of the family is old enough to be meeting someone's parents."

"She's graduating from college next year, Dad. She's old enough." Lydia pursed her lips. "Though saying that, I guess I see what you mean. I'm not sure I'm old enough for her to be that old."

Paul chuckled and patted her knee again. "Why don't we go see if you mother needs any help, though I'm certain she doesn't. Maybe we can sneak a taste or two of something." He winked and set his book aside then tugged Lydia to her feet. "She'll be glad you made it."

Lydia schooled her expression to hide the wince and followed after her dad. At least she'd only have to deal with one perfect sister, though it would have to be Priscilla. Only half way into chastising herself for that thought, she smiled as her dad snuck his arms around her mom and kissed her cheek.

"Oh, Lydia. You *did* make it." Mary grinned and slapped playfully at her husband's hands so she could gather Lydia into a hug. "I'm so glad." Leaning back, she looked her daughter over critically. "You've lost more weight."

Lydia opened her mouth to deny it but her father stepped in. "Now Mary."

"Oh Paul, hush. A mother is allowed to make a comment like that now and again. Besides, I imagine we can fix that today. I've made enough for six armies. And Priscilla brought about twice that along with her. Though I've no idea why." She frowned, then shrugged at Lydia. "Regardless, I hope you have room in your fridge, because I'm going to have to send stuff home with you, I can already tell."

"Can I help with anything, Mom?" Lydia looked around at the efficiently organized kitchen as her mother shook her head.

"No, I've got it under control. We'll be eating soon. But you can pull up a stool and stay out of the chaos if you like." As she spoke, war whoops from the other room morphed into wails, accusations, and the sound of Priscilla laying down the law.

Lydia winced and slid onto a stool, accepting the chocolate covered peanut butter ball her dad slipped to her under the counter as he padded back to the den.

"Go ahead and eat it." Mary chuckled as Lydia tried to look innocent. "He's been sneaking those Buckeyes all morning. That's why I hid most of the batch. I made extra, too, because I invited the renters downstairs, but they had other plans. I'd also hoped Kevin would be joining us, but he's already left for London."

"London?"

"Mmm, some big install for work." Mary poured more cream into the potatoes she was mashing. "He didn't mention it?"

Lydia shook her head and idly pushed around the individual sized turkey shaped salt and pepper shakers that had sat at each place setting for Thanksgiving since she was a child.

"Oh. Well." Mary tasted the potatoes. "I think he's going to be gone until the new year, possibly longer, depending on how things go." She paused in her mashing and studied her daughter for a moment. "You look tired, are you sleeping all right?"

"I've had a few long nights lately...but that should be over soon."

"Just take care of yourself, Baby. Now, I've been meaning to mention the new look. Where'd you have it done?"

Lydia reached up and patted her new hairstyle. She still wasn't used to it being this short. "Actually, Laura did it."

"Laura? Laura Stephenson? You went to *A Cut Above?*"

"Laura Willis...Stephenson is her married name I guess?" She felt heat creep across her cheeks. "That slipped my memory. But no, I didn't go to her salon. She came over to do it."

A pleased smile lit Mary's face as she scooped potatoes into the serving dish. "Good. That's good." She offered the spatula to Lydia who eagerly licked creamy potatoes from the handle as her mother laughed. "You would never lick a cake beater, but I could always count on you to clean up after potatoes."

Mary turned as the oven timer buzzed. Slipping on her oven mitts, she bent and removed a glistening golden turkey from the oven and carefully settled it onto the stovetop. "Run and tell your father it's time to carve, would you?"

Lydia slipped off the stool still licking the spatula and poked her head into the den. "Dad? Turkey time."

Dan glanced at his watch and then at the countdown timer on the screen. He frowned as Paul pushed out of his chair rubbing his hands together in anticipation.

"How long will it take to carve, Dad? Any chance I can finish the game?" Dan craned his neck to see around Paul as he stopped in front of the screen.

"Unlikely, but I'll try to get you as close as I can." He gestured at the remote. "That'll record though, if you can figure out what button to push. Maybe Lydia can show you." He snagged the spatula from her and licked off the last of the potatoes, laughing at her pout. "Go help your brother-in-law, then see if you can round up your sister and the imps."

Lydia sat next to Dan, snatching the remote from his hand. After a quick study, she pushed the record button and got the game set, then poked Dan's shoulder. "Go find your wife and kids, I'm going to make sure the table is set."

Dan frowned at the remote before he got up. "You're sure it's recording?"

Lydia shooed him. "I'm sure."

She poked her head in the dining room. Everything looked set. Maybe her mom needed help putting out the food. Lydia wandered back into the kitchen.

Paul eyed the turkey sitting on the kitchen counter and made an appreciative noise as he ran the knife down the file, sharpening its edge. "I don't know how you do it, Mary. This could be on the cover of a magazine."

"You say that every year, Honey. Did you notice Lydia's new 'do? Laura did it."

"Really?" He carefully sliced into the turkey, neatly separating a leg from the rest of the bird and transferring it to a platter. "It's lovely, Lydia. I didn't realize you were still friends."

Lydia gave a non-committal grunt. "Thanks. She did a great job—though I'm still struggling to get used to it."

She watched her parents exchange a look. What was that about?

Mary turned and stuck a spoon into the potatoes then hefted the bowl and pressed it into Lydia's hands. "Set that out, would you?"

"Sure." Lydia began ferrying dishes from the kitchen to the table.

After the family gathered and said grace, Lydia elbowed her sister in the ribs.

"Ow." Priscilla shot Lydia an annoyed glance. "What was that for?"

"Oh, sorry." Lydia smiled innocently. "Must've slipped, muscles get tired with all the prep work I had to help with." She sighed dramatically. "If only there'd been some extra hands in the kitchen."

"Next year, you can chase the kids and I'll do the food service."

Lydia scooped stuffing onto her plate. "Uh-uh. I'm no sucker. Besides, next year..." She trailed off at Priscilla's murderous look. Oh. Her sister hadn't mentioned the pregnancy to her parents yet. Great. "I might have other plans."

Her mother shot her a curious look.

Lydia shrugged. "Well, you never know."

Food and conversation engulfed the table. Lydia was content to let it swirl around her, answering questions here or there, adding a joke or a jibe when called for, but still staying on the fringes and observing. She caught her mother's concerned looks and her father's studied insistence that everything was normal. Invisible weights piled onto her shoulders. Would she ever meet their expectations?

When the dishes had been cleared and the pumpkin pie held court in front of her father's place, Lydia cringed internally. This was the worst part of the whole meal—the mandatory thankful-fest.

Paul smiled and cut the first slice, slipping it onto a plate and heaping whipped cream on top. "Who's first?"

The kids all squirmed in their seats at Priscilla's brisk head shake. "I'll go first, Dad."

She scooted her chair out and went to the head of the table. Leaning over she kissed his cheek and reached for the pie.

Paul held it out of reach, his eyes sparkling. "Not so fast, Missy. Thanks first, pie second."

Priscilla laughed and reached around him to dip a finger in the whipped cream. "All right. This year, I'm thankful for my family." She smiled and looked at her parents, then her children, and finally at her husband. "And more than that, I'm thankful that God has seen fit to allow that family to expand. Again."

She reached for the pie but instead found herself enveloped in her father's arms.

"Oh Honey, what great news." He held her a moment then kissed her forehead and looked down the table at Dan. "Congratulations."

Mary grabbed her next, laughing as she nearly toppled the pie off the plate. "How exciting. When are you due?"

Priscilla kissed her mom's cheek then went back to her seat with her pie and forked up a big bite. "May 14th. That'd be a nice Mother's Day present, wouldn't it?"

Lydia felt the smile on her face stiffen. That was only three days off from what her due date would have been. It had to be obvious, didn't it? She swallowed bile and waited for someone to ask her what was wrong.

The buzz of new babies continued around the table. Paul shook his head and simply passed out slices of the pie. Were they going to skip the whole tradition of sharing thankful thoughts? At least she wouldn't have to make something up. Lydia looked down at the pie and felt her stomach clench. She dipped the tines of her fork into the whipped cream but couldn't bring herself to take a bite. With a sigh, she pushed the pie to the middle of the table.

"What's wrong with it?" Priscilla looked down at her empty plate. "It tasted fine, and since you didn't actually cook it, it's not likely we'll all die of food poisoning."

Lydia wrinkled her nose. "Ate too much, I guess." She shrugged and struggled to keep her voice light. "Mom's turkey always wins over supermarket pie."

"I always make too much and then your father complains about the leftovers. I'll be sure to send some home with you."

"That'd be great, Mom." Lydia smiled and poked at the pie, digging little trenches in its side.

Priscilla tapped the back of Lydia's hand with her fork. "Hey. Don't abuse it. In fact," she eyed the pie speculatively, "let's not let it go to waste." She grinned and pulled the pie toward her. "After all, your niece," Dan cleared his throat and Priscilla amended, "or nephew deserves her own piece."

Lydia frowned at her sister. "You're going to gain fifty pounds again, aren't you? Then I'm going to have to listen to you whine for two years about how you hate exercising."

Priscilla shrugged and continued eating the pie.

Dan winced. "You're not the only one who has to hear the complaining, I get to live with it."

"Fine, fine. Here, in front of all these witnesses, one of whom is a pastor, I solemnly vow not to whine about my weight for two years." She paused and scooped up the last bite of pie. "Maybe this time it'll be three."

Everyone groaned. The kids squirmed in their seats and were finally shooed off to play. Paul and Dan cleared the table and settled back in front of the television.

"Can I help with the dishes, Mom?" Lydia leaned on the counter watching her mother efficiently prepare neat take home packages for Priscilla and herself.

"No need, sweetheart. It relaxes me. You go watch the game."

Lydia rubbed the back of her neck. "Actually, I think I might go home and have a nap. Besides having eaten entirely too much, I think I feel a migraine coming on."

"You do look pale. Here," she pushed a parcel of food into her arms, "take this." Mary hugged her tightly and pressed a kiss to her cheek. "Be sure to tell your father you're leaving. We'll see you Sunday?"

"I should be at church, yeah."

"Lunch?"

"Not sure yet. I'll let you know."

"All right. Thanks for coming, Honey, I love you."

Lydia's smile didn't reach her eyes. "I love you too, Mom."

She turned, arms full of food, and went to find her dad.

Paul was sleeping in the recliner with the game blaring. Dan and Priscilla looked comfy curled up on the couch watching through half-shut eyes. Lydia leaned and pressed a light kiss to his cheek. "Bye Dad, I'm going to head out."

He opened an eye and smiled. "Thanks for coming Lyddie. Drive safely."

"I always do." She shifted the package of food to the crook of one arm and waved to her sister and brother-in-law. "See you."

"Need help with that?" Dan tore his eyes from the TV.

"I got it. It was good to see you."

"We're only three hours away, Lyd, you should come visit more often." Priscilla snuggled deeper into Dan's shoulder. "Let us know when you can take a long weekend, ok?"

"I'll see what I can do." She slipped from the room, bee-lining for the front door. Pulling it closed behind her she stood in the crisp afternoon and closed her eyes, breathing deeply. If only there was someone she could talk to.

Kevin dropped his bags in the front hallway and let out a gusty sigh. The flight had been a killer. He dropped to the sofa, soaking up the details of home. His jetlagged brain might be foggy, but his spirits lifted as he looked around the familiar space. It was good to be back in his own place. Scrubbing his face, he checked his watch; 4:30 was too early to call it a night, no matter what time his body thought it was.

He toed off his shoes and padded into the kitchen. The last email he'd gotten from the college kid he'd hired to house sit said that he'd leave food in the fridge. Kevin earnestly hoped the boy, *what was his name?* He paused, hand on the refrigerator handle and concentrated, "Joe? John?" He shook his head. "No idea. I hope his memory is better than mine though." He tugged open the door. A smile grew on his face at the sight of fairly well laden shelves. Browsing for a minute, he grabbed a yogurt container and spoon and settled on a stool at the counter.

His eyes landed on the calendar by the phone. "How can it be May?"

He scooped yogurt into his mouth as he thought through the last months. The project in London had gone well, though it had taken him into the middle of January to get all of the problems with the install worked out. By mid-December it was obvious that things were taking longer than anticipated so he'd asked Laura and Matt to find him a house sitter. That had turned out to be a good call. The week he'd been tying up all the loose ends in London, he'd sat in on a conference call with his boss and a development team working out of Mumbai. They'd needed onsite supervision. Since he was at the end of one of his projects and was closer than anyone else he'd been the natural choice to send.

The three months he'd spent in India had been productive professionally and personally. He'd had a chance to meet the Christian aid workers the church supported, as well as help on the weekends at the shelter for women and children, though the bulk of his work was in their administrative offices. It had been a fascinating study in the differences between the castes. He'd worked in the office all week and stayed in a hotel that catered to tourists. On the weekends he spent time with those who truly had nothing to their names. As a result, he'd felt a tug for mission work of some sort forming in his heart and mind. He planned to spend some time praying to see where it might lead.

The trip to a conference in Australia in mid-April had been scheduled before he left for London. Since things were back on track in Mumbai, he rearranged his flights and was able to present his paper and do some networking. Though there'd been considerably more downtime at the conference, the travel was beginning to catch up with him. As a result, he hadn't done as much sightseeing in Sydney as he had hoped.

Through it all, he'd spent the majority of his spare time thinking about Lydia and wondering how she was doing. He'd tried to avoid sending her email unless she sent one first. Maybe it was petty, but he hoped to make her miss him even a fraction of how much he missed her. With Brad out of the picture, he wanted to remind her that he was still waiting...but not so obviously that it scared her into someone else's arms. That had been part of the problem in the first place...he'd been too pushy. Someone as strong-willed as Lydia was going to have to be coaxed. If it wasn't already too late. Although her messages to him continued to be breezy and friendly, the conversations he'd had with Matt and Laura painted a different picture. Had he managed to miss the window of opportunity?

He stood and tossed the empty container in the garbage and the spoon in the sink. There was nothing to do about Lydia right now, and it was too good to be home to spoil it with worry. "God has it under control."

The verbal reminder helped calm his thoughts. He grabbed the portable phone and wandered into the living room, sinking into the couch and propping his feet on the coffee table. Punching in numbers, he listened to the ring on the other end.

"Hello?"

"Hey, Mom."

"Kevin." There was a pause and he imagined his mother looking at the caller ID to see what number he was using. "You're home."

"I am. And boy does it feel good."

"I bet. Have you eaten? Can I bring something over?"

"I just had some yogurt. Honestly, I'm not really hungry. I don't think my body has any idea what time it's supposed to be." He yawned. "I'm actually trying to decide when I can let myself go to bed."

His mother's laugh echoed over the line. "If you have to try and figure it out, you're probably safe doing it. Your father and I have been enjoying all the photos and can't wait for a more detailed trip report."

"Give me a few days to get back into a routine and we'll put something together. Maybe we can include Matt and Laura and do it all at once?"

"Absolutely, we love having Jennie over. Go get some sleep, Sweetie. You sound dead on your feet."

"You don't have to tell me twice. Love you."

"Love you too, Baby. Night."

Kevin dragged himself off the couch and headed toward the stairs. He glanced at his luggage. It wasn't going anywhere—he'd get to it later. What he needed was a hot shower and bed.

CRINO

Kevin opened bleary eyes and squinted at the digital readout of the clock across the room, "Two a.m., great."

He rubbed a hand over his face and flopped onto his back, wriggling until he was comfortable. He had almost dropped back to sleep when the phone on his nightstand buzzed. Sighing, he reached across to grab it. Hadn't he turned it off? With a finger poised on the off button, he saw Lydia's face on the screen. Should he answer it? A yawn cracked his jaw. No...he needed sleep. Had she forgotten he was coming home? Didn't matter— her voicemail would be there in the morning. He turned his phone completely off and burrowed back under the covers.

CRINO

Lydia slipped her phone back into her purse and set it on top of the clothes she'd neatly folded and placed on the counter. Why had she called Kevin? It wasn't as if he could get her out of this situation. It wasn't as if she wanted him to. *It's good he didn't answer.* She clutched the skimpy motel towel around her chest and leaned forward to look herself in the eye. The buzz of the overhead fan that had come on with the light did nothing to drown out the television and footsteps in the room outside. She ignored them and stared at her reflection in the mirror.

In her mind's eye, she saw a miniature of herself jumping up and down, frantically waving her hands over her head, mouth moving. But she couldn't hear even the faintest whisper anymore. She mentally brought a spiked heel down on the head of that miniature version of herself and made her lips curve into a smile.

Dropping the towel on the floor, she dug through her purse and tugged a prescription bottle free. Unscrewing the cap, she shook two pills into her hand and tossed them back. She slid her feet back into the strappy sandals she'd worn to the bar that night, flipped off the light, and left the bathroom.

The man reclining shirtless on the bed looked up from the TV, a slow smile spreading across his face, "Well, now, Darlin'. Looks like you have the same thing in mind as me." He nodded to the TV where Lydia caught a flicker of naked flesh cavorting in a swimming pool.

She made her laugh playful to cover her roiling stomach. "We'll just have to see who's better at it then, won't we."

❧

The sun shone through a break in the blinds and crept up the wall, finally waking Kevin. Stretching, he turned to see the clock.

"Well," he pushed himself to a sitting position, "just in time for lunch."

He nabbed his phone from the night stand and made his way downstairs. The gurgling in his stomach grew more insistent now that he was up and moving.

Setting the phone on the counter, he opened the fridge and pulled out ingredients for an everything omelet. His phone beeped and buzzed as it booted, signaling new voice and email messages. He could deal with those while he ate.

"Seems like a lot of fuss for a Saturday." He paused in the act of cracking an egg into a bowl and frowned, turning to double check the date on his phone. Nodding, he went back to fixing his meal. "Saturday. Nothing like a good night's sleep to get things back in focus."

Deftly, Kevin poured the beaten eggs into a pan and swirled them around. He waited a little then stirred them slightly to get more of the eggs on the heat. When those had cooked, he wiggled the pan and, holding his breath, made a quick shake, watching with a smile as the eggs flipped and landed back in the pan. "And he's back, ladies and gentlemen."

Adding his own soundtrack of roaring fans, Kevin spread shredded cheese and peppers on the eggs, then flipped half of the omelet over them before putting it on his waiting plate. Checking to make sure he'd turned off the stove, he carried his omelet to the counter and frowned. Did he want coffee, too? He pursed his lips, then shook his head and instead found a soda in the fridge.

"All right," he forked up a bite and sighed happily as the melted cheese hit his tongue, "let's see what all the fuss is about." He dialed voice mail and hit the speaker button.

"Hey man," Matt's voice filled the kitchen, "Laura talked to your mom last night. She said you were back in town but heading to bed so we didn't buzz you then. Thought you might be up early and want to hit the courts to run off some of that jet lag." Matt laughed. "Guess you're still snoozing away though. Heard the plan for trip photo viewing is TBD. Keep us in the loop. Also—I'm betting you really need a hair cut by now. I promise not to scalp you. Come by sometime. Gotta run man, catch you on the other side."

Kevin snorted and ran a hand self-consciously through his hair as he deleted the message. It was shaggy, no question. He'd been planning to hit up his usual barber, but it'd be nice to see a friendly face. Maybe he should swing by Matt's salon. He took another bite as the next message began to play.

"Hi Honey." His mom's voice now filled the kitchen. "I didn't want to wake you with the house phone, but I just wanted to say again how happy we are that you're home. Give us a call when you're up and let's plan that show and tell. Can't wait to see you."

Scooping up the last bite of omelet, he deleted the message and pressed on to the next. When there was no sound, he frowned and picked up the phone and heard

Lydia clear her throat. "Hey, um, it's just me…I guess I got confused with the time differences, thought I might catch you awake. Call me back, if you want. It's not a big deal."

Kevin set the phone down and stood. He stretched and carried his plate to the sink. A quick glance in the dishwasher revealed that it was empty so he rinsed the plate and set it inside. Eyeing the phone, he leaned back against the sink and drank his soda. Finished, he rinsed out the can and crushed it before two-pointing it into the recycle bin across the room. Leaving the phone on the counter, he went back to the entry hall and grabbed his bags.

"First things first. Or last things first, who can say." He carted the bags upstairs and dumped their contents in front of the washer in the laundry room. "At least this I understand."

His mother's voice in the back of his head stopped him from just dumping everything in as one big load. He quickly sorted the clothes into light and dark piles and got the first load started. He snagged the bags and went back to his bedroom to dump out the various gifts and souvenirs.

He smiled as his gaze landed on the little stuffed Paddington Bear he'd picked up in London. He threw on an old pair of jeans and a t-shirt and stuck his bare feet into a ratty but comfortable pair of loafers. He grabbed the bear, one of the boxes of chocolates, and a tea canister he'd seen in a London shop. He eyed the miniature Taj Mahal made out of inlaid marble for a moment before adding it to the pile. Juggling the pile of gifts, he snagged his wallet, keys, and phone and headed out the door.

☙❧

Kevin's senses were assaulted with the sweet smell of coconut mixed with pungent peroxide and who knew what else as he opened the salon door. He barely heard the cheery jingle of the bells on the door over the hair dryers and conversation. It was clear that Matt's ears were more attuned to the bells from the way his head jerked up from the computer screen he studied at the front desk. He jumped out of the chair and crossed to the door to grab Kevin in a back slapping hug. "The world traveler has returned. Welcome home, man."

"Thanks. It's good to be home." He dangled the backpack stuffed with gifts at eye level. "I come bearing gifts."

Matt reached up and tugged Kevin's hair. "A chance at your hair is gift enough. Let's go get you shampooed."

"I didn't really come for…" He trailed off at Matt's steely glare and let himself be pushed into a shampoo chair.

"I'll leave you in Jessica's capable hands and go set up my station." Matt paused and ran a hand appraisingly through Kevin's hair. "Give him the deep conditioner and let it sit for five."

"Oh I really don't…" Kevin sighed as his head was gently tugged back into the bowl and warm water started flowing over his scalp. He squinted up at Jessica. "I really wasn't planning on a cut, or the whatever it was he said, so you know, you can just leave it."

Jessica shook her head. "He's right, you need the deep conditioner. Besides, he's the boss. Doesn't pay to ignore his requests." She grinned, snapped her gum, and then looked around guiltily. "Don't mention the gum, would you?" She continued without waiting for an answer, "How's that water temperature feel?"

Kevin groused silently through the shampoo and conditioner. It just didn't pay to do nice things like bring people gifts from overseas. He'd worked himself up by the end of the shampoo and found himself glaring at his reflection with Matt's hands in his hair.

"You know, I only came by to bring you presents. Not to have you brow beat me into a chair so you could hack at my head and make me look goofy."

"Still jetlagged and grumpy, I see. Don't make me break out the seaweed facial."

Kevin shot Matt a look of horror in the mirror. "You wouldn't dare."

"I absolutely would, and you know it. And right now, you really could use it." He waved a hand. "Don't worry, we'll discuss that later. For now," he snapped a cape around Kevin's neck, "just close your eyes and tell me about your trip, this'll be over before you know it."

Kevin sucked in a breath and narrowed his eyes at his friend's reflection. "Remember that we're adults now, please? I have to work and everything; I can't have another swim team experience."

"I shave half of your head one time while you're asleep and you never let it go."

"Gee, I wonder why that is." Kevin closed his eyes as Matt began sectioning and snipping at his hair. Squinting one eye open he watched the scissors for a minute. "Couldn't you use the trimmers like my barber does?"

Matt sent him a bland look in the mirror.

Kevin cleared his throat. "Any new word on Lydia? She called last night, or this morning I guess, but I didn't get it in time. I guess she doesn't know I'm home yet?"

"I figured you'd let her know. I could've left a message, but really unless it's time for Laura to do her hair, we never see her these days. She's looking more like herself but from what I've heard, she's out all hours doing who knows what." Matt frowned. "I guess I shouldn't say that. I don't know for sure what's going on. All I really know is that she's not with any of the people she used to hang out with and she's not hanging with us old married people." He made a mocking grin. "So I don't really know what she's doing. Honestly, we'd planned to ask you what was going on."

"I was worried you'd say that. We've traded emails and voice mails, but we've only managed two or three actual calls in the months I've been gone...I thought maybe being really low key would catch her interest, you know? Now...I don't know. She makes everything seem like it's fine, but then I hear from you and Laura…and I'm not sure what to think."

"I know what you mean. I've never seen a life as perfect as she tries to make hers seem. Except on TV." He shrugged and kept snipping. "When I'm finished with your hair you can ask Laura if she knows any more. I take it that means my prayers that you meet and fall in love with an amazing Christian woman in one of your ports of call weren't answered?"

"Sure they were, the answer was no." Kevin met Matt's eyes in the mirror. "Lydia's for me, Matt. I don't know how else to put it. I've tried to get away from it. I've prayed to get away from it. But I keep circling back to her being who God has for me. I'm doing my best to wait on His timing."

"Then we'll do what we can to help you wait and pray that she'll get back in His will so the two of you can be together." He set the scissors aside and flipped on his hairdryer to blow the hair away from Kevin's collar. "You may now vocally admire my genius with hair."

Matt grinned and unsnapped the cape.

Kevin leaned forward and turned his head from side to side. "Not bad, man, not bad at all." Cautiously he ran a hand around the back then smiled when he found no bald spots. "Maybe you can give my barber a run for his money after all."

"High praise indeed. Come into the back and we'll find Laura so you can distribute the goodies."

Lydia rolled over and pried open an eye, taking in the generic low-rent motel décor. She groaned and patted around on the nightstand to find her cell phone. Reaching for the switch at the base of the lamp, her arm knocked something to the floor. She flipped on the light and rolled to peer over the edge of the bed. Why was there cash splayed on the floor? Scooping it up, she pushed herself to a sitting position and arranged the bills into a tidy stack.

"Three fifty..." Lydia closed her eyes as the tiny voice in her head shouted nasty epithets. Swallowing the bile rising in her throat, she clenched the bills in her fist and tossed them in a wad on the bed. She threw back the covers and hurried to the bathroom and the hottest shower she could stand.

Wrapped in a towel, Lydia dug more pills out of her purse and swallowed them. About half way through the shower she'd dredged up sufficient anger to replace the shame that burned in her gut. She cleared the steam from the mirror and tugged on the clothes she'd worn the night before. Justifications and accusations warred with one another in her head.

She slapped her brush down on the counter and fumed at her reflection, startling when her phone buzzed with an incoming call.

"Oh for crying out loud, it's four o'clock in the morning." She glanced at the caller ID and frowned as she saw her mother's number. She debated a minute then cleared her throat and tried to sound sleepy. "Mom? What's wrong?"

"Lydia. I know I woke you, I'm sorry, but it's just so exciting. She's here."

"Who's where?"

Her mother's laugh tinkled over the line. "They're calling her Mary, after me. I finally have a namesake and she's the most precious thing you've ever seen."

Her mother rambled on and Lydia's heart sank as she listened to the statistics on her new niece.

"How's Prissy?"

"Just beaming, as you would imagine. And Dan is over the moon and your father." Mary laughed. "You'd think the man had no other grandchildren. He's smitten."

Lydia forced a smile into her voice. "Give them all my love. I'll try to swing by as soon as I can though maybe I should wait til everyone's back home."

"Oh don't wait. Can't you come to the hospital? Not now, obviously, you should go back to sleep, but later on?"

"I'll see what I can do, Mom, but I have a pretty full day planned." She didn't even flinch at the lie. So far her plans for the day consisted of going home and taking another long shower.

Mary couldn't quite hide the disappointment in her voice. "Oh, well of course. I know Priscilla wasn't due for another two weeks, so you wouldn't have thought to try and keep things clear this early. Hold on a second." Lydia heard snippets of a muffled conversation but couldn't make out any words. With a laugh, her mom came back on the line, "Your father is going to take me and Dan out for something to eat, so I've got to run. Please try to come by—I know it would mean so much to your sister. And you just have to see Mary. Ok, ok, I have to run. Love you, Lydia."

The phone clicked in her ear. Lydia set down the phone, fighting a sudden wave of nausea. Blinking back tears, Lydia sank to the rim of the tub, lowered her head to her knees and focused on forcing air in and out of her lungs. Deep breaths turned into sobs and she crumpled to the floor. There should be two new babies in the family, not just one. Images of a newborn and her aborted child deluged her.

The backup alarm on her cell phone beeped. Lydia struggled to a sitting position and wiped at her eyes, smearing snot and mascara across her cheeks. Hiccupping, she pushed herself to her feet and scrubbed mercilessly at her face to clear the smears. Her eyes were swollen, her face blotchy, but she barely noticed. She forced herself to meet her own gaze in the mirror as her eyes filled with tears. Loathing for the person in the mirror filled her heart. As more tears leaked down her face she spun out of the bathroom, pausing to stuff the crumpled heap of bills into her purse.

Flipping the deadbolt to her apartment, she leaned against the door and let her purse fall to the floor. At least she hadn't run into anyone she knew. After kicking her shoes in the direction of the coat closet she made her way through the bedroom and turned on the shower. While she waited for the water to heat, she shook a few pills from a different bottle into her palm and swallowed them.

When the heat of the water began to fade, Lydia turned off the tap and tugged on old sweats and a t-shirt, bundling her hair into a towel. Between the shower and the drugs, she'd finally found a place of disconnectedness. She went to the refrigerator and frowned at the contents. Sniffing at the milk, she fixed a bowl of cereal and sat at the table.

"Eight thirty." She sighed and poked at the floating O's in her bowl. Pushing the bowl away, she went into the living room and snagged her phone out of her purse. Flopping back into the chair at the kitchen table she checked her messages.

"Nothing from Kevin. His turn, I guess." Opening the first of the six new texts she found herself face to face with the scrunchy red face of a newborn wearing a pink knit cap. She hit delete and the next, a photo of her beaming sister and brother-in-law holding the baby filled her cell's screen. Punching delete again she snapped her phone shut and dropped it on the table before another photo could pop open.

Lydia carried her bowl to the sink and dumped the cereal down the disposal. Her cell rang. Frowning at the unfamiliar number she answered anyway.

"Hello?"

"Lydia, Baby." She could barely make out the words. They were clearly shouted in an attempt to rise over the loud ringing and clanging in the background.

"Brad?" She glanced down at the readout on her phone again but she still didn't recognize the number.

"That's right. Wait a sec." She heard him mutter followed by loud, female giggling. "Sorry. Hey, thought you'd want to be one of the first to know—Staci and I got married in Vegas this morning."

"Ah..."

"Anyway, we're going to head to Hawaii after a few days here, impromptu honeymoon and such. Staci's already called the leasing company to okay it, so they're gonna drop a key off at your place. You'll take care of her cat and plants, right?"

"Wha…"

"Awesome." A cacophony of clanging broke out in the background. "Woo! Gotta run, my sexy bride just hit the jackpot."

Lydia stared at her now silent phone. What just happened? When someone knocked on her door she walked over in a daze. The maintenance man smiled and waved at her through the peep hole. Sighing, she unlocked the door.

"Morning, Jake."

He grinned, showing off the gap between his tobacco stained teeth. What was left of his silver hair was cropped short in the hairstyle he'd had since his days in the Marine Corps during World War Two. "Miss Lydia." He stuck out a key. "Manager called and said you needed a key to 17C?"

Lydia shook her head and twisted her fingers together. "I can't do it, Jake. They just called but," she shook her head again, more vigorously, "they didn't give me a chance to say no, but I can't."

Jake poked the key out further. "Now, now, Miss Lydia. Knowing that lot, that poor cat's half starved already. You gotta' do the right thing."

Reluctantly, Lydia reached for the key, pausing before grasping the end. "You wouldn't have time for a little extra work, would you? I'd pay you."

Jake shook his head and pressed the key into her hands, pursing his lips. "Sometimes you hafta do what hasta be done." He patted her hand, closing her fingers around the key. "You're a good girl, Miss Lydia, it shows. Go on and feed that poor kitty."

He nodded his head crisply and shuffled down the hall, adjusting the volume on his crackling walkie-talkie.

Lydia sighed and shut the door. She stared at the key in her hand then dropped it on the table and went back to find her phone. She'd make sure the stupid cat was cared for, but she wasn't going to be the one to do it. Three phone calls later, she had a college student from church set up to pick up the key and house sit. Best of all, he was willing to negotiate payment terms with Staci when they got back.

If only going to see the new baby could be outsourced, too. Lydia sighed and sank into the couch. She stared at the blank TV for a few minutes before flipping it on and idly switching channels. She settled on an over-scripted so-called reality show about police women in some city she didn't recognize. She leaned forward and dropped the remote on the coffee table then twisted around a bit to get comfortable. Before long, her eyelids had closed and she was sleeping fitfully, dreaming of being chased through a dark, endless maze by a maniac with a screaming baby in one hand and a roaring chainsaw in the other.

The banging grew louder and more insistent. Lydia struggled out of sleep and frowned at the television. The same women were racing around their city, sirens blaring, but the clock underneath said it was almost two in the afternoon. The banging came again and Lydia pushed herself off the couch and yanked open the door.

Puzzled, Lydia looked at the clean cut young man in the hallway with a small bag propped against the wall.

"Miss Brown?" He cleared his throat and offered a tentative smile. "I'm Jackson Trent? From the church? You said to pick up the key at two?"

Lydia rubbed her eyes. "Jackson. Right. Sorry, I was napping and time got away from me."

"Happens to me all the time. Up cramming all night."

"Hang on a sec and I'll get the key. I think I left it in the kitchen." She left him standing in the doorway and shuffled to the kitchen as she stretched and tried to work a kink from the arm of the sofa out of her neck. Standing in the middle of the kitchen she frowned and looked around. No key. She filled a glass of water and went back to the living room smiling absently at Jackson.

He stood politely outside the door.

"It's here somewhere, give me a minute." She sipped the water and set it on her coffee table. With fists on her hips she cocked her head and spun slowly, her eyes roaming over the various surfaces where she would have dropped a key. When she reached the door she laughed, slightly embarrassed. "It's around, I promise."

"No problem." He darted a glance at the table just inside the door and the lone key sitting on it. Nodding toward that key he cleared his throat. "Is this it?"

Lydia looked at the table and rolled her eyes. "Yes. Sorry, never at my best when I wake up." She slipped the key off the table and dropped it into Jackson's outstretched hand then leaned out the door and pointed down and across the hall. "17C is down there—you can't miss it."

Jackson held the key and drew in a breath. After a second he shook his head almost imperceptibly and smiled. "I'll be back if I can't find it. Thanks for this, though. I just finished another house sitting job and wasn't really looking forward to crashing at my sister's for any longer than necessary."

Lydia drew her eyebrows together. She didn't really care, but the polite thing to do was listen. Right?

"It's an imposition. She puts up with it, cause, well, I'm her little brother. But they barely fit in their apartment when it's just them. I try to stay out of the way as much as I can, but it's easier to actually get studying done when I have quiet…and that doesn't happen with four kids under ten." He grinned. "Anyway. Thanks."

He grabbed the handle of his bag and started down the hall.

"You're welcome, though you're really doing me a big favor."

"Then we'll call it square. You don't know how long she'll be gone, do you?"

"Sorry, no. It was a fast and…strange… conversation this morning."

"Gotcha. Well, I'll go start now then and enjoy the quiet for as long as I can." He made a half-salute and turned back down the hall.

Lydia watched til he put the key in the right lock then shut her door. "One down." She frowned at the clock. "No time like the present, I guess."

She went down the hall, and checked her hair in the bathroom mirror. She winced and dragged her brush through the tangled mess then pulled it into a tight ponytail, glad it had grown out enough to do that again. She traded the sweats and t-shirt for jeans and a polo and dabbed on just enough makeup to look like she'd been out with friends. Shaking three more pills into her hand and swallowing them, she dug around in her closet for comfortable sandals. Snagging her purse and sunglasses, she checked for her cell phone and keys then headed to her car before she could talk herself out of getting it over with.

Traffic was heavy, though that was to be expected on a pretty spring Saturday. Lydia darted between cars on the Beltway, zipping back and forth through the lanes. Several annoyed motorists tossed unfriendly looks and gestures at her as she wound her way around to I-95 and pointed the car south. Glancing at the dashboard clock she sighed. It was three hours on the best day down to the Williamsburg area where her sister and husband lived. Squeezing between two cars in order to gain half a car length in the mostly stopped traffic, she turned up the radio and muttered.

South of Fredericksburg the traffic thinned out and Lydia was able to pick up some speed. Setting her cruise control, she dug around in her purse with one hand until she came up with a small prescription bottle. She frowned as she shook it. With a sigh, she tossed it back on the seat and hit the button on her cell phone's Bluetooth. Enunciating clearly she said, "Call Danny."

The other line rang a few times before the slurred male voice picked up. "Lyddie, baby. What's happening?"

"Running low again, D." She thought of the three hundred fifty dollars she'd earned at the hotel. "I've got cash though."

"Well now, that's almost too bad. I enjoy our alternative payment plan. Still, cash is more helpful in the long run. How much you need?"

"Whatever three hundred will get me."

There was a pause and she heard him typing on his keyboard. The sound stopped and he sucked air between his teeth. "That's only about thirty tablets, Babe, even with the steepest discount I can manage for my best customer. How fast are you running through them?"

"Doesn't matter. I can scrounge up more when I'm empty."

"You really ought to consider moving out of prescription, girl. Buzz lasts longer, cheaper overall."

"Just tell me when on Monday I can pick up the thirty."

"If you're waiting til Monday I can hook you up with double if you'll do a little entertaining for a friend who'll be in town. Drinks, dinner, that kind of thing. Monday night? He's been anxious to meet you, but I didn't think I'd be able to swing it."

Lydia stomped the accelerator and squeezed into the left lane in front of the car that had been beside her. Continuing to floor it, she zipped around the semi she'd been following then back into the right lane, ignoring the vigorous honking from both vehicles. "For that, triple."

"Fine. I'll text you deets."

Lydia ended the call and pulled the Bluetooth headset out of her ear. Tossing it on the passenger seat, she cranked her radio and emptied her mind of all but the thrill of driving fast. She refused to think about what waited for her at the end of her trip.

Kevin frowned when Lydia's voicemail picked up. He glanced at the clock on the stove and waited for the beep. "Hey Lydia, it's about 5:30 on Saturday, sorry I missed you last night. I'm actually home. I've been trying to get the laundry and all that kind of stuff taken care of today. So anyway…gimme a call. I'm heading over to my folks' in a few minutes to do pictures and all that and was hoping you could join us—Matt and Laura will be there too, so it's turning into a welcome home party of sorts. But…maybe another time. Anyway, give me a call. Oh, this is Kevin, by the way."

He ended the call and set his phone on the counter. The ball was in her court now. He tucked his hands into his pockets and headed upstairs to gather his laptop, portable projector and the rest of the gifts he'd bought.

Lydia made good time the rest of the way. She fumed when traffic briefly slowed to a crawl and everyone hugged the bumper ahead of them. As she passed the speed trap she sent up a quick prayer of thanks. Not that she deserved to get out of a ticket. A few minutes away from the hospital, she shook the last pills from her purse stash into her mouth, washing them down with the last of the jumbo diet soda she'd succumbed to in Richmond.

It was six when she pulled into a parking spot near the door of the hospital. Lydia flipped down the visor and practiced smiling at herself, checking to see that it came across as genuine. Good enough. She snapped the visor back into place and slipped from the car. She absently pressed the lock on her key fob as she strode into the building.

"May I help you?" The elderly lady behind the information desk smiled.

"Oh, um. Yeah, that'd be good. My sister just had a baby?"

"Congratulations, Auntie. Her name?"

"I guess that'd be helpful, wouldn't it? Priscilla Snyder."

The woman nodded and consulted her computer, tapping a few keys and scrolling through the information. "Maternity, room E-18. Go down this hallway," she leaned over the counter and pointed, "take the fourth left and then follow the signs to the red elevators. You'll go up to 4 and then make an immediate right to land in Maternity."

"Can't miss it, right? Thanks. I'll be back if I get lost."

She only missed one turn, and easily got back on track thanks to good signage. At the main desk for Maternity she signed in and verified the room number with the nurse on duty. Looping her visitor's badge around her neck, she pushed through the double doors and drew in a quick breath at the sounds of babies crying. Her insides seemed to solidify into one squirming mass. This was harder than she'd thought it would be. She leaned against the wall and squeezed her eyes shut until she felt steadier on her feet. With a deep breath she steeled herself and walked stiffly toward her sister's room.

Her mother's laughter drifted down the hall. Her father's quiet chuckle followed and then her sister and Dan said something not quite decipherable. Her heart sank. Her parents were still here.

Fixing a smile on her face, she peeked around the doorframe and knocked lightly. "Got room for one more?"

"Lydia." Her mother beamed and ran to the door to tug her into the room. "Come and look at this precious little girl."

Lydia rolled her eyes at her sister who was laughing and went to look into the bassinet next to the hospital bed. The baby was wrinkled, red, and bald, her face relaxed in sleep. Tiny lips were twitching as if seeking a food source.

"Nice work, sis. Though I think she's going to be waking up any minute, the lips are going."

Mary chuckled. "I'm surprised you remember that, Lyddie."

"It only takes one episode of a nephew trying to nurse for that to be indelibly imprinted on the memory."

As if on cue, the baby scrunched up her face and let out a scathing wail. Dan scooped her out of the bassinet quicker than Lydia would have dreamed possible and handed her to Priscilla. In seconds, the only sound was a quiet sucking as the baby ate.

"I'm so glad you were able to make it." Her father patted the seat next to him.

Lydia sat, leaning to rest her head on his shoulder. He slipped an arm around her shoulders in welcome.

"Me too, Daddy." What was one more lie in the grand scheme of things?

Mary dropped onto the seat next to Lydia and reached over to pat her knee. "We'll take you to dinner in a bit. They kick us out of here at 7:30 anyway. Can you wait that long?"

"Sure. That sounds nice." She let her eyes wander the sterile room, trying to avoid watching her sister and the baby. She cleared her throat. "Have you been sitting here all day?"

Mary smiled. "I could sit for days at a time with a newborn, dear. You know I love babies."

"Dan and I have gone out for a bit here and there. Got something a little nicer than what the cafeteria serves for lunch and so forth. Found a nice coffee shop with Internet access, too."

"Dad." Lydia shook her head. "I think you may have an Internet addiction."

"Just needed to make sure Steve was ok to preach tomorrow and that sort of thing."

Lydia shot him a look. 'That sort of thing' included a good deal of online news reading. He wasn't fooling anyone.

"What? People should be informed about what's going on in the world."

"Sure, Dad. You stick to that story."

Mary laughed and stood, her arms already outstretched for the baby Priscilla was burping. "Here, let me do that. And then Lydia should have a chance to hold her, at least for a few minutes."

Priscilla dropped a kiss on the baby's head before handing her and the burp cloth to Mary. "When do you go home again? I'd like to get to know my little girl."

Mary laughed as she walked slowly around the room bouncing and patting the baby, cooing quietly into her ear.

Priscilla fixed her gaze on Lydia. "So what were you up to today?"

"Some shopping and stuff with some of the girls, but I couldn't really get out of it. I've bailed on them too many times recently, so they made me swear. Then I had a little work that I needed to catch up on and it turned out that I had to arrange a cat sitter as well."

Her sister arched a brow.

Why had she said that?

"For whom?"

"Oh, just a neighbor." Why couldn't her sister just drop it? Take a hint?

"That wouldn't be Staci, would it?"

"Fine. Yes. It's Staci."

Priscilla and her dad exchanged looks.

Priscilla spoke first. "Why on earth would she think you'd do her any favors? And more to the point, why would you?"

"I didn't really have much of a chance to get a word in...before I realized it, they'd hung up and I was left holding the bag. I couldn't let the cat suffer, could I?"

"They?"

Lydia bit back a curse. "Brad was actually the one who called. Apparently he and Staci have eloped and were off on their honeymoon."

"What? And they called you?" Priscilla looked ready to hunt them down and shake some sense into them.

"Oh Lyd, I'm so sorry." Her dad patted her knee gently, his face a mixture of compassion and irritation. "Even if I never wanted him for you, I know you were serious about him. Breaking up is bad enough, but to have him marry so quickly is just insulting."

"Well at least someone will benefit from it. I got the name of a college student, Jackson I think, from the church office, and he seemed pretty pleased to stay in Staci's apartment." Her dad knew she was serious? How much did he really know...or guess? Nothing. It had to be nothing. He would've said something if he really knew.

A grin split her father's face. "Jackson's a great kid. He house sat for Kevin while he was out of town. Nice that he can find another place so soon."

"What? Wait..." She glanced between her mom and dad. "Kevin's back in town?"

They both nodded.

Mary pursed her lips. "I know he was going to get in touch with you. Are you sure he hasn't called?"

Lydia checked her phone. "No, he has...wait." She paused as she scrolled through her missed call list. "He called while I was on my way down here. I must've had the music up too loud." She smiled sheepishly and tucked the phone back into her purse. "Looks like he left a message, but I'll grab it later." She stretched out her arms, "If I'm going to get to hold that little darling, you'd better give her up now, Mom, cause they're going to be coming around to kick us out shortly."

Mary slid the burp cloth onto Lydia's shoulder then transferred the baby with a quick kiss.

Lydia looked down at her new niece and met the serious gaze with one of her own. "How long til she smiles? She's very stern." She glanced up at Priscilla and Dan. "Maybe she knows what's waiting for her at home."

Dan laughed. "Even the slightest inkling about her siblings would account for that stern look."

"Who's watching them? Your folks?"

Dan nodded. "Since your mom and dad could come today, they took the monsters and tomorrow your folks will switch. And Pris and I get a two day vacation where we remember what it was like to only have one."

Everyone laughed, startling the baby who started to fuss.

"Ooh, that's my cue." Lydia hurried to her sister and deposited the baby in her waiting arms. "I don't do crying. Auntie privilege." She grinned and looked at her mom and dad. "You two ready? I'm getting hungry and should probably start the trek back home as soon as we're done eating."

Disappointment flashed across Mary's face but she said nothing. Instead she aimed a querying look at Paul. "Ready dear?"

"Absolutely. It'll be nice to have a slightly more comfortable seat for the bulk of tomorrow. Hospital rooms are not designed for the visitors." He winked at Priscilla as he leaned over to kiss the baby and then his daughter. "Nice job you two." He pulled Dan into a fierce hug before offering Mary his arm. "Now, where do my girls want to eat?"

"Before I go, can I use your restroom Pris?" Lydia nodded toward the door of the private bathroom.

"Absolutely."

Lydia shut and locked the door. She did need the facilities, but as she set her purse on the counter she spied a large prescription bottle nestled in her sister's makeup kit. Just what she was hoping to see. She checked the label. Jackpot. Leave it to Priscilla to be prepared with left over pain killers. She opened the container and shook some of the pills into her hand, eyeing the level of remaining medication. Enough to get her through, but not enough to be missed. Perfect. She dropped all but two of those pills into the empty bottle in her purse. She swallowed the two she kept out, washed her hands, and checked her hair.

"Thanks." Lydia stepped back out into the room. "You never know what you're going to get at a restaurant.

At least in the hospital you know they're clean. Congratulations again, you two."

"Thanks for coming down, Lyd. Be safe on your way home, ok?"

"Always. So, Dad, where are we eating?"

As Lydia sped back toward I-95 under the thin light of a slivered moon, she dug in her purse for another pill. Dinner had been relatively uneventful, though from her mother's probing questions, Lydia wasn't doing a very good job convincing her everything was all right. Mom had made brief attempts to ferret out the truth, her questions becoming less and less subtle despite the under the table kicks her dad was giving. Fingers closing around the bottle, she thumbed off the lid and shook six pills into her hand, pausing for a moment at the sight of them in her palm. What was she doing? Getting by. She had it under control She washed them down with the melted ice in her cup and waited for blissful numbness to take away the agony of holding that new baby.

Lydia stomped on the gas and her car shot forward. She zipped closer to the bumper of a car going much too slow for the left lane. Waiting a fraction of a second, she darted into the right lane, neatly cutting off the car that was hovering nearby. If they wanted to keep her from passing them, they needed to step up their game. With a grin, she pushed her car faster and continued weaving in and out of the light traffic. She slowed slightly on the ramp to 95, and then gunned it around another slowpoke, tapping the brake and instinctively starting to swerve back into the left lane when she saw the even slower car that had been obscured from view. The driver of the car in the left lane laid on their horn and Lydia jerked the wheel back to the right while stomping the brake. The car began to wobble and skid. She should be making smaller adjustments to try and regain control. She jerked the wheel again. Burning rubber filled the air and her tired squealed on the pavement. The steering wheel seemed to take on a life of its own. She fought the spin. One side of the car began to lift and tilt. The car landed on its roof with a crunch of metal and continued to spin until it slammed into something solid and unmoving. The force of the impact sent the contents of her purse flying everywhere. Her pills! Lydia's head cracked against the steering wheel.

She roused briefly several times; her blurry vision tinted a flashing red, nose accosted by the pungent odors of automotive fluids leaking. Sirens and moans were the only audible noises. Something or someone was tugging her. Why wouldn't they stop? It hurt. A strangled whimper worked its way past her lips. When the EMTs strapped her to the back board and loaded her into an ambulance, Lydia gave in to the pain and quit fighting the blackness.

♋⁊♋

Kevin's phone vibrated. He slipped it out of his pocket to check the readout. His parents, Matt, Laura, and Jennie were all busy exclaiming over their various gifts and rehashing their favorite pictures from his trip. He glanced up and smiled at his mom who was looking at him, brows raised.

"It's Lydia. I'll take it in the kitchen, be right back."

He made his way through his parent's living room to the kitchen as he answered the call. "Hey, Lyd. It's not too late if you want to come by."

"Hello?" The voice on the other end was male, and very clearly not Lydia. "Is this a Mr. Kevin McGregor?"

Kevin glanced down at the number on his phone. He hadn't misread it. Who was this? "It is. Can I help you?"

"Sir, you're listed in the cell phone of a," papers shuffled and in the background, Kevin could hear someone being paged over an intercom, "Ms. Lydia Brown as her emergency contact."

"I am? Wait. Emergency contact…Lydia. Is she ok? What's going on?" Kevin pulled a chair out from his mother's kitchen table and sat, digging in the basket in the center of the table for a piece of paper and something to write with when the man began speaking.

"This is Sergeant Hicks with the Virginia State Police. I'm afraid there's been an accident."

The man continued on, but Kevin lost several seconds to a droning buzz between his ears. Time seemed to stop. After a moment, everything snapped back into focus and he scribbled the name of the hospital and her currently known injuries on a notepad bearing the caption "Don't worry, be hoppy!" and a picture of several Rastafarian frogs playing steel drums.

The other end of the line had gone quiet.

Kevin cleared his throat. "Can you let her know I'll be on my way as soon as I can, but it'll be about an hour before I'm there? I can call her parents on the way."

"I'll let the doctors know."

Kevin ended the call and sat for a minute staring unseeingly at his notes. He pushed away from the table and swallowed the hard lump in his throat, dragging a hand through his hair as he made his way back to the living room.

"I've gotta go."

Everyone stopped talking and looked at him questioningly.

"Lydia's been in a car accident. The State Trooper who called from the hospital wasn't too specific, but he'd been on scene and didn't seem as worried about patient confidentiality as a doctor would have been." Kevin managed a weak smile. "So I have at least a vague notion…" His eyes met his mother's concerned gaze and held it. "It sounds bad, Mom."

"Oh Honey." She was off the couch and had him in her arms, her hands rubbing his back soothingly as she had when he was a little boy and couldn't sleep. She leaned back and met his gaze then glanced at Matt and tilted her head. "You'll take him, won't you Matt?"

"Mom."

"Absolutely." Matt interrupted and shook his head at Kevin. "Don't argue. Let's go…if you say you're ok to drive, I'll let you, otherwise you'll have to trust your baby to me."

Kevin chuckled weakly and shut his eyes, pressing his forehead to his mom's. "I'm ok, but I'd appreciate the company." He brushed his mother's head with a kiss and dug into his pocket for his keys. "I'll be back for the computer and stuff later, ok?"

His mother shooed him out. "Of course. Go. Stay in touch though, please. Let us know what we can do."

Kevin nodded and turned to go, his lips twitching into strained smile as he spied his dad and Laura clasping hands, heads bowed. Jerking his head at Matt, he strode out to his car, scrolling through his contacts to find the number for Lydia's parents.

By the time Matt and Kevin were on I-95 south, Lydia's parents were on the way from their hotel in Williamsburg. It was likely that they'd make it faster than Kevin and Matt. Saying they didn't want him to feel obligated just because he was in Lydia's phone, they had tried to convince Kevin to wait and come down after church the next day. They'd given up without too much fuss when they realized that he wasn't going to be easily deterred.

"She'll be all right, Kev."

Kevin kept his eyes intent on the heavy traffic that was, at least, moving freely through the rapidly darkening night. Heavy clouds were rolling in from the west, blotting out the few stars that usually managed to shine through the ambient light of the suburbs. The first fat drops of rain splattered on the windshield as the interstate narrowed from six lanes to four and the speed limit increased to 65. Kevin accelerated, keeping his speed just at the limit, his fingers drumming with impatience on the steering wheel.

Matt craned his head to look at the speedometer and chuckled quietly. "You can do five over without any fear of getting pulled, you know that, right?"

Kevin cast a serious look at his friend. "I don't speed. You know that. Not since the accident in high school. You could've been killed—we both could've. As it was…well, I don't speed. Not even when it feels like an emergency."

"I understand…but that wasn't your fault either, man."

Kevin nodded, keeping his eyes on the road. "Maybe. But the sinking feeling in my gut is pretty much the same." His face twisted with misery. "She has to be all right."

"I know. And even better than that, God knows. I can't believe that He would've made it so clear to you that she was who He had planned for you if it was going to end this way."

"Do you…" Kevin sighed. "Do you ever wonder if I'm just hearing what I want to hear? Maybe I'm just misunderstanding?"

Matt was silent for a while before answering. "There was a time I did. But seeing how God worked to bring Laura to me," he paused again and shrugged, "when you're truly seeking God, well, I think He makes Himself known. And I don't doubt that you're truly seeking Him. I don't think I've known anyone as faithful about that as you are. And…" he shifted to stare out the windshield.

"What?"

"Well, if He releases you from this, then I think you'll know that, too."

Kevin swallowed the lump in his throat but said nothing.

Several minutes passed before Matt spoke quietly. "Sorry, Kev. It's something Laura and I have talked about from time to time, when you're hurting the most. It hurts us to see you go through everything Lydia throws at you."

"I get that." Kevin forced himself to relax his death grip on the steering wheel. "And I appreciate the place it's coming from. You're a good friend. And, well, you're not the only one who's had that thought."

Matt's eyebrows shot up but he said nothing.

They spent the rest of the drive in silence. Kevin alternated between praying for Lydia and asking for wisdom.

As they made their way through Richmond to the hospital, Matt followed their progress on his phone's GPS and spoke only to indicate when a turn was coming up. Kevin pulled up to the main entrance and took a slip from the Valet, patting his pockets for some sort of tip. The young valet waved him off, gesturing to a large sign indicating that tips were not allowed.

Nodding, Kevin stuffed the valet ticket into his pocket then joined Matt inside at the information desk.

"Ma'am, the police called because he's her emergency contact. We'd just like to be in the general vicinity, even if we can't see her right now." Matt's voice showed the effort he was expending to remain polite to the stern faced woman behind the desk.

"Sir, I'm sorry. It's immediate family only on that floor."

Kevin laid his hand on Matt's arm as he pulled out his phone. "Hello, Mary? It's Kevin. We're at the hospital, have you made it here yet?" He paused and nodded. "Matt came down with me." He paused again as Mary chattered nervously in his ear. "Seventh floor? Grey stripe. Got it. We'll be up in a few minutes; can we bring up some food or coffee?...Great. We're on our way." He ended the call and glanced at the woman behind the desk. "Thanks for your help. I really appreciate it."

She opened her mouth to protest but snapped it shut at Matt's look. Kevin jerked his head toward the hallway and the sign hanging from the ceiling that advertised both a coffee shop and elevators. "This way, I think."

Kevin and Matt wound their way through the halls, stopping at a 24-hour coffee shop to get sandwiches, chips, and large, refillable cups of coffee for the four of them. When they arrived at the waiting area, they saw Mary sitting, pale, hands twisting in her lap. Paul was standing, staring sightlessly out the window. Neither noticed them for several seconds. Then Matt cleared his throat and they looked up.

"Oh, Kevin." Mary stood.

Paul turned as she spoke and patted her shoulder, murmuring. "Rest a bit, Mary." He crossed the room and helped with some of the food, gesturing to the end tables that separated every fourth chair. "Pull some of those around, would you, Matt?"

Matt nodded and tugged the tables around to make an approximation of a booth. He glanced around the otherwise empty room. "Quiet tonight, at least."

Mary nodded absently and patted the chair next to her as she looked at Kevin. "Sit down, Honey."

When he sat, she slipped an arm through his and squeezed his hand. "I'm glad you could come, though you didn't need to."

Paul nodded his agreement.

"I had to be here. You understand." Kevin unwrapped a sandwich and stared at it before poking the soggy bread. With a sigh, he set it aside and opened a bag of chips instead. "Have you heard anything yet?"

Paul shook his head and drank deeply from the coffee Matt handed him. "They've been in once and explained what the Trooper probably told you on the phone. She has a head and neck injury. They can't determine the severity of it until she's conscious." Mary's breath caught at Paul's words. He patted her knee and leaned over to press a kiss to her hair. "A couple of broken ribs, one of which may have punctured her lung, and they're concerned about her spleen."

"And a broken leg." Mary whispered, turning to look at her husband. "Don't forget the leg."

Paul nodded and set down his coffee. "And a break in her right femur that they think will need surgery. It will probably need a plate and some screws, to mend properly."

Kevin let out a breath he hadn't realized he was holding and dipped into his chip bag. Eyeing the potato chip he tried to sound convincing. "She's going to be ok."

Paul and Mary looked at each other for a long moment, then Mary spoke. "They're saying it's likely drugs were involved."

Kevin looked at Mary blankly. "I thought it was a single car accident?"

Mary nodded slowly.

Matt's eyes widened and he looked from Mary to Kevin, watching his friend's face.

"I don't…" Kevin shook his head. "Drugs?"

Mary rested a hand lightly on his back and rubbed in small circles.

"They're not certain, but they're doing tests." Paul sighed and shook his head, his expression that of defeat. "We're thanking God no one else was injured, or worse."

Kevin gave up the pretext of eating and dropped the chips onto the table. He glanced at Matt and then at Lydia's parents. "How could we have missed drugs? I mean, I know I've been gone, but still…" He frowned.

Had she sounded high in her voicemails? Something had been off in some of them…could it be? "Oh man. Knowing it's there, I can see it."

Paul nodded slightly as Mary shut her eyes, color draining from her face. Matt simply sighed.

"Laura and I knew something was up and, well," he cleared his throat, "I actually followed her one night. When I saw what was going on, we let it drop…I never thought drugs were part of it."

Kevin looked up at his friend quizzically. "What was going on?"

Matt shook his head.

Paul fixed Matt with a firm gaze. "Could it possibly shed any light on her medical condition?"

Matt slowly shook his head. "No. But she ended up," he glanced apologetically at Kevin and Mary then stared out the door, down the sterile hospital hallway. His voice was pained and quiet as he finished the sentence, "at a swinger's bar."

Kevin stared incredulously at his friend before pushing himself to his feet. "I can't…" he glanced at Paul and Mary and shook his head, "I can't be here."

He raked a hand through his hair and stalked from the room.

Kevin strode blindly through the hospital halls, pulse pounding in his ears, stomach in knots. When the thundering of his blood slowed, he stopped and glanced at the signs on the wall. The chapel was straight ahead. He snorted. What good would that do? Just keep walking—explore the halls. Seemingly of their own volition, his feet carried him into the dimly lit space filled with simple pews. There was an abstract stained glass window at the front of the room, lit from behind, and a plain table that was probably intended to stand as an altar. But there were no other symbols or decorations to imply a denomination, or even a particular faith.

Sinking to the pew in the back corner, Kevin slid forward to his knees and rested his head on the pew in front of him. He knelt for several minutes, his mind filled instead with images of Lydia, unable to focus on a specific prayer. Why had God given him the vision of him and Lydia standing as man and wife if it was never going to happen? For so long, he'd had that security—even while Lydia and Brad had been together, there'd been peace, a reminder of God's promise. But now? His mind rebelled even as blurred images of her in bed with other men shattered his heart.

"Oh, God," he whispered, "I'm not strong enough to be Hosea."

CR><

It was more than two hours before Kevin found his way back to the waiting area where Matt and the Browns remained. They sat in silence, flipping idly through books and magazines, the crinkled wrappers of more food strewn across the end tables.

Matt looked up when Kevin came in and shot him a concerned look.

Kevin managed a tight smile that got nowhere near his eyes as he sank into a chair. "Any news?"

"Nothing new." Mary looked up and smiled sympathetically at him before glancing at Paul. She let out a quiet chuckle when she realized he'd fallen asleep reading his magazine. "He always could sleep anywhere." She slipped the magazine from his lap and draped her coat over his legs like a blanket. "You should go ahead and go home, Kevin. We'll call you as soon as we know anything."

Go home? Kevin stared at Mary for a minute then nodded. "All right. It's probably better."

Matt blinked and drew his eyebrows together.

Mary paused before offering a gentle smile. She reached for his hands. "Thank you for always being here for her, and for us." She held his gaze and waited until he nodded. "No matter what, you'll always be a member of the family to us." She leaned forward and kissed his cheek. "Now, you go home and get some rest." She glanced at Matt and her smile broadened. "And you go home and kiss that little girl of yours and tell her I can't wait until she's old enough to be in my Sunday school class."

"She asks every week about that. I think she has to wait another year though." He stood and slung an arm companionably around Kevin's shoulders. "What's the likelihood I can talk you into letting me drive? You have no idea how much I miss a real car. Laura talked me into that minivan, and I see its use, but honestly," he rolled his eyes, "it has the get up and go of a dead turtle."

Kevin dug the keys out of his pocket. "You're pathetic, man. Pathetic." Laughing, he jangled the keys before cocking his arm back, "You catch 'em, you drive. Go long."

"Dude, you're not…" Matt tore down the hallway after the keys, nearly toppling over one cart and getting the stink eye from several nurses. He nipped the keys out of the air just before they hit the floor and shook his head at Kevin as he ambled down the hallway.

"Punk."

"You're getting slow. Must be the fumes from all the hair dye."

Smugly, Matt tucked the keys in his pocket. "We can talk about slow if you ever manage to tear yourself away from your computer long enough to make our Sunday afternoon football games. Then we'll see who's slow."

They bantered the rest of the way to the car. As Kevin clicked the seatbelt of the passenger seat he looked over at Matt, expression suddenly serious. "Thanks, Matt."

Matt started the car and looked over at his friend. "At the risk of sounding like an insincere bumper sticker, it's all in God's hands and it'll work out for the best. There's no other way for it to go, because you seek His will with a dedication I've never seen in anyone else." He pressed his lips together. "Even if you are too chicken to come out and play ball with the big boys."

Kevin shook his head, a smile tugging at his lips, and turned to stare out the window as the night rushed by.

CʒʒꙨ

The morning came entirely too quickly. Kevin lay in bed staring blearily at the ceiling listening to the music of his alarm play quietly. He should get up and get a move on if he was going to make it to church. Why wouldn't his limbs work? With a sigh, he reached out an arm to silence the music, then rolled over and pulled the covers over his head.

He surfaced again around eleven. This time he threw his legs over the side of the bed and propelled himself into the shower. He stared at his reflection in the steamy mirror. He wasn't going to shave. One more day wasn't going to make a difference. "Besides," he muttered, "it's not like there's anyone to impress."

With a sigh, he pulled on jeans and a t-shirt, grabbed his phone, and headed down to the kitchen. He saw the email indicator on his phone as he fixed coffee. His parents had brought his laptop back for him, leaving it plugged in on the kitchen island. He paused to boot his laptop before opening the fridge to stare at the contents.

With an over sized coffee mug steaming in one hand and his laptop balanced on the other arm, Kevin nudged open the door to the deck and settled himself in a chair. He stared out at the backyards in his neighborhood. There were a few kids playing, but mostly it was a quiet Sunday morning. He could see silhouettes of people moving around in some of the windows, families getting home from church or just starting up after a lazy morning. He sipped his coffee and forced his attention back to his computer.

The first message he opened was from the Browns. Kevin skimmed it, frowning as the words sank in. He glanced at the clock in the corner of his screen. They probably weren't busy with lunch or anything. He grabbed his phone and dialed.

"Hello?" Mary Brown answered.

Kevin could hear the hospital sounds in the background.

"Hi Mrs. Brown." He winced, "Mary. It's Kevin. I was checking my email and saw your note. Have you heard anything more?"

"Not yet, but we're hoping that the doctor will come find us again soon. I'm just thrilled that she's conscious, at this point. Though, well…" her voice was heavy and weary, "it's likely they're going to end up pressing charges."

Kevin swallowed and leaned back in his chair. "So it's not possible there was any mistake? She's definitely using drugs."

"So it seems." Mary sighed. "I'm not sure how we missed it. Though to be honest, I don't understand how it happened in the first place." Her voice caught. "We taught her better."

"You can't blame yourself, Mrs. Brown. Lydia's an adult, whether she chooses to act like one or not…What can I do?"

"We were going to wait until church was over to call." There was a hint of reprimand to her tone. "But we wondered," she paused to clear her throat, "we wondered if you had any friends that practice this type of law. She has to take her lumps, but, well, if we can help then we'd like to try."

"I think I might know someone. I'll give her a call. Even if she can't help, she's sure to have a recommendation. You're sure you don't want to try and find someone in the congregation?"

"Paul and I know we have to notify the elders, and actually I think he's already sent out an email with the basic details and asked for a conference call this afternoon, but," she paused and Kevin could hear her struggling against tears, "we're just hoping that this won't be the end of his ministry. So we'd like to involve as few people as possible in sorting out the mess."

"I can't imagine that anyone would see this as a reflection on either you or Dr. Brown. Lydia's not a child. She isn't in your household anymore."

"Thank you, dear heart. I appreciate that, especially knowing how this is costing you, too. But you have to be realistic; there will be those who want him to resign, and others will leave the church. The fallout, no matter what way you look at it, is going to ripple through the whole of the body."

What did you say to that? She wasn't wrong. Trite reassurances weren't useful—or believable.

Mary spoke again. "God will see us through it, and, I pray, use it somehow for His glory. Though I'll admit right now I don't see how that's possible. Now," she made her tone more brisk, "I believe I see the doctor coming, so I need to go find Paul. If you'd email or text us information on an attorney, you'll be doing more than you can imagine."

"I'll get on it right away. I wish there was more I could do."

"I think we all wish that right now. I'll call you back if the doctor has anything more to tell us."

Kevin hung up and set the phone down on the arm of his chair. He stared out across the neighborhood. Would he ever have a family with Lydia? How could he now? Pulling his thoughts back from where he'd rather not dwell, he drafted an email to a college friend who had gone on to law school. They still exchanged Christmas cards and the occasional email, but as college friends often did, they had drifted apart despite both living in the Metro DC area.

That task completed, he sorted through the remainder of his email, firing off a few quick replies to coworkers who didn't have enough to do on their weekends, or who figured he was still out of town and had nothing better to do with his.

He set the laptop aside and went inside for a refill. Glancing at the clock, he poked his head in the refrigerator again, this time coming out with a couple of cheese sticks. He paused to grab the bag of chips off the top of the fridge and headed back outside. Coffee sloshed over the top of the mug as he set it down on the deck. Kevin frowned at the puddle and dropped the rest of his food on the chair before turning back inside to grab a handful of paper towels. He heard his phone start to ring as he pulled the towels off the roll under his cabinet. Narrowly avoiding kicking the coffee over completely as he grabbed at his phone, he answered it just before it would roll to voice mail.

"Hello?"

"Well, well, well. Kevin McGregor. Emailing me about a criminal defense attorney. On a Sunday no less." The low, throaty voice was full of amusement. "My how things do change."

Kevin snorted out a laugh and sat, rescuing the chips from being smashed at the last second. "I see you're still a workaholic, Allison. Checking corporate email on a Sunday morning...why aren't you in church?"

"I was, actually. But the sermon was nearly over and when I happened to see the email was from you, I begged out of the lunch plans I had with friends. So." Her voice became all business. "Please start by telling me that the 'friend' you're referring to in the email is not a euphemism for yourself."

"No. Not me. I'm currently sitting on my back deck having lunch and talking to an old friend on the phone."

"I object to the term old."

"Noted. No it's really a friend. Do you remember," he paused, cleared his throat and started again, "Did I ever mention Lydia to you?"

"Sure. Lydia Brown, pastor's daughter, light of your life, and crusher of maiden hopes the world wide. What about her?"

Kevin closed his eyes and steeled himself to say the words. "She's who I'm calling for. Or, well, for her parents. But she's in trouble. And it sounds like it could be serious."

Allison paused. "I have to ask, Kevin. And maybe it's not professional, but I have to ask, because it's going to influence whether or not I can take her case. Are the two of you together?"

"No. Never did manage to work that out. Now...I guess the best way to put it is that in the last twenty four hours, I've gone from being very sure about one thing to completely unsure about nearly everything."

"I'm sorry. I…I really can't imagine." Allison paused again and Kevin heard her typing in the background. "We can do this two ways. You can give me the details you know and contact information for her parents, or you can send my information their way and have them get in touch with me. If we do the latter, try to explain that the sooner I know everything there is to know, particularly if there is already talk of charges, and the sooner I can speak to Lydia, the better potential there is for me to be able to do something to help."

"I told Paul and Mary I'd send them contact details, so let's stick with that plan. They know more at this point than I do anyway, since they've been at the hospital talking to the doctors."

"Which hospital?"

Kevin gave her that information, as well as the room number and directions to the waiting area so she wouldn't have to deal with the visitor's desk if she decided to make the trip. "I'll text Mary with your name and number when we hang up."

"Fair enough. Tell them I'm home and waiting for their call, they don't need to wait until business hours."

"Thanks, Allison. I really appreciate this."

"Hey, it's what I do. I hope I'll be able to help. But you know I can't promise anything, right?"

"I know. But I can't think of better hands for her to be in."

"Tell them to call as soon as they can. And Kevin? You know you don't have to have a friend who needs a criminal defense attorney to call me, right? I like to eat dinner sometimes, too."

Kevin blinked. What did she mean by that?

"You don't have to say anything. I'm just putting that out there, since it seems like your ears might be a bit more receptive these days than they were in college. Anyway." Her voice was hurried, tinged with embarrassment, "I'll be waiting to hear from the Browns. Bye."

The phone clicked in his ear and Kevin sat, bewildered. Women were odd creatures. Shaking his head, he sent Mary a text with Allison's contact information and a link to her webpage so they could check out her firm and be sure that they were comfortable with that choice.

When that was done, he found himself sorting through memories of college. He'd had six really good friends throughout his time in school: Matt, Laura, Allison, Scott, Steve, and Jim. There'd been others who drifted in and out, usually as dates for one of the group, and occasionally just someone who clicked on their own for a bit, then wandered off. But there'd never been anything between him and Allison; it wasn't something that had even crossed his mind. He'd been too focused on Lydia. With a sigh he pushed that line of thinking away and focused on the pile of work email that had been getting only emergency attention while he was out of the country. If his inbox was any indicator, it was going to be a long, busy week.

Kevin scanned the tables in the restaurant then smiled at the hostess. "I don't see them yet. Can we go ahead and get on the list?"

"How many?" The petite brunette behind the podium smiled flirtatiously and glanced from Kevin back to her seating chart.

"I think they said there'd be six, altogether." He nodded absently at her and peered around one more time to be sure that he hadn't missed seeing the Browns.

The hostess' smile faded slightly when he didn't engage further. "I can seat you now, if you'd like." She made a mark on one of the tables and gestured to a server standing nearby. "Forty-seven." She looked back at Kevin. "Just follow Marie. Can I have your name for when the rest of your party comes?"

"Thanks. Sure, um, McGregor. Kevin." He laughed. "But they'll probably see me. They always do."

Kevin settled into a seat that gave him a clear view of the door and ordered a soda. He took a minute to enjoy sitting without someone asking him for advice or yelling at him about production problems. If he'd had any inkling how busy this last week was going to be on Sunday he might have tried to come down with some rare disease before Monday morning.

Before he could daydream about a deserted island, Matt and Laura came in and glanced around. He saw them point at him and laugh with the hostess for a moment before joining him at the table.

"Ah. Feels good to get off my feet." Matt sighed as he sat next to Kevin.

Laura jabbed him in the ribs as she took the seat next to his. "Seems to me you spent most of the day in the back doing paperwork. In a chair. I'm the one who had back-to-backs all day." She rolled her eyes and grinned at Kevin. "How're you? Haven't heard a peep from you all week."

"I was just starting to think that being stranded on a desert island wouldn't be such a bad way to go, after all. Then you showed up and I have to admit I'd miss you." He glanced at Matt. "And I guess since you insist on dragging him along with you everywhere you go, him too." Kevin grinned. "Busy week. Apparently I was the only one who could do anything in our division, so being out of the country for so long was a major slowdown in the productivity department."

Matt and Laura laughed together.

Laura reached over to pat Kevin's hand. "It's hard to be indispensible, isn't it?"

"Honestly, I hadn't realized that I was until this week. But it's better than the other option."

"That, my friend, is very true." Matt held up a finger. "To demonstrate the point, I was in the office doing the aforementioned paperwork when my lovely wife came in and greeted me with 'Oh, hi honey. I didn't realize you were still here.'"

Laura and Kevin chuckled.

"Well now, that's a sound I've been longing to hear." Mary Brown scooted around the table, stopping to give each of them a hug on her way to the empty chair on the other side of Kevin. She pressed her cheek to his and whispered, "I was worried when we didn't hear from you at all this week."

Kevin winced and reached up to lay his hand on her cheek. "Sorry, Mrs. B." He caught her frown and hunched his shoulders. "Sorry again. It's been a crazy week at work trying to sort out everything from my trip. I appreciate all the updates you've sent though."

"Always trying to make time with my wife." Paul Brown ruffled Kevin's hair and held the chair out for Mary then settled into the seat next to hers.

Kevin held out his hand. "Good to see you, sir."

"Sir? Oh dear." Paul held his hand to his heart. "There really are aliens and they've gone and abducted poor Kevin."

Everyone at the table joined in the laughter as the server came for drink orders, "Still expecting one more?" She indicated the last chair.

Kevin glanced curiously at Paul and Mary who both nodded. When the server had left he eyed the Browns. "All right. Who are we missing? Lydia can't possibly be up and about already."

Sorrow flashed across Mary's face before she could school her expression. "No. Sadly no. Probably not for some time." She glanced over at Paul who squeezed her hand. "In fact, well, that's part of…"

"Let's wait until we're all here, Mary." Paul gently interrupted. "I'm sorry to say it's not all going to be joyful socializing this evening." He glanced across the restaurant and caught the eye of the woman standing by the hostess scanning the tables. "Ah, here she is."

Allison strode to the table. She was still dressed for the office in a charcoal skirted suit and black blouse. Her patent leather peep-toe stilettos matched her attaché case and added a flair of femininity to the ensemble. Chocolate brown hair skimmed her shoulders in a ruler straight bob and the pink of an eraser could be seen peeking out from behind her ear. The only jewelry she wore was a simple gold cross on a chain that Kevin knew had been a gift from her parents when she went off to college.

Laura squealed and jumped up from the table. "Alli!" The women embraced and looked one another over adoringly.

"You're looking great." They said in unison, then laughed.

Paul stood and held out her chair. "Allison, good to see you again." He smiled and nodded to the table. "I believe you know everyone?"

"I do." She smiled at Matt. "You're looking good, Matt. Hair styling appears to agree with you."

Laura laughed. "It does, though he spends most of his days in the office doing paperwork. It makes him cranky."

"The trials of the small business owner. But I did manage to con Kevin into letting me whack at his hair last weekend. So you can see my genius in action."

Kevin shook his head. "Hey Al."

"Betty."

They grinned, Matt and Laura laughed. Paul and Mary looked at them quizzically.

"It's a song." When they continued to look perplexed, Allison sang a few lines. "Paul Simon? Never mind."

Kevin hung his head. "I'll never know why you continue to be willing to sing in public. I believe you have previously undiscovered sadistic tendencies."

"Hey!" Allison grabbed a sugar packet and threw it at Kevin.

He dodged the missile, chuckling.

"None of my attempts to teach you to throw ever caught on, I see." Matt added.

Allison narrowed her eyes at both of them as pink stole across her cheeks. "My apologies. It's obviously been too long since I've seen these two. If I'd known they hadn't matured at all since college I would have come prepared."

The Browns chuckled. Paul started to speak but the server came over to get a drink order for Allison.

"I think we're probably all ready to order?" Paul shot a querying glance at Allison.

"Sure, start there," she pointed at Paul, "and go around that way," she circled the long way around the table, "and I'll be ready when you get to me."

When the food orders were taken and the menus collected, Mary glanced at Paul and nudged him with her elbow.

Paul cleared his throat. "So. I was starting to say when Allison arrived that this wasn't purely social." He reached up and rubbed his neck with one hand. "You all know about Lydia's accident, obviously. And I'm assuming you all know about the other, the..." he trailed off for a moment and Mary patted his arm gently. Finally he continued, "The drugs." He cleared his throat again. "Apparently they have reason to believe that this is a long standing pattern of abuse. Four to six months, is their guess based on her tolerance of the pain meds they're using for her injuries. They're pressing charges."

Paul's voice broke and he swallowed convulsively.

Allison looked at him sympathetically. "Mr. Brown, would you like me to explain?"

Paul nodded.

Allison reached under the table for her attaché and pulled out a sheaf of papers. After glancing at each person around the table and meeting their eyes, she looked directly at Kevin as she spoke. "Ultimately it comes down to a DUI charge. As it's her first offense, even with the suspected long term abuse, we have some wiggle room. I sincerely do not believe she'll end up going to jail. If they press for the mandatory five days, given her current physical condition, I believe we can make a case for that to be served in the hospital." She shuffled a few papers then returned her gaze to Kevin. "What will be the best legal argument and, in my opinion it's also best for Lydia, is to have her voluntarily submit to rehab. If we go to the prosecutor with that and time served in the hospital, I believe she'll be able to avoid a formal trial. No one else was injured in the wreck, so the court can afford to appear lenient to someone who is willing to make a commitment to sobriety."

"Will she?" Kevin's voice was subdued as he looked at Mary and Paul.

Mary sighed. "Right now she's still denying everything and is angry and feeling persecuted."

Paul took a minute to bless the meal that the server delivered.

Mary continued. "She's so angry about everything right now; it's hard to get her to see past it. But she's going to need to, soon."

Allison nodded. "The sooner we can get the ball rolling the better it will be for everyone. Honestly, it'll be best if I can go talk to the prosecutor before much longer so that they don't spend lots of time putting together a case. The less investment they have in it, the easier it's going to be for them to take our very reasonable suggestion." She paused to take a sip of water. "And it is reasonable. I've made essentially this same deal for several other first time offenses."

Laura looked at Allison. "What can we do?"

"I can't really say I know her all that well yet. We met in college a few times, and then recently in a professional setting though that was…" Allison hesitated. "Let's go with uncomfortable. Regardless, it seems to me that the one most able to convince her to play ball is going to be Kevin." She shot him an apologetic smile.

Kevin fiddled with his silverware for several seconds, trying to get the knife to align perfectly with the spoon and edge of his plate. "I just don't…" He frowned and picked up the knife, running it through his fingers before setting it down and folding his hands in his lap. "I can try."

Mary reached over and laid her hand on his arm. "We appreciate it, Kevin. And we know how hard it is for you."

He met her eyes and saw the understanding and concern in them.

"I can't promise anything."

"No one expects you to, Kev." Matt spoke up. "Lydia's a big girl and needs to make her own choices. Which she's been doing. Now they've caught up with her and we're all trying to help. But ultimately?" He nudged Kevin with his elbow. "This is all on her and has been from the start. If she'll let us help her through the consequences then great. But if not, that's her choice too."

"Matt." Laura whispered.

"No, Laura. I know what you mean and maybe it's harsh. But if you can't see that Kevin is starting to blame himself for this whole thing, then you're not looking." He fixed Kevin in his gaze. "Or am I wrong?"

"I might have entertained the thought that I pushed her to this once or twice."

Everyone around the table erupted in a flurry of denials.

Allison pitched her voice over them. "Ok, hold on. Hold on." Gradually everyone settled down and she continued, "First," she ticked up a finger, "basic counseling for the loved ones of an addict might not be a bad idea for you and for anyone else involved with Lydia. Because Matt's right, these are her choices, and ultimately no one is responsible for them but her. That said," she ticked up a second finger, "if it's too much for you to go and talk her into this, there are other options."

"No...no, I can try." He glanced at Allison. "And I also understand that it's not my fault," he looked at Paul and Mary, "or either of yours. Still, sometimes it's hard to remember that." Blowing air out of his cheeks he looked down at his mostly untouched dinner. "I'll go down tomorrow and see what I can do."

Allison nodded and pulled out her Blackberry to make a note. "If you'd give me a call when you're finished and let me know how it went, I'd appreciate it."

"Will do."

"Do you want us to go with you?" Laura pursed her lips in concern.

Kevin shook his head.

Mary patted his arm again. "Will you call us after you've gotten in touch with Allison?"

"Of course." Kevin smiled at Mary. "We'll get her through this somehow."

Allison flipped through a few more pages in her file and glanced at her Blackberry before slipping them all back into her briefcase. "That's really all I've got. Until Lydia's on board with some sort of plan…" she shrugged, "there's not much more I can do."

"We understand. Thank you, Allison." Paul smiled across the table.

"Well then." Matt cleared his throat and Laura elbowed him fiercely, her head shaking frantically. He looked at her and whispered, "What?"

"Do you really think it's appropriate?" Laura whispered fiercely back at him.

Matt grinned, nodding, and cleared his throat again. "As I was saying, before I was so grievously wounded by my wife's stray elbow."

Laura made a face and started to elbow him again.

He caught her arm and tucked it into his own. "To end the evening on a slightly happier note, we'd like you all to be the fourth or fifth to know that Jennie won't be an only child for too much longer."

He turned and beamed at Laura before dropping a kiss on her forehead.

"Now that's fantastic news indeed." Mary clapped her hands in joy. "Oh, congratulations."

The rest joined in, letting the conversation slide into more cheerful waters while they finished their meals.

α

In the parking lot, Allison hung back as Kevin bade Matt and Laura farewell and promised to call them or stop by after his visit with Lydia. He was unlocking his car when she tapped him on the shoulder.

"Kev?"

He turned and smiled wearily. "Hey. Thought you left already."

"I wanted one more quick word, after everyone else was gone." She twitched her fingers over his arm, pulling back and adjusting her purse strap on her shoulder instead of touching him. "The counseling I mentioned really isn't a bad idea. I know you've always been in love with her." A flash of pain shot through her eyes before she was able to replace it with friendly concern. "There's no shame in talking to someone about it."

"You sound like my mom." He sighed. "I've got an appointment next week. The thing is," he stared up at the stars as they peeked through the wisps of clouds overhead, "if it was anyone but Lydia, I'd want to talk to Paul. But that doesn't seem like a fair choice for either of us right now. And that makes it worse. Because I blame her for that, too. But thanks."

"Maybe it's not fair to tell you this, but you should know there's a selfish motivation behind me helping her and wanting to see you back to normal."

Kevin looked confused.

"So blind. Did it never occur to you that someone might feel about you the way you feel about her? I didn't realize I was such a good actress." This time she did lay her fingers on his arm. "For right now though, let that go and just do what needs to be done to get her the help she needs."

She smiled wistfully at him before walking off, leaving him standing there, mouth agape.

After a minute, Kevin got into the car and put the key in the ignition. Still stunned, he leaned his forehead against the steering wheel and tried to organize his chaotic thoughts into a prayer.

Peeking around the doorframe, Kevin tapped on Lydia's hospital door. "Knock knock?"

Lydia looked away from the cooking show on the muted TV and managed a weak smile. "Come on in."

Kevin pushed himself into the room and looked around for a place to sit. After a slight hesitation, he snagged the doctor's stool and rolled it up to the bedside before fiddling with the height adjustment. When he was settled, he forced a smile and looked at Lydia. Her hair was dull and stringy. The only color in her face and neck were the yellowing bruises from the accident. Her cheeks looked sunken and if it weren't for the tremors that shook through her body, she could pass for lifeless.

"You've looked better."

"I can always count on you to boost my ego." Her eyes raked over his face. "Though I could say the same about you today. Did you have to check the bags under your eyes or did you somehow manage to carry them on?"

"I've had a rough night or two this past week. Not everyone gets to laze away in a five star resort you know." He gestured to the sparse private room in the rehab side of the hospital with a view of the adjacent building.

"I always knew I was destined for the glamorous life." Lydia reached to brush an errant hair out of her eyes. The handcuff keeping her in bed rattled on the side rail.

Kevin watched it slide up and back and raised his eyebrows. "New jewelry too, I see?"

Lydia shook the cuff with scorn. "Just in case I decided to get up and walk out of here, I guess. As if I could." She indicated the cast on one leg and the tubes hooking her up to various IVs.

"Any idea when you'll be well enough to go home?"

"My home? Not for a while. Maybe to Mom and Dad's in another couple weeks." Under her breath she added. "If they'll have me."

Tentatively, Kevin squeezed her hand. "You know they will."

"No, I don't. From what I gather, they're trying to pack me off to some *rehab* place in the Smoky Mountains." Her voice dripped with scorn. "All because of a little car accident that had nothing to do with anything else."

"Little car accident?" Kevin stood and paced over to the window, trying and failing to keep his voice calm. "Do you have any idea how much worry you've caused? How scared people have been?" He glanced over his shoulder and shook his head then returned to staring out the window. "No, of course you don't. Because you're Lydia and the world revolves around you." He stalked back to the bed and lowered his face toward hers until they were nearly nose to nose. "Well I'm here to tell you, it really doesn't, Lydia. And here are the facts. You're headed to jail and you stand to lose your license. I don't suspect that you'll keep your job with a DUI on your record, especially when it's for illegal prescription drugs and not alcohol. Your father could have lost his job because of you, if the elders at the church hadn't understood that at some point, grown children are responsible for their own actions, regardless of how well they were raised. Your mother's heart is broken and she blames herself, wondering what she did that could possibly have caused this."

Trembling, he paused to take a breath. "So for once in your tiny little life, move outside of what makes you feel happy and important and do what's right. Call your attorney. You know, the one your parents who love you hired for you, and agree to whatever it is she recommends. Because if you don't, you're simply solidifying your place as the world's most self-absorbed, spoiled princess." He leaned back and shot her a look of disgust. "You know, they wanted me to come and try to talk you into the plan but I find I really don't care anymore. Do what you want, Lydia, it's all you know how to do anyway."

He strode out of the room without looking back.

CR&O

Kevin sat on his deck with his feet propped up on the railing, looking unseeingly up at the sky. The phone was in his lap, but he hadn't been able to make himself call the Browns or Allison to tell them about his disastrous meeting with Lydia. He'd spent the whole drive home fuming at her attitude, focusing on the soul crushing hurt she'd caused him. It was only in the past several minutes that he recognized that he hadn't handled things as well as he might have. He rubbed his temples and sighed. "Always best to kick someone when they're down, Kev. Smooth." He shook his head and looked at the phone, starting guiltily when it rang.

"Hello?"

"Dude. Don't you answer your doorbell anymore?"

"Matt?" Kevin stood and strode through the house to the front door, hanging up the phone as he pulled the door open for his friend. "What are you doing here?"

Matt grinned and dropped his phone into his pocket. "Checking up on you, clearly."

He shouldered his way inside and headed for the kitchen.

Kevin followed and shook his head when he saw his friend half-buried in his refrigerator, muttering. "Make yourself at home."

Matt pulled his head out of the fridge and arched a brow. "Hmm. All signs point to pissy." He grabbed a soda off the top shelf and shut the door. "I take it that means your talk with Lydia did not go well."

"What kind of word is pissy? Girls get pissy. I object to the term pissy just because I might want someone to ask before helping themselves to my last soda."

Matt popped the top and took a long swallow. "Ahh. Refreshing, too. Goes down smoother knowing it's the last one." He grinned and wagged a finger. "I'm adding argumentative to my list. And I'm also noting that while you object to the term pissy, you didn't comment on the other, leaving me to surmise that I am, in fact, correct."

Kevin grabbed a napkin off the counter and wadded it up, throwing it at Matt before stalking back out onto the deck. Dodging the missile, Matt let it stay where it landed on the kitchen floor and followed him out onto the deck.

"So. Wanna talk about it?" Matt plopped into the other deck chair and leaned back, letting his gaze wander over the houses and up to the sky that was rapidly filling with ominous clouds.

"If I say no will you go away?"

"No. I'll just find other ways to fill the silence."

Kevin muttered something unintelligible and turned to scowl at his friend.

"Sorry? Didn't catch that." Matt simply grinned and finished off the soda.

"You're a dork, you realize that I hope?"

"Hey, when you've got it, you've got it. Now, what happened?"

With a sigh, Kevin related the incident at the hospital. When he finished, he raked his hands through his hair and leaned forward to prop his chin on his knees dejectedly. "As you see, I'm not sure that it's possible to have done a worse job. And what's even worse than that? I'm not really sure I care. And that's what I feel guilty about. For so long I knew," he met Matt's gaze, "really knew in my mind and heart, that she was it. She was who God has for me. And now?" He shook his head and shrugged. "I'm starting to question if I even understand how to hear Him at all. How was I so wrong?"

"Maybe you weren't. Aren't. Weren't. Whatever." Matt rolled his eyes. "What I'm saying is that maybe she still is."

Kevin shook his head.

"Seriously, Kevin. Life's not without bumps. So maybe yes, Lydia is the woman God has for you. And maybe part of that is the two of you overcoming this bump and ending up on the other side, better people. I mean, look at me and Laura. We didn't have a perfect courtship." He scoffed. "It's not every guy who has to figure out a way to convince his future in-laws that he's not playing for the other team and trying to use their daughter as a nod to respectability."

"But that was just them being stubborn and playing into stereotypes. Plus that was them, not Laura."

"Sure, but she'd been engaged before. And I guess I owe Lydia a little thanks. She sorted that engagement out so that Laura saw his true colors before she walked down the aisle. But there was history there, man. And it took some getting over. But when it's the right person, the person God has for you, then the forgiveness comes."

"I hear what you're saying, I do. But…right now? I can't see it."

"That's fair. But promise me you won't write her off completely unless God gives you the go ahead."

"Wasn't it you not long ago saying exactly the opposite to me?"

"I'm just saying you need to be sure that any decision you make is because it's what God's telling you. Admittedly, it's going to be a hard road if you stay the course. But that's not the right reason to turn away from her."

Kevin nodded and snapped his mouth shut on a response. After several minutes, rain began to splatter on the deck. Glancing up at the sky he stood and jerked his head toward the door. "Come on, let's go find something to eat and then you can help me make some phone calls."

Lydia glanced over disinterestedly when another knock sounded on the door frame.

"Hey there, just stopping by to make sure you're doing ok." The perky volunteer whose nametag proclaimed "Hi, I'm Becky" smiled and waited expectantly for an answer.

"Sure. Great. No problem." Lydia took a deep breath to calm the clutch of nausea that was her constant companion, and turned to look out the window.

"Can I get you anything?"

"No, really. I'm all right." Lydia swiped at the sweat beading on her forehead. "Though you could put the remote back where I can reach it if you don't mind." She nodded to where it rested near her feet.

"Sure thing." Becky took the remote and laid it on the rolling table within easy reach of Lydia's handcuffed arm. She considered the cuffs a minute then looked at Lydia, chewing on her lower lip.

Lydia followed her gaze with a sour smile. "DUI. Drugs. No one but me was hurt, but I guess I'm the example du jour."

"Oh. I knew that. Hospitals are like small towns if you're here every day. I," she frowned and shook her head, "Never mind. Sorry to intrude."

She spun and headed quickly for the door.

"What?"

Becky turned and managed an apologetic half-smile. "I've been where you are. So…if you ever wanted someone to talk to." She saw Lydia's expression darken. "Like I said, never mind."

Becky slipped from the room and Lydia listened to her shoes clop down the hallway.

Lydia almost called out for her to stay but bit off the words at the last minute. *She couldn't possibly understand.* She flipped the TV channel, willing her mind off the cramps that wracked her abdomen and muscles.

Gritting her teeth, she lowered her head to her pillow. A headache had plagued her unmercifully since they took her pain pump three days ago. She winced as the pain kicked into high gear. With unsteady fingers she clutched the remote and struggled against the shaking. She bit her lip, drawing blood, and fought to keep from crying out.

Mary Brown set the phone back in its cradle and padded into the den where Paul was sitting on the couch, sock feet up on the coffee table, flipping channels idly. He glanced up and smiled when she entered and patted the space next to him. She settled in and rested her head on his shoulder.

"That was Kevin."

"I gathered." He clicked the mute button before setting the remote aside. "I also gathered that his talk with Lydia didn't go well."

"No. And I can't really say I'm surprised, but I thought he'd have the best chance of any of us at getting through to her. I mean, they're friends and have been for forever. I've always clung to the hope that she'd finally see him, really see him, and stop chasing the bad boys. Do you think I pushed her to this?"

Paul shook his head and turned so he could see her face. "No. We're not responsible for her, Mary. As much as I want to think that somehow we could have done something differently to keep this from happening, it's not true. We did our best. We raised her to know better. She went off course somewhere along the line and now we need to be there to help get her back."

Mary wiped at a tear that trickled down her cheek. "I know you're right. I just don't understand any of this."

"Neither do I, Honey. All we can do is pray and hope that we hear the direction He wants us to take and then follow through."

"It just feels like so little when my baby girl needs so much."

Paul grabbed her hand and squeezed. "I know, Baby." He kissed the top of her head and rested his cheek on her hair, silently begging God to show him what to do.

CRBWD

Lydia lay in the hospital bed flipping channels and trying to avoid watching the clock. The middle of the night was the worst time in her hospital room. She couldn't sleep, but there was very little noise on the floor to keep her distracted, and there were really only so many infomercials a person could watch. This left room for her brain to kick into overdrive, and without the fuzz of a high, she had no choice but to watch her idiotic mistakes dance in slow motion through her memory as she spiraled deeper into guilt. Worse, Kevin might have had a point. The guilt made it hard to get angry again, and without the anger to sustain her, she felt herself sliding into despair. Prison. She didn't want to go to prison. Or rehab for that matter—but maybe it was the better option. Isn't that where losers like her belonged? Her thoughts, coupled with the constant waves of nausea and pain as her system purged itself of drugs, stretched the nights into interminable hours of torment.

Shoes squeaked quietly in the hallway, not slowing as they passed her door. Lydia caught a flash of the outfit and chewed on her lip before calling out hesitantly. "Becky?"

The squeaking stopped and Becky poked her head through the doorway. "Need something?"

Lydia shook her head and Becky turned to go. "No. Wait." She sighed, looking defeated and lost. "Were you on your way somewhere?"

"Nope."

"Could you...could you come in and talk to me for a little?"

"Sure." Becky slipped in and pulled the visitor's chair closer to the edge of the bed.

Lydia turned off the TV and sat silently for a minute. "What did you mean that you'd been where I am?"

"Just what it sounds like, actually." She offered a grim smile. "I was handcuffed to a hospital bed facing DUI charges about three years ago. Except," she swallowed and closed her eyes, "I wasn't quite a lucky as you."

"Lucky?"

"I wasn't the only one injured in my accident." She paused and wet her lips. "My daughter, Sarah, she was seven and the light of my life. She was all I had after John, my husband, her father, was killed in a convenience store robbery. He was a cop. Losing him, well, I didn't cope so well. And Sarah, she paid the highest price. Even before the accident." Becky stopped and looked at Lydia.

"It started easily enough with sleeping pills to help with the insomnia. No one could fault me for having trouble sleeping after a tragedy. But it just seemed to escalate, and nothing eased the sucking hole that I felt right here." She tapped her chest. "I blew through the life insurance and had to turn to, well, creative means of paying for what I needed. I'd been so proud of the fact that John and I were virgins when we married and then? None of it seemed to matter, I just needed to find the haze that made the pain ebb for a few hours." Becky looked down at her hands. "I wish I could at least say that I'd always found someone to take care of Sarah so she didn't know what was happening."

"What happened to her?"

"She died. Not instantly, though I didn't know that until after I came out of a coma. She lingered for about two weeks while I was out for almost six. From what I've been able to research, the injuries she had would have made every breath a misery." Tears slipped down her cheeks. "When I realized, really realized, what I'd done, I tried to end it." She flipped over her arms to reveal long, jagged scars up both arms. "But I couldn't even manage to do that right." With a wry smile she shrugged. "I didn't have a choice about getting help at that point and I fought it every day for weeks until I finally realized that it wasn't going to get better unless I really wanted it to."

"I'm sorry."

"Don't be. It's why I come here. I want to be able to tell people that it can get better. And usually it's more believable when it comes from someone who isn't looking down from atop a medical degree, silently clucking their tongue that you got to this point in the first place."

"I'm glad someone else has noticed that."

"Well, I think they try to hide it. But really, they don't understand how people end up here most of the time. At least not the ones that they think were predisposed to succeed in life. Still, there are more of us than you'd think. Most are just managing to keep their nose above water and not end up here. So," she eyed Lydia, "want to tell me what happened?"

Lydia focused on the darkened TV for several minutes, clenching her teeth against a flare of pain from her leg. Closing her eyes she began in a strained whisper. "I had everything. I think, maybe, that was part of the problem. But I'm not sure I even realized how much I had. All I felt was the pressure to be as good as my sisters. To meet the expectations of the church as to what a pastor's daughter should be. To succeed and set myself apart and prove myself somehow. So when Brad caught my eye, I figured I deserved him, and that he'd be the perfect man to help me finally be enough. Turns out he was just as interested in me, and, well, we looked good together. Barbie and Ken, you know?" She shook her head. It sounded so stupid when she said it out loud. Was she really that vain? That vapid?

"We met at church, so for the longest time things were exactly what you'd expect a pastor's daughter and her boyfriend to be like. I loved him. He said he loved me. We got engaged...though he made me promise that I wouldn't tell anyone until he could afford a ring. But since we were engaged, I figured there was no harm in sleeping together because we were going to get married. It's not like I was sleeping around."

Hesitantly, Lydia looked up. Seeing the compassion in Becky's eyes, she took a deep breath and kept going. "Brad was an expert at excuses for not getting me a ring: new tires for his car, loaning money to his brother, emergency travel to see a friend from college going through a rough time. They all seemed reasonable. And then I found out he was cheating on me. It finally clicked that the engagement was simply a farce designed to convince me that sex was ok. And I had fallen for it."

Becky reached over and patted her leg gently. "You're not the first girl to do that, and unfortunately, you won't be the last."

Lydia nodded and leaned forward so she could swipe at her cheek. "Anyway, I ended it and thought, hoped, that I could just get on with my life. Until I realized I was pregnant." She closed her eyes and rested her head back against the pillow. "All I could think about was how angry my parents were going to be. How I'd managed, yet again, to not measure up. And how disappointed Kevin, my best friend, was going to be. I knew I'd let them down when I started sleeping with Brad, but it wasn't in their face and, well, I'd thought when we were married it wouldn't matter. But you can't hide a pregnancy, especially when you're not even with the man who did it to you anymore. So before I could change my mind, before I could really even think about it—certainly before talking about it with anyone, I had an abortion."

She swallowed the lump in her throat and looked around for her water. After taking a long drink she continued. "They make it sound like it's a simple, easy thing. But it's not." Her voice cracked. "It's just not. I couldn't vacuum anymore—the sound was just too much like the procedure...and the thought of the suction." She closed her eyes, shuddering. "I couldn't hear a baby or see a pregnant woman. And they are everywhere. I knew what I'd done, but rather than face it, I started looking for ways to numb the pain. The drugs were easy. Selling myself for them, well, it got easier each time. After all, I was already damaged and unredeemable; at least I didn't have to feel it when I was drunk and high." Tears coursed down her cheeks. "Now I've let down my whole family. And Kevin? He's written me off for good and I never even gave him a chance. He was supposed to be my fallback plan."

Becky tilted her head and fixed her eyes on Lydia. "So what are you going to do about it?"

"They think they can keep me out of jail if I volunteer for rehab. It's what everyone thinks I should do, and in my heart I know they're right, but it doesn't feel like enough. In so many ways...I guess I think I deserve to go to jail. To pay, somehow."

"You've already punished yourself enough, Lydia. And as a pastor's daughter you know that punishment isn't required, only repentance."

"How can anyone possibly forgive me? I took the life of an innocent child."

"So did I and I promise you, it's nothing you'll ever forget or stop regretting. But you can move through it, you can be forgiven and set free."

"You really think so?"

"I know so. I'm living proof. Did they say where they want you to go to rehab?"

Lydia pushed the papers on her nightstand around until she found the flyer Kevin had brought and offered it to Becky.

"Go. The folks here," she tapped a picture of a cabin in an idyllic mountain setting, "they've been where you are too. They even have special group sessions beyond the addiction counseling. Even one specifically for after abortion counseling."

Lydia raised her eyebrows. "You realize how hokey that sounds, right?"

"Yeah, I do. But I'm telling you, I saw the results with some of the women who were there when I was. It's incredible. And if that's what's at the root of your pain, and it sounds like it is, well, it'll be good for you too."

"I'll think about it."

"Do that. Pray about it, too."

Lydia watched Becky leave and stared at the flyer for the rehab center. "Pray about it...I don't know if I remember how."

Kevin woke to his phone ringing. He rolled over and glanced at the caller ID. Clearing his throat he answered. "Hello?"

Allison was alert and cheerful on the other end of the line. "Good morning. I'm surprised I caught you at home. I'd planned to leave a message."

"What time is it?" Kevin pushed himself to a sitting position and looked over at his clock.

"Just after nine. Tell me I didn't wake you up."

"Ok, you didn't wake me up." He rubbed his eyes. His blinds were completely closed, keeping the morning sun from getting in and waking him. He was going to kill Matt. Or maybe thank him. "So, what's up?"

"I got a call from Lydia this morning. She's agreed to go along with the plan. I'm not sure what you said to her, but it certainly seems to have done the trick. So, thanks."

"It wasn't me. When I left she was furious and I figured she'd do anything other than what you recommended, simply to spite me."

"Hmm. Well, something or someone changed her mind." Allison shuffled some papers in the background. "She's even agreed to give us the name and number of her dealer, though it seems he's been rather insistently calling her phone, so I think the police were already on to him. Still, every little bit of cooperation helps. I'll try to get the deal on the table as soon as possible. The faster we can get things rolling, the more likely we are to get a positive result. I've already talked to Mr. and Mrs. Brown, and they said I could let you know."

"Thanks. It's good news for Lydia, certainly." He paused and took a deep breath. "About the other thing you mentioned."

"Please don't, Kevin. I should have kept my mouth shut and I really don't want things to be awkward between us."

"No, I don't want you to think that. I actually, well, I was going to see if you wanted to maybe have dinner Friday?" With Lydia out of the picture, it was time to try and move on.

"Are you sure?"

"Yeah. Yeah, I am. Seven o'clock?"

"That should work. I'll let you know if something changes. Do you want to meet somewhere?"

"Sure. Why don't you choose a place near your office and let me know the address. That way I know you'll actually make it on time. I've heard stories about the hours lawyers work."

Allison laughed. "All right, I'll send you an email later today. Bye."

"Bye." Kevin clicked the off button and stared at the phone for several seconds. With a bewildered sigh he pushed himself out of bed toward the shower and a late start to his day.

❧

The week passed in a blur of meetings and phone calls. Between work projects, possible new assignments, and trying to stay on top of Lydia's situation, Kevin scarcely had time to think. He kind of liked it that way. Less thinking cut down significantly on the confusion he was feeling about going out with Allison on Friday.

"It's not like you haven't dated before." Kevin looked at himself in the mirror. Did he need a tie? Frustrated, he dropped the tie on his bathroom sink and sighed. "Why does it feel like I'm being unfaithful?"

He glanced once more at his reflection. The pale pink dress shirt, open at the collar, and black slacks would have to do. He couldn't bring himself to fuss with a tie. He was nearly out the door when the phone rang.

"Hello?"

"Hey Kev, it's Matt."

"Hey. What's up?"

"Just seeing what you're up to tonight. We were wondering if you wanted to grab dinner, maybe a movie? We've actually managed to score a sitter tonight, so we could even eat somewhere that doesn't serve macaroni and cheese."

Kevin grinned at his friend's enthusiasm. "Sorry, but I'll have to take a rain check. I was actually on my way out the door."

"Oh?"

"Yeah. Um. Dinner with Allison."

"Oh really? Interesting…You sure about this?"

Kevin closed his eyes and rested his head against the door jamb. "No. Not really. But I've got to do something to start moving on."

"So you're giving up?"

"No. I'm…I don't know what I am. I'm hurt and I'm reeling and I feel like I'm being unfaithful to Lydia, which is a laugh given the current situation. Still, what do I have to lose? I'm having dinner with a friend who has, apparently, had a crush on me for years. Seems like if I don't do this, I'll always wonder if I should have."

"That's a lot of feeling, dude. Have you been watching daytime TV while you're working again?"

Kevin snorted out a laugh. "You're such an idiot."

"That wasn't a no." Matt was laughing on the other end of the line.

"I'm hanging up now." Kevin pulled the phone away from his ear then quickly added. "Hey, Matt?"

"Yeah?"

"Thanks, man."

"Let me know how it goes."

The drive into D.C. was as uneventful as possible for a Friday night in early summer. Though he'd been trying to sort through his thoughts the whole way, Kevin was no closer to any conclusions. He slipped his car into a spot in a garage a block from the restaurant and glanced at his watch. He wouldn't be too late. With any luck, Allison was running late as well and he'd still manage to beat her there.

Turning the corner, Kevin spotted Allison hurrying toward the restaurant door and called out.

"Allison." He waved to catch her eye.

Allison laughed and slowed. "Oh thank goodness. I was so worried I was going to be late and never hear the end of it."

"Well," Kevin glanced at his watch, "technically you are late. But I promise not to say anything if you won't."

Allison stuck out her hand. "Deal."

"Deal." Kevin shook her hand once and reached for the door. "After you."

She smiled at him over her shoulder and went in, holding up two fingers for the hostess at the podium.

The hostess greeted them and led the way to a small table in a back corner of the busy restaurant. She gave them menus, named their server and disappeared back toward the front of the room without a backward glance.

"So." Kevin glanced down at the menu then snapped it shut. "How was your week?"

"To use one word: crazy. I had to call in a few favors to keep the DA from using Lydia as an example to the world. Apparently someone in the office has an axe to grind with Christians and was in heaven at the thought of a pastor's daughter taking a big fall. I finally managed to convince them that there were bigger fish to fry out there and that really they'd be doing more harm than good if they kept up their crusade. Of course, you can't do it all in short, civilized phone calls, you have to write it all up using twelve words when one would've sufficed. And that's just the one client, and she's nowhere near my most interesting case right now."

She turned to the server who appeared at the table.

After ordering sodas and an appetizer, Allison leaned toward Kevin. "What about you? Slay any really interesting code whatevers this week?"

Kevin raised an eyebrow. "Code whatevers? You're really up on your technical jargon these days, Allison. Sadly, no. No slaying this week of any variety. Though I do have a few clients who make that a very tempting prospect." He glanced down at the menu and flipped the page before shaking his head and snapping it shut again. "What's good here?"

Allison made a few recommendations and kept up her side of the conversation with anecdotes from work. Kevin tried to keep pace but his attention kept slipping back to Lydia. After the server cleared their plates and left a dessert menu for them to consider, Allison watched Kevin over the top of her glass for a minute.

"This isn't going to happen, is it?"

"What do you mean?"

"This." She gestured between them. "Us. I appreciate you trying, I do. But I can see you're not really here for me. With me."

Kevin blew out a breath. "I'm not even sure I was trying all that well, I'm sorry. I think I was trying to prove to myself that I could move on with life. But, well…Maybe I need to give myself some more time."

Allison slowly shook her head. "I don't think time is going to fix anything, Kevin. You've been waiting for her since you were kids. I don't think that's going to change." She reached across the table and rested her hand on his. "I hope she realizes what she has soon."

"Thanks. I wish you were wrong."

"Me too." She glanced at the check that Kevin had finished paying and stood. "Thanks for dinner, anyway."

Kevin stood and walked with her to the door. Outside, she stretched up and pressed her lips to his cheek. "I'll do what I can for her, for both of you."

He watched her turn and stride purposefully down the sidewalk. Shoulders slumped he tucked his hands in his pockets and wandered back toward his car.

ॐ

Kevin turned off the ignition to his car and looked at Matt's house. There were still lights on downstairs and their car was in the driveway. Glancing at the dashboard clock he frowned. It was probably too late to stop by. Still, he found himself easing out of the car and heading up the steps to knock lightly at the door.

He saw Laura peek through the sidelight window and sheepishly raised a hand. She grinned and flipped the deadbolt, pulling open the door.

"Kevin." She grabbed him into a hug and tugged him into the house. "What a nice surprise." She glanced at his outfit and waggled her eyebrows. "My my, don't we look handsome?"

Kevin smiled as a weight lifted from his shoulders. "For all the good it does me since my one true love went and married my best friend." He winked. "When are we going to bump him off and run away together?"

"I heard that." Matt poked his head through the kitchen door. "And I was getting out a third dish for ice cream."

Laura laughed and took Kevin's hand. "Come on into the kitchen. We find that's the easiest place to be when Jennie's sleeping. Much less chance of waking her. Plus it's closer to the ice cream."

"I never could turn down ice cream."

Matt placed a bowl in front of Laura, then Kevin and snagged the container and a spoon for himself. "So. How was the date?"

"Miserable." He recounted the stilted conversation and Allison's grasp of the situation at the end of the meal. "And the worst part of it all is that she's right." He ran a hand through his hair. "I can't escape the idea that Lydia's it. Even though right now? I want nothing to do with her."

Laura squeezed his shoulder sympathetically, raising her eyebrows at Matt.

"Why don't you hang here tonight? Then you can see Jennie tomorrow morning and maybe we can talk Laura into pancakes."

"I think I'd like that. Thanks."

"Oof." Kevin grunted as his eyes popped open to see Jennie bouncing on his stomach.

"Uncle Kevin!" She bounced and grinned then crawled up to rest her face on his. "Pancakes!"

Kevin laughed and reached around to tickle her ribs. "Where? Are these pancakes? Yum."

Jennie giggled and squirmed down to the floor. "No. Pancakes in the kitchen." She toddled in that direction chanting "Pancakes!"

Kevin smiled and shook his head as he swung his legs to the floor. He stretched and letting out a jaw cracking yawn. A good night's sleep provided a lot of perspective. Maybe things weren't so bleak after all. He sniffed. There were indeed pancakes in the kitchen. He tugged on his pants and slipped his arms into his shirt, leaving it unbuttoned over his undershirt. He took the time to fold the sheets and blankets and tuck the pull-out sofa back into couch mode before shuffling barefoot into the kitchen.

Matt looked up from the stove. "I see the siren song of Jennie led you to the food?"

Kevin looked at the frilly 1950's housewife-style apron his friend wore over sweatpants and a sleeveless t-shirt and held up a finger. He darted back to the living room and grabbed his phone. Returning, he snapped a photo of Matt flipping a pancake expertly in the air. "Morning, dear."

Matt laughed and grabbed for the phone, nearly dislodging the bowl of pancake batter from its precarious position on the counter. "Gimme."

"Nope. This is going online first chance I get." Kevin laughed and slid the phone into his pocket. "Hairdresser *and* breakfast cook, in an apron no less. Do your in-laws know?"

"Low blow man." Matt narrowed his eyes at Kevin.

"Do my parents know what?" Laura slipped into the kitchen, planted a kiss on Kevin's cheek and Jennie's head then twined her arms around Matt as he cooked.

"That he looks so pretty in an apron?"

Laura laughed. "Well…"

"Don't. Don't you dare." Matt interrupted.

Laura talked over him. "They should, as they gave it to him for Christmas last year."

Kevin let out a whoop of laughter while Matt fixed Laura with a scowl. "I'm spitting on both of your pancakes."

"Flavoring." She winked at Kevin and went on tiptoes to kiss her husband. "Morning, Baby."

Grumbling under his breath, Matt finished making the pancakes and set the platter in the middle of the table. After saying grace, Matt dropped a pancake onto Jennie's plate while Laura made a small mound of butter and a puddle of syrup next to it.

"You two are really perfect, you know that?"

Laura smiled. "Perfect what?"

"Parents? Married people? Take your pick." He took a bite of his pancake with a nod to Matt. "I want that."

"I know." Matt looked at Laura lovingly. "And I really do believe that God has it for you. You just need to wait. Which is easier said than done."

"I guess at this point I'm kind of getting used to it. But after this recent turn of events...I don't think I'm ready anymore." He looked down at his plate and pushed his pancake into the syrup. "I don't know how to recover from this, guys."

Laura reached over and rested her hand on his. "I don't have any sage words of advice to offer, Kevin." She glanced over at Matt before continuing. "When my first engagement ended, I think I was probably in a similar place emotionally. The best advice I got was to really seek God and focus on my relationship with Him...then everything else would fall into place." She patted his hand and returned to eating. "It's a lot easier to say than do though, especially when you're hurting."

Kevin nodded and mopped up the last of the syrup from his plate and chased the bite with a big swallow of coffee. "Thanks."

Matt deftly caught Jennie's fork as it started to crash to the floor. "Hey, that's what friends do. You've been there for us more times than either of us can count, why wouldn't we return the favor? Besides, now it's your turn to do the dishes."

"All right, fair enough." He looked around the lower cabinetry. "Where's your dishwasher?"

Matt grinned and tossed his apron at Kevin. "Go find a mirror, man. We're old school around here."

Even though it was Saturday, when he got home Kevin spent some time in his office dealing with email emergencies that had cropped up overnight. One conversation, consisting of nearly twenty replies back and forth, caught his eye and he frowned, scrolling back to the top to begin reading from the start. Reaching the end he shook his head and checked the time as he grabbed the phone and dialed his boss.

"Hey Charlie, it's Kevin. Sorry to bother you on a Saturday, but.."

"Just saw the email?"

Kevin leaned back in his chair, propping a foot on his desk. "Yeah. I thought I got everything in Mumbai straightened out. How did it get messed up again so fast?"

"No idea, but if I can figure it out, heads will be rolling. As of right now though, we've got a major work stoppage on that end of things, and you know there's no room in the schedule for that to be going on."

"What do you need me to do?"

"I was going to wait to talk with you on Monday, but since you called me, how do you feel about going back out there for a semi-long-term assignment?"

"Define semi-long-term."

"At least two months, possibly six. Everything points to the issue being with the management team, not the folks actually doing the work. We're looking at bringing someone we know and trust into the management equation to evaluate and axe as needed. Your name was the only one that came up."

Kevin ran a hand through his hair and frowned. "I'll need to think about it a little. Can I get back to you?"

"Sure. Like I said, I wasn't going to approach you about it until Monday, so you can at least have the weekend. But it'd be good to get you out there as soon as possible, before the client starts to notice and things really hit the fan."

"All right. I'll plan on coming into the office Monday instead of working from home and we can sit down and go over more details about what needs to be done and so forth."

"Sounds good. I've got some early morning meetings on the books, but I should be free right before lunch for the better part of the afternoon. And if I'm not, I'll have Elise clear things out so I am. See you Monday."

"Yeah. Have a good rest of the weekend." Kevin ended the call and set the phone back in its cradle. Closing out his email, he shut down his work computer.

It was coming up on noon. On cue, his stomach growled and he headed down to the kitchen to find a snack.

A glob of jelly fell on the floor as he lifted his hastily made peanut butter and jelly sandwich to take a bite. Chewing, he grabbed a paper towel off the roll and wiped it up, grumbling.

"I really need a dog…though I guess it's not overly fair to a dog if I end up in India for the next six months." He furrowed his brow, lining up positives and negatives of an extended trip. Sandwich finished, he looked out at the sunny day. A bike ride would be just the thing to clear his mind. It was good weather to hit the trail along the Potomac and see where it took him.

Kevin dropped his laptop by the door and kicked off his shoes. Days in the office always seemed longer than days at home, even though he ended up working more hours from home than he ever did on site. He headed to the kitchen and filled a glass of water as he dialed his parents.

"Hey Mom."

"Hi Baby, how was your day?"

"Long and busy. I went in to the office today." He spotted the flashing light indicating that he had answering machine messages. "Which I guess you figured out since I'm betting at least one of the blinking lights on my machine is from you."

"You know me too well. I was just calling to say hello. I had hoped to catch you yesterday but I guess you had a busy weekend, too?"

Kevin perched on one of the stools at his island and set the glass down in front of him. "Yeah. It's looking like I'll be heading back to Mumbai for another extended stay, probably only a month, but it could stretch beyond that, depending on how accurate I was with my guesses on personnel problems."

"It feels like you just got back in town, honey. Though I guess it's been over a month. Just with Lydia..."

"Five weeks. Yeah." He spun the glass in little circles, trying not to spill the water. "Lydia's part of the reason, really, that I'm thinking another trip out of town would be a good idea."

"What do you mean, Kev? Don't you want to be there when she gets out of the hospital?"

"She's not going to be going home, Mom. There were some details that I kept to myself. I don't know why. Or, I guess I do, but...she's got to go to rehab Mom."

"Well, of course, physical therapy."

"No, Mom. Rehab. For drug addiction."

His mom was silent and Kevin heard his watch ticking the seconds off. Finally she sighed. "Oh Baby. Why didn't you tell me?"

"There's more. She was...she wasn't always paying for the drugs with money."

"What do you...oh. Oh, Kevin, Honey. What are you going to do?"

"I don't know, Mom." His voice was full of anguish. "I get so angry when I think about it, but even with that simmering in my brain, I can't get away from the fact that I love her. That she's the one God has for me. Though right now, that seems more like a curse than a blessing. No matter how much I love her, right now I also want nothing more to do with her." Bitterness tinged his voice and he stopped and took a deep breath. "So maybe getting away while she tries to get straightened out would be better for both of us."

◌◦◦◦

It was July before all the details of the assignment to India were worked out. Given the expected duration, Kevin's company found a short term rental apartment rather than spending money on a hotel. Kevin was only marginally hopeful that it would be a decent living arrangement. With the time lapse, it was clear to everyone in the Mumbai office that a shakeup was on its way, and the frantic emails and phone calls had already started as people tried to shift the blame to another business unit.

Kevin reclined in his airplane seat. At least he'd had the miles to upgrade to first class for the final long leg of his trip. What was the best approach to use when he reached the office the next morning? Every time he tried to focus on work, his thoughts strayed back to the Browns and their clear disappointment with him at his refusal to see Lydia off to rehab. He had pled busyness with the upcoming trip, but the lie had sounded thin, even to him. They had to understand, didn't they? Maybe someday they'd be willing to forgive him.

He was having nightmares every night featuring Lydia doing all manner of things with a series of unknown men all the while sporting a wedding band that matched his own. The moisture evaporated from his mouth as the vivid images formed. He pressed the flight attendant call and asked for another bottle of water and a blanket. Maybe the discomfort of the airplane would keep him from sleeping deeply enough to dream.

At the airport in Mumbai, Kevin collected his luggage and took a taxi to the address he'd been given. The high rise apartment building was in what seemed to be a good area of town from what he remembered, and it was a reasonable distance to the office, though he might need to look into buying a bicycle. He paid the cab and headed up to what would be his home for at least two months. Dropping his bags inside the door he glanced at the fully furnished apartment and nodded with relief. They had sent him the specs, six hundred square feet and so on, but seeing it eased his fears. The furniture was in good shape and all the fixtures were things an American would be comfortable with.

Given that the Mumbai office knew part of why he was here, he had half expected them to put him somewhere guaranteed to exact revenge for any firings that needed to take place. After a look around, he dragged his suitcases to the bedroom, washed up enough to not feel guilty about getting between fresh sheets, and fell into an exhausted slumber diagonally across the bed.

Lydia watched her parents wave from their car and drive away. She gave herself a firm mental shake and turned, smiling weakly at the nurse standing next to her.

"Let's get your bags to your room and get you settled." The woman's nametag indicated her name was Rose. She was a fifty-something, robust woman who exuded an air of no-nonsense efficiency.

Lydia gathered her things and nodded mutely. At least she'd passed the physical therapist's test before coming here and only needed a cane to get around. She hadn't been looking forward to being on crutches in rehab.

Rose spun on her heel and led the way, chatting amiably about the various rooms and their functions as they passed them.

"And, here we are." She knocked once and pushed open a door, revealing six twin beds and matching dressers arranged three across in a dorm room configuration. "Home sweet home for the next little while." She indicated the bed farthest from the door. "That one will be yours, closest to the bathroom. Just drop your bags here and let's get you unpacked."

"I can do it." Lydia walked to the bed, looking around. It was worse than being back in college. At least there you'd had a semblance of privacy. Here...there was none.

"Sure you can, but they pay me to help." Rose grinned and began unzipping the first suitcase, briskly pulling stacks of clothing out and setting them into the nearby dresser. Lydia noticed that her fingers expertly checked each item for contraband as she did so. When all her bags were unpacked, there was a small mound of items sitting to the side.

"Where do I put those?" Lydia indicated the pile.

"Can't have these here, sorry. We'll lock them up and you can get them back when you check out."

Lydia closed her eyes and nodded once, shoulders slumping. Why was perfume on the proscribed list? She was going to miss the little pick me up that smelling good always brought her.

"Now then, it's nearly supper time, but you have a bit of free time. This evening is group; you've been assigned to Dr. Melanie with the rest of your roommates and the girls in the room on the opposite side of your bathroom." She indicated the door in the center of the wall by Lydia's bed. "There are twelve of you sharing the bathroom. Come and let's have a look."

Lydia followed behind Rose, taking in the six toilet stalls and locker room style shower. A row of sinks lined the other long wall. She sighed heavily.

"Oh now, it's not as bad as all that. Plenty of room for all of you to get ready at the same time if necessary, though your schedules won't be entirely the same. It all depends on where you are in the program and what individual needs you have." Rose smiled and patted Lydia on the shoulder. "You'll be settled in no time." She led the way back into the bed room and glanced at her watch. "Now then, why don't I show you the way down to the dining hall and you can hang out in the TV lounge until they ring the dinner bell."

"Sure." Lydia looked at her bed. Should she take something with her? What though? There was nothing she needed. She grabbed her cane and limped after Rose. What had she gotten herself into?

⚜

Dinner was a noisy affair. Lydia held her tray with one hand, leaning on her cane with the other. She looked at the tables of cheerfully chattering women. Were the seats assigned?

A petite brunette nudged her elbow and grinned. "Hey. You're Lydia, right?"

Lydia nodded, drawing her eyebrows together in confusion.

"I'm Rachel, you're in the bunk next to me. Plus I think you're the only new admission today, so it was pretty easy to figure out who you were. Come on." She tilted her head toward a table in the far corner. "You can meet the rest of our room. You don't have to eat with your roommates but we all get along pretty well, so we figure we might as well."

Rachel set her tray down at an empty spot and patted the table. "Here, sit by me. Girls," she raised her voice to the table's attention, "meet our newest roomie, Lydia. Lydia, the girls."

Lydia slipped into her seat and offered a tentative smile. "Hi."

The startlingly pretty blonde girl to her right looked around. "I'll start the intros. I'm Jessie. Been here three months going on what seems like forever." The other girls laughed at her tone. "Though I think I'm probably going to be heading home next week. At least, that's the hope." She spun a plain gold band around on her left ring finger. "I have a six month old baby girl at home. I'd really like to get to know her before she's old enough to realize that she spent a lot of her first year without me."

"I'm Charlene." The tall, plump girl with mousy brown hair sitting to Jessie's right extended her hand across the table. Lydia shook it and smiled. Charlene continued. "I've only been here about two weeks, started the same day as Lucy and Dacia." She pointed to the two girls across the table.

The olive skinned girl raised her fingers and muttered. "Lucinda, hi." She brushed her long, straight dark brown hair back over her shoulder and continued eating.

Rachel laughed. "Don't talk our ears off now, Lucy."

Lucinda chuckled.

"I'm Dacia. Not quite as talkative as Lucy, but close." The short, extremely freckled girl gave a tight lipped smile and bent back to her food.

"As you can see, we're a pretty diverse bunch. So you're likely to get along with at least some of us, most of the time. Jessie is on the 'do whatever it takes' plan for recovery. The rest of us are on the more standard 'four to six weeks' plan. What about you?" Rachel shot Lydia a curious glance.

"Um. The more standard plan, I think. At least, I only packed for about a month. I guess we'll see what happens."

"Did they tell you your schedule yet?"

"Just that after dinner is group."

Nodding, Rachel shoveled food into her mouth. "Yeah, they'll probably wait until tomorrow morning to get you into a rotation." She pursed her lips. "Wonder where they'll stick you for rec." She eyed Lydia's build. "You look like you could hold your own on a volleyball court."

"I can play about as well as anyone who got through high school gym class, but I can't say it's a consuming passion." She hoisted her cane above the table. "I should say I used to play. I'm guessing this might get me a pass though." She puffed out her cheeks and slowly expelled a breath. "If I had to guess, my recreation is going to be more physical therapy."

The girls around the table laughed and Rachel bumped Lydia's shoulder with her own. "That's too bad. Most of us don't even have high school gym class competency, you could have ruled the court."

"So," Lydia cleared her throat and took a drink of water. "Group? What's that like?"

The girls looked at each other and shrugged. Rachel, who appeared to be the table spokesperson, spoke up. "Kinda like you'd imagine if you've seen any TV with rehab facilities as part of the plot." She grinned and spoke in a peppy voice. "Hi, I'm Rachel, and I'm an addict."

The other girls all chanted back. "Hi, Rachel."

Lydia smiled slightly.

Rachel scraped the last bit of food off her plate and into her mouth. "It's not really that stilted, or that bad. But it's all 12-step based, you know? Which is fine, I mean, it's helping me, it's helped Jessie a lot. Right, Jess?"

Jessie nodded. "It has. I thought it was hokey, and really only came here because David, that's my husband, said I had to get help or lose him and Clara. At the time I was so angry, but now, I'm grateful." She spun the wedding band again and sighed. "But gosh I want to go home."

"Anyway, I don't know that anyone can accurately describe group. You've just got to do it, you know?"

Rachel looked around at the quieting dining room. "And from the looks of things, they're getting ready for announcements, so your wait's almost over."

As she spoke, someone at the front of the room stood and cleared her throat. "If I could get your attention, ladies?"

Several chairs scraped the floor as people turned to face the front of the room and the low level babble died off.

"Thanks. Now a few reminders." The woman continued and Lydia listened with only partial interest while she looked around the rest of the room. Everyone looked like middle to upper middle class housewives or single women on the career path. She had expected to see more of the typical street junkie, though with what she was sure this was costing her parents, maybe it was out of their reach financially. A pang stabbed her chest. Where were they getting the money? Just one more thing she'd done to hurt them.

Everyone pushed their chairs out from the table and grabbed their trays. Rachel nudged Lydia and raised a brow. "Come on, girlie. We're not on KP tonight, so that's something at least. All we have to do is bus the table and then I'll show you where group is."

She led Lydia to the row of trashcans and recycle bins, showing her what went where before they put their dishes on the conveyor belt into the kitchen. Then she grabbed a wet sponge out of a tub full of warm, soapy water.

"Grab another. I'll wipe the table, you get the chairs. The other girls are getting the floor." She nodded to the four girls bringing brooms, dust pans, and mops over to take care of their area.

Lydia took her sponge and wiped down all the chairs. They washed their hands before heading out of the dining hall and down a hall she hadn't seen yet to where she assumed group would take place. She was dreading having to share her private life with this group of virtual strangers. Why had she agreed to this? Was it really any better than jail? How much hope did she really have?

Kevin made a point of getting in touch with the women's and children's shelter where he'd helped during his last stay in India. He was grateful to them for the sense of belonging they'd given him. Maybe spending his weekends with them would help fill the time and help him stop thinking about Lydia. It was avoidance...but what else was there to do? He just couldn't face it. If all went as planned, work during the week and helping out the shelter on the weekends would leave him too tired for dreams or serious contemplation.

His first week in the office went about as well as he'd expected it to. Everyone was overtly hostile and in full blame shifting mode. Even his coworker from the London office commented on it. All Kevin could do was shrug and continue outlining the plan for restructuring and damage control. At the end of the day, he hoped to be able to convince people that the client was the more important aspect of the whole fiasco, but it was evident that certain personalities would never bend enough to make all the changes that were needed. Kevin started keeping a list of those employees. He hoped that he'd be able to track improvement, but if not, he wanted to make sure the right cuts ended up being made. He urged the London manager to do the same so they could compare notes when it came time to actually start letting people go.

Marvin and Tina, the Christian couple who ran the shelter, were glad to have him back in town and put him to work early Saturday morning untangling their email system. Someone, it seemed, had a propensity for opening attachments without scanning them and had managed to install a handful of viruses. None were serious, but they were bogging down the system and making their already slow computers nearly glacial in speed. When he'd finished that, he had a list of IT chores that appeared to have started the day after he left. He kept at that until late, taking them up on their offer to stay the night and worship with them the next morning.

Church was a different experience for Kevin. As he sat, surrounded by those who had nothing but who came to worship full of joy and ready to praise God, he reflected on how he'd come to take his faith for granted. The sermon was short and plain, but the message challenged him nonetheless. When the service was over, he remained in his seat as everyone shuffled away.

"Can you join us for lunch?" Marvin smiled and settled into the seat next to Kevin.

Kevin glanced at his watch. "Well, I had hoped to get a bit more done at the office before heading back to the apartment."

Marvin shook his head and smiled apologetically. "We don't open the office on Sundays. It's hard to convince those who have to work a full day for every scrap of food that goes into their families mouths to have a day of rest if we who are provided for so lavishly do not."

"That makes sense. In that case, I'd love to stay for lunch if it's not an imposition."

"Sharing a meal is never an imposition. Let me tell Tina to set one more place. Though I suspect she already has." He grinned and indicated the door that led back to their main living area behind the space they used for worship. "Join us when you're ready. People trickle in and out most of the afternoon, so if you want to stay here to pray for a while, that's not a problem."

"Thanks. I might do that." Kevin clasped his hands in his lap and stared at his intertwined fingers as Marvin left. Slowly he slid to his knees and rested his hands on top of the chair in front of him and lowered his forehead.

"God," he whispered and paused, his mind reaching for words that wouldn't come. Water filled his eyes. "I don't even know how to pray anymore. What to say. For so long it was Lydia, and I felt so sure that I heard You saying we would be together and do great things for You. But now, I don't see how that's even possible. Either part. I've been faithful to You and to her and she..." he stopped as he felt a tear slip down his cheek. Clearing his throat he squeezed his eyes closed tighter. "She hasn't. You know the details, I only know pieces. But those pieces, I don't know how to get past them. I don't even know that I want to. I know in theory You can use everything, anything, to Your glory, but looking at this mess, I have to wonder why You'd want to."

He knelt for several more minutes. Why wouldn't peace come? Or at least some kind of answer that made sense.

"I need the wisdom to know Your will." When his stomach rumbled and his knees began to express their displeasure with the concrete floor, he pushed himself to his feet and made his way to the lunch table.

Lydia spent most of her first week saying as little as possible in the counseling sessions. Every now and then, when there was no graceful way to avoid it, she would speak and slowly her story, or most of it, trickled out. When her parents had dropped her off, she'd insisted they not get out of the car but drop her and go. It had been petty, but she hadn't been able to make herself do otherwise. After unloading her bags, her dad hugged her and whispered in her ear.

"It doesn't do any good for you to be here if you don't want to get well. I hope you'll try. Know that we love you no matter what."

Those words consumed her.

She didn't want to be here, she just didn't have any other choice. As to being well…if the guilt and pain were gone, then she was all for it. But she needed to be free of the haunting memory of what she'd done. And addiction had, at least, done that. She could go back...she'd simply need to be more careful. Her roommates and counselors treated her differently than the other patients. Was her disconnection from the process so obvious? Some days she was irritated by it, other days it made it easier for her to keep up the farce of saying what they wanted to hear. She just wanted to go home.

Rachel was the most persistent. She was also the roommate with the most overlap in schedule, which made her persistence easier and more irritating. At lunch, midway through the first week, Rachel sat next to Lydia and grinned, dropping several slices of lemon onto her tray.

"Hey!" Lydia looked down at the lemon that landed in her mashed potatoes.

"Ooops." Rachel grinned and speared it with her fork. "We won't use that one. These, however," she gestured to the slices that had avoided all food, "are going to give you that little lift you've been pining for."

Lydia arched a brow.

"A little bird told me that you brought perfume." She shook her head. "Clearly you didn't read through the reams of information they sent you prior to your stay. Not that any of us ever do. Still," she waved the fork that still held the potato laden lemon, "there is no reason you can't still get at least a whiff of that pleasure. Allow me to acquaint you with Eau de Rehab." She set down the fork and selected a slice of lemon from Lydia's tray. "Observe."

With that, she used her knife to score the rind of the lemon, then she dabbed the lemon, rind first, below her ears and on her wrists. "Voila!"

Rachel thrust her wrist under Lydia's nose.

"Um." Lydia sniffed, "Nice?"

"It's the best we can do. Some girls use things other than lemons, but I find citrus to be the most long lasting and pleasing. Oranges will do in a pinch. You might have to reapply at each meal, but hey, if life gives you lemons, right?"

Lydia couldn't stop the laugh that bubbled up. "If I were cynical..."

"Which you are," Rachel interrupted.

"If," she emphasized, "I were cynical, I'd think you made that whole thing up just to trot out the life-gives-you-lemons line."

"Fine. See if I share any other rehab survival secrets."

"Does it really work?"

Rachel shrugged. "In so far as it does, yes."

Lydia laughed. "Gee, what an encouraging response." She picked up a lemon slice and eyed it. After a minute she shrugged, scored the rind and rubbed it on her pressure points. Sniffing her wrist she eyed Rachel. "Better than nothing, I suppose, but it's sure not Estee Lauder."

"That it isn't."

"Thanks."

"No problem." Rachel took a few bites in silence. "What do you have after lunch?"

"I actually have a free hour. I thought I might find something to read. You?"

Rachel groaned. "I have extra chores due to the fact that Dr. Gilbert despises me."

Lydia wrinkled her nose. "Lucky you. I'll try to avoid getting on his bad side."

"Don't be, as he calls it, 'sassy' and you'll be fine."

The administrator stood and called the ladies to attention at that point, making a few announcements before dismissing them to their afternoon activities. Lydia helped with cleanup then, with a half wave to Rachel, started off in the direction she'd been told would lead her to a library of sorts.

It was more like a lounge with a couple of bookshelves. No one was there at the moment though, so it provided her with much needed solitude. She spent a few minutes glancing at the books on the shelves, finally settling on a cozy mystery that she hadn't read before. She continued her perusal of the room, stopping to look at the bulletin board. Her eyes were drawn to a flyer for a special seminar on Saturday about healing after abortion. Glancing around to be sure no one had come in while she was browsing she pulled one of the tabs off the bottom and tucked it in her pocket. She could ask Rose about it later. Then she chose a big chair and flopped into it, throwing her legs over the side, and began to read.

Lydia didn't get a chance to talk to Rose until Saturday morning at breakfast. She'd kept the slip of paper from the flyer and had stopped herself from bringing it up to Rachel or one of the other girls several times. Lydia hadn't checked the box on the pre-intake form about an abortion. Her dad was faxing it with her reservation and there was never going to be a good time for him to find out about that. She'd do her best to keep it from him at all costs. Of course, that now meant that if she wanted to go to this workshop, she'd have to figure out a way to get in. Or come clean.

"Rose." Lydia whispered as the nurse walked by her in the line for food.

Rose turned and retraced her steps. "Morning, Lydia. How are you settling in?"

"Fine I guess. Um." She glanced around to make sure no one was paying attention before tugging the scrap of paper out of her pocket. "I saw this in the library and wondered if it was something I could go to?"

Rose took the slip and looked at it. "Of course. I'll make sure you're on the attendance sheet." She flipped the paper over and scribbled a room number on the back. "Just go on over after breakfast. They plan to start around 9:30, so you'll have plenty of time to eat. I'll make sure any of the groups or activities you're signed up for today know that you'll not be coming."

Breakfast was quiet. Most of the girls from Lydia's room had a free day and were expecting family visits or planned to go on one of the many hikes or horseback rides that the facility offered. Lydia had told her parents not to plan on coming back for a visit until she got in touch with them, so she wasn't expecting anyone to come see her. The thought caused a pang of hurt as she thought of Kevin. She sighed and shook her head. That ship had sailed. Not that she'd wanted to be onboard it anyway. He hadn't even come to say goodbye.

"Who?" Rachel plopped down next to Lydia with a cup of coffee.

"Who what?"

"Who didn't come say goodbye?"

Lydia felt heat rush to her face. "I didn't realize I said that out loud." She looked down at her barely touched breakfast. "Just a friend, um, his name's Kevin."

"Just a friend Kevin, huh?" Rachel winked, using air quotes around "just a friend."

"Doesn't matter. Like I said, he didn't come say goodbye."

"Maybe he'll come visit."

"Doubtful. According to my parents, he's gone to India. Where at least the people who do bad and shameful things are driven to it by poverty." Her voice dripped with bitterness.

Rachel winced and sipped her coffee, saying nothing.

"Sorry." Lydia muttered.

"No sweat. Men." She put as much exasperation as possible into her voice and glanced at Lydia out of the corner of her eye.

Lydia laughed.

"That's better. Now," Rachel set the nearly empty coffee cup down on the table and twirled it, "what *does* your day hold?"

After a minute of silence, Lydia bit her lip and pulled the slip of paper out of her pocket and slid it across the table.

"Oh, great seminar. I've been twice. Thought about going today, actually, but there's that horseback ride up to the waterfall on the far edge of the property and I thought some nature might be good." She frowned. "Wish I'd known you were going though, I would've changed my mind."

Lydia blinked. How was Rachel able to be so open about something like that?

"What?" Rachel glanced over her shoulder to see if someone was standing there. "Do I have a coffee mustache?"

"No. I just...you're so matter of fact. Aren't you mortified?" The last came out as a whisper.

"I was the first time I went. And it took a while for me to work up the courage to even ask about going, so you've got me beat there." She lifted a shoulder in a half-shrug. "But you're in for a treat. This," she tapped the paper, "is what really got me to a place where the rest of what we do here could help. I probably owe these ladies my life."

Lydia looked skeptical.

"I know, I know. But give them a chance." She craned her neck to see the clock on the wall behind them. "You probably ought to get going. See ya tonight."

Lydia glanced at the clock and tucked the paper back into her pocket. She grabbed her tray, made a cursory swipe at the table, and quickly sorted her trash and dishes. She left the dining room and turned down what she hoped was the right hallway.

She ended up being about five minutes late, having gotten turned around in the halls of the complex. Thankfully, everyone was still milling around a small table of refreshments. Having just finished breakfast, she took the packet she'd been given and found a seat at a table in the back corner. She had just started flipping through the papers in the folder when a chubby older woman with short silver hair dressed in a simple black pantsuit and turquoise blouse moved to the front of the room and clapped her hands.

"Ladies, if everyone could take a seat, we can go ahead and get started."

21

Everyone moved to a seat, most choosing one a good distance from any of the other attendees. Lydia didn't see anyone she knew among the thirty-ish women attending, though she recognized all the faces from the dining hall.

"Great, thank you." The woman smiled again and took a sip of water. "My name is Jillian Simmons and I'm the director of the Pregnancy Resource Center in this area. I've been working with women facing unplanned pregnancies for about six years now. I started as a volunteer, just looking for something to do a couple of hours a week while my kids were in school and it rapidly turned into something that I knew I was called to do. With me today are Michelle and Charity." She gestured to two women who were also dressed in sharp pantsuits. Each gave a little wave. "These ladies work with me at the Center and both have been on the side of the table where you're sitting right now."

She paused to meet the eyes of several of the women in the room. Lydia quickly looked down at her agenda and idly drew a wavy line under the heading "Opening Remarks."

"We're here today to talk about post-abortion recovery. We assume that everyone here has either had an abortion themselves or knows someone who has. You don't have to tell us which category you fall into, but we will split into small groups periodically throughout the day, one group for those who have personally experienced an abortion and the other for those who have been touched by abortion another way. Since you choose which group you want to go with, if you aren't ready to openly admit an abortion, please feel free to choose the other group. All we ask is that you remain in the same group throughout the day and that you remember that everything said in this seminar remains confidential." Jillian paused to look around the room again. "This room, and your breakout spaces, need to be areas of safety, so even though you may know the woman sitting next to you or you may see her in other groups during your stay here, please remember that anything shared here is for that woman alone to choose to share elsewhere. Now, before we start with a discussion of what post-abortion stress is, let's take a minute to pray and ask God to have His hand on this gathering."

Jillian bowed her head. Gradually all the other heads around the room bowed. For several moments it was silent, then Jillian began to pray quietly. "Heavenly Father, Thank you bringing each of these women here today. You know why they are here and what they need. Open our ears that we would hear You. Open our hearts that we would know You. Have your hand on the leaders and the participants today that all we say and do would be to your glory, Amen."

A quiet chorus of amens followed. Jillian turned and nodded to Michelle who in turn pushed a button on the projector. A slide bearing the title "What is Post-Abortion Stress?" filled the screen and Jillian continued. "If you'll take out the top sheet of your notebook, you'll see a note page to follow along. Please feel free to ask questions as we go, or jot a note and come find me at a break if you'd rather not ask in front of the group."

Lydia pulled the note sheet out and began doodling along the edges as Jillian spoke. She filled in each blank as the talk continued. The symptoms listed were easily identified in her own life. Guilt? Check. Anxiety? Lydia snorted quietly, double check. Becoming numb? Check, check, check. Drug and or alcohol abuse? Well, look where she'd ended up. The one that really hit her, though, was anniversary syndrome. As Lydia took notes, she finally consciously pieced together that the due date of the baby she'd aborted, coupled with the birth of her sister's baby in that same timeframe, is what pushed her over the edge. She bit her lip to keep her tears at bay, though she noticed several other women wiping at their eyes.

"Now that we know what post-abortion stress is, and hopefully you've been able to decide if you've experienced any of those symptoms, let's take a few minutes to discuss the other half of this equation. The men involved." She smiled and looked around the room. "Obviously since this is a women's rehabilitation center, we don't have any men here with us today, but I want to make you aware of the fact that the fathers of the babies who were aborted can and often do experience post-abortion stress as well." She paused to take a sip of water and indicate that the slide should be changed. "We aren't going to belabor the issue today, but those same symptoms we just discussed may be evident in the men in your relationships. And," she paused, holding up a finger to emphasize the point, "friends and family members may experience post-abortion stress too. It may not only be the fathers of the babies, but your own parents or good friends may hurt too. Hopefully as time goes on, you'll be able to share with them the healing you've found and help them to recognize a need for this healing in their own lives. There's a list of resources, both state and national, in the back of your folder that I hope you'll pass along as you recognize the need."

Jillian paused and took another sip of water then glanced at her watch. "All right, let's go ahead and take a five minute break. During that time, please take a moment to sign up for one of the breakout groups. There are two clipboards over by the refreshments; please put your first name on the sheet for the group you want to work with."

Jillian stepped back from the front of the room and switched on soothing music at a low volume. The women sat for a minute, looking around nervously.

Gradually, one after another, they stood and made their way out of the room, presumably toward the restrooms, and over to the sign ups on the tables against the wall. Lydia blew out a breath and crossed the room. She pulled a bottle of water from the cooler under the refreshment table and looked at the two clipboards.

"Decision time." She muttered. Hesitantly she reached for the pen tied to the clipboard for women who have had an abortion and printed her name. She dropped the pen quickly when she was finished and scooted to the far side of the table.

Jillian finished a quiet conversation with her helpers and stepped back to the front of the room. "All right, ladies, if you could all take your seats we'll get going again. Now that we know what post-abortion stress is, and you've learned how it is personally affecting your life, the obvious question is: what next? How do I heal? So let's take a minute to consider steps to healing."

The slide now showed a seven point list. Jillian started at the top and briefly touched on each one. Lydia doodled on the accompanying note page, filling in blanks as needed. Why had she decided to do this? She could be swimming, or reading, or doing extra chores.

Lydia half listened as Jillian continued. "In addition to remembering that you're not alone and understanding that recovery takes time, you need to remember that it is ok," she paused and shook her head, "not just ok, but *necessary* for you to grieve. And you may have to give yourself permission to do so."

The slide changed again to show a big pit in the ground with labels down both sides and an arrow indicating a path from the left, down the hole, and then back up the other side. "Grief is a cyclical process. This graphic is one illustration of that process." She pointed to the top left side. "Here is the loss – and it applies to any sort of grief, but in our context, this is the actual abortion. From there, you slip down the slope into shock and denial, next comes anger, then depression. And remember, you may circle through each of these stages for awhile before moving to the next. So you may be in denial, then move on to anger, and then go back to denial before moving back into anger and so forth. My point is that waiting it out, expecting the cycle to end, isn't going to get you back to a meaningful life." She tapped the upper right side of the pit. "You have to work through each phase. So, after depression you have bargaining and then finally acceptance. Another item of note, acceptance doesn't mean you'll never think about it or hurt again because of it. It simply means that you're ready to move on from your grief. The life you have once you reach acceptance will not be the same that it was before your abortion."

Lydia sighed quietly and circled the last stage. She didn't expect it to be the same. Nothing was going to be the same, not since the accident had pulled her whole family into her private business and landed her here. She tucked the grief sheet back into her notebook and snapped it shut, pushing her chair back from the table slightly. She glanced over her shoulder at the door, it would be so easy to get up and go…somewhere. Lydia frowned, but where? Her roommates had all made plans for the day. She didn't want to spend an entire free day with any of them anyway. This is probably as good as it was going to get. She turned back to the front and crossed her arms over her chest. She'd just sit through the rest of the seminar.

"We'll be looking at forgiveness more closely in a bit, but notice how it touches three of seven steps to healing. You won't heal without letting go of bitterness and hurt. You'll have to forgive yourself and others." Jillian nodded and the slide changed again. "Now, it's time for our first small group session. We've split you into three groups based on your sign ups, Michelle and I will each have a group of ladies who have personally experienced abortion, Charity will lead the group of those who have been touched by abortion in another way. If you signed up on that clipboard, please go ahead and follow Charity now."

A handful of women stood, gathered their belongings, and quietly filed out of the room in Charity's wake.

"Next, if I call out your names, please follow Michelle, otherwise just stay seated." She rattled off several names and the women all followed Michelle from the room. Lydia looked around to see there were still a handful of women waiting.

"Great." Jillian smiled and settled into a chair at the front table. "If you'd all move in closer, bring your folders and a pen, but you don't have to bring anything else."

Lydia grabbed her things and moved forward, trying to sit as far away as she could without seeming to be antisocial. Most of the other ladies continued to give everyone a good bit of personal space, so the circle was loose, not confined to one table.

Clearing her throat, Jillian held up the paper with the grief cycle illustration printed on it. "Let's take some time to go over this, answer any questions you might have, and then spend some time sharing our stories and identifying where we are in this cycle." She paused, nodding once. "And yes, I say we, because I've been in your shoes. Maybe not for the exact same reasons, but I had two abortions in graduate school. They turned my world upside down. Looking back, God has made something good from my rebellion and sin, but when I was there," she glanced at the chart, "I spent most of my time spinning between anger and depression. It took a suicide attempt to get my attention and force me to admit that I needed help. But even then, no one would consider that my abortions had anything to do with my rage and depression. I got back on my feet, mostly, but it wasn't until I found forgiveness for the abortions that I truly healed." She met the eyes of each of the women in the group. "Now, were there any questions?"

No one had any, so Jillian turned to the woman sitting closest to her and asked if she'd like to begin. One by one, each woman shared. Some went into great detail, others as little as possible. When Jillian looked at Lydia enquiringly, Lydia winced and looked down at her hands.

"Is it mandatory?"

"Of course not. If you're not ready to share, you certainly don't have to."

"I don't think I am. Though," she glanced at the grief cycle and pursed her lips, "I think I'm probably in the depression stage at this point." Lydia smiled sardonically. "After all, I'm not in rehab because I'm making smart choices." Some of the other women chuckled. "Though I can't rule out anger, either. I was glad you said they're fluid stages."

"You're not the first to be comforted by that." Jillian looked at the group. "Thank you, all of you, for sharing what you did. I hope that as we continue you'll see that understanding what you're going through and talking about it sets you on a path toward healing." She glanced at her watch. "Let's take about a ten minute break and then we'll round everyone back up for another general session."

Lydia took her folder to her place at the back table and hurried from the room. She ducked into the closest restroom and locked the stall door. Sitting down on the closed toilet lid, she buried her head in her hands. How had she ever thought this would be a good idea? Rachel's encouragement at breakfast came back to her. Maybe it was worthwhile…but it was hard. With a glance at her watch, she peeked out of the stall. Slipping through the still empty restroom, she hurried to the nearest bank of phones with outside lines. It was Saturday, a free day, maybe they'd be turned on. Dialing her parents, she held her breath as it rang. She was about to hang up when her mother answered.

"Hi, Mom...it's Lydia."

"Hi Sweetheart. I didn't know you'd have phone access. What a great surprise. Let me get your father."

"No Mom, please don't. I just wanted to hear a friendly voice."

"Well, you found one. Should I ask how you are? How your roommates are?"

Lydia rested her hip on the phone booth's shelf. "I guess it's ok. They're ok. I can't say I love it here, but I've heard stories about places that are terrible so...I guess I just want to say thanks. I'm going to pay you back."

"Oh Baby, get better, that's all the reimbursement we want. And, well, it's not just the drugs, not that we don't want you off them, but something had to have happened for you to turn in that direction. I hope that you'll remember your value and how much you're loved and let God fill whatever caused that hole."

"Thanks, Mom...I should probably go."

"So fast? Are you sure you don't want to talk to your dad?"

"Not right now. I'm kind of taking a seminar today. We're on break."

"Ok. Call again when you can, honey. Even if it's only a few minutes. We love and miss you."

"I'll try. Bye." Lydia set the phone back in the cradle and hurried back to the meeting room, slipping quietly into her seat. Leafing through her folder, she found the handout that matched the slide currently being displayed. Michelle was talking now about anger and its destructive nature. She wove passages from the Bible into her talk, as well as personal anecdotes and Lydia found herself making notes and listening carefully. After another half hour, the women split into groups again.

Jillian held a sheet of paper that had dandelions drawn on it. "What I'd like you all to do is take about five minutes and draw in the roots of the anger weed in your life. These, like Michelle talked about, are the people and situations that cause your anger about your abortion. Maybe it's your partner who forced you into the decision or wasn't supportive of any other choice. Maybe it's your family or friends who you felt would be disappointed with you and thereby you felt trapped. Maybe it's the doctors and nurses who didn't give you other alternatives. There aren't any wrong answers here. Spend some time reflecting and drawing and then we'll share and discuss."

Lydia looked at the drawing and slowly penciled in a long line under the mounded earth, she labeled it in dark, capital letters "Brad". Considering it, she underlined it twice. She drew another line and looked at it. After several minutes she wrote her own name next to it. She added a third line for her perfect sisters and a fourth for Kevin. She looked at the line for Kevin and scribbled it out. If she was going to be honest, and fair, she wasn't mad at him, she was mad that he knew about the drugs and that surely he hated her now. A tear slipped down her cheek and landed with a splat on her paper.

"All right, does anyone want to share?" Jillian looked at the group. A few women volunteered. Lydia noticed that most of their roots were similar and fell into the categories that Jillian had mentioned at the start of the exercise. Did that make her feel better...or worse?

Several of the cafeteria staff came in as they were finishing up and began laying out trays and chafing dishes. "Excellent, lunch is right on time. Let me go and tell the other groups to wrap it up and we'll eat before we continue. We'll start back up with sessions in about 45 minutes if you don't want to eat in here."

Lydia wandered over to see what they were setting out. It looked as good as the cafeteria fare. Might as well just hang out here. Especially since she didn't have anyone to sit with in either place.

Everyone kept mostly to themselves during lunch. The few women who had been sitting together at the start chatted quietly, but everyone else stayed near their belongings, flipping through the material or staring into space. If she ever did anything like this again, she was going to bring a book.

When the lunch had been cleared and everyone was back in their seats, Jillian stood again. "Now that we know what our roots of anger are, it's time for the hard part. Forgiveness."

Lydia listened as Jillian talked about God's command that we forgive as we've been forgiven and also about the destruction that unforgiveness and bitterness can wreak in your own life. She thought back through the decisions she'd made, starting with believing Brad when

he'd said they were engaged. If she had to be brutally
honest with herself, and really, what better place to do
that than rehab, she had suspected on some level that a
ring would never materialize. Still, she didn't want to
forgive him, or herself. She doodled idly around the edge
of her notes. She didn't deserve to be forgiven.

"You may feel like what you've done, whether
that's an abortion or something else, is too terrible to be
forgiven. But I promise you, Jesus has already died for
that sin. And if He's already paid the price, then how can
you refuse the forgiveness freely offered?" The slide
switched, revealing the image of a cross. "The ground at
the foot of the cross is level. No sin is worse than any
other in God's eyes. Let Him give you freedom and
peace."

Jillian paused for a moment meeting the eyes of
those who were looking up. "All right, let's move on to
our next topic, breaking soul ties. First, it's probably
helpful to define what a soul tie actually is." She smiled
and the slide switched again. "A soul tie is the bond that
forms between two people when they're intimate. It
doesn't necessarily have to be physical intimacy, either.
Close friendships can create soul ties between those
friends. Clearly, not all soul ties are bad, but when a soul
tie is made because of sinful behavior, then to truly break
free from that behavior, the soul tie must also be broken.
The good news is that you can break these soul ties. You
first need to confess any sin that was involved in the
creation of that tie, then forgive the other person
involved. Next, you want to renounce any promises you

made with that person and get rid of gifts that you exchanged. Finally, pray for God to remove any vestiges of that soul tie from your life."

Jillian perched on the edge of the table at the front of the room. "I know it sounds easy, and on the surface it is, but expect it to be hard. You may have to return to the process a few times to free yourself completely, depending on the strength of that tie. Now, rather than breaking out into our groups, let's take a break. As part of that time, though, spend a few minutes jotting down the names of anyone you feel you have an unhealthy soul tie with. Then, if you're ready, spend some time praying about them, asking to have the ties broken and your soul repaired. We'll meet back here in twenty."

Lydia closed her folder and stood. She noticed a few of the other women were also making their way out of the room and relaxed. She passed them and found a door to one of the outdoor courtyards. Looking around and seeing no one else, Lydia walked around several planters and found a concrete bench in the sun. She settled on it and closed her eyes, turning her face upward to the warmth and focused on simply breathing, willing her mind to clear.

When she felt like she'd collected her thoughts, and that it had been about twenty minutes, she slipped back into the room. Jillian had already started on the next topic and was explaining the purpose of the memorial service they were about to have.

"As the music plays, feel free to come to the front and light a candle in memory of the aborted child. As you do, ask God to heal you from your past. Of course, there's no requirement to come forward if that's not something you feel comfortable doing."

Jillian moved to the end of a front table by a small CD player and sat. She fiddled for a moment and quiet music began to play. Charity used switches at the back of the room to dim the lights. A small cross had been placed in the middle of the table at the front. Michelle made her way to a pile of votive candles, placed it near the foot of the cross, and lit it. She stood there for a minute with her head bowed, tears sliding down her face. After a bit, she sat next to Jillian who grabbed her hand and patted it.

Alone and in pairs, the other women began to come forward to light candles. Some whispered names, others knelt, weeping. Lydia watched, fighting with herself. As the music wound down, she finally slipped from her seat and lit a candle. She stared at the flame as it flickered for several heartbeats before closing her eyes. She let the reality of what she'd done wash over her. Swallowing the lump in her throat she went back to her seat and buried her face in her hands.

The music had been over for several minutes when Jillian stood and spoke quietly. "Thank you for coming today. If you'd like more information or want to talk with any of us further, our contact information is in the back of your folder. We'll be praying for each of you over the next several weeks."

The three women began quietly packing up, leaving the memorial candles at the foot of the cross. Lydia took a final look, the image of the cross surrounded by flickering candles imprinting itself on her brain. She gathered her things and slipped from the room. Maybe it'd still be empty. She had almost an hour and a half before dinner and she wanted to escape into sleep.

Kevin's Monday started off with a bang. He'd figured out the primary culprit of the office debacle and, as anticipated, an altercation ensued. The incompetent fellow thought he was untouchable since he had an uncle higher up in the local management structure. The uncle, when presented with the details of how his nephew had colossally messed up, simply shook his head and stated that he supported Kevin in whatever actions he felt were necessary. Kevin let the man know he was on notice and presented him with a list of improvements needed and the timeframe for those improvements to be accomplished. His emailed resignation letter came in less than an hour.

Kevin forwarded the email to the appropriate personnel and let HR know that they shouldn't bother with a counter offer. Resigning and taking paid leave was the best decision for everyone involved, especially the company. He hit send on the last email detailing the event and leaned back in his chair and rubbed his temples. His phone chirped, signaling a text message. With a groan, Kevin reached for it.

"Thinking of U. C how trendy I am? Miss u. Praying for u. <3 Mom."

Kevin smiled and texted back. "Perfect timing. You're very hip. See how unhip I am? Miss and love you and Dad. Prayer definitely a good thing."

A few minutes later he got another text from his mom, "Lull."

Kevin laughed aloud. "I think you meant LOL. Which is exactly what I did. Though a lull right about now would be welcome. Back to the grindstone I go."

He pulled his laptop closer and opened the project plan to look at the personnel records of those attached to the current fiasco. Who was he going to find to fill the recently created vacancy? "Not that anyone could be worse, of course." He muttered as he began scrolling through resumes.

The rest of the week flew by as he interviewed potential replacements from within. There were a few qualified people on board, but they were all critical in their current roles. Plus, none of them expressed any interest in the transfer. They'd have to use external advertising to fill the position. Kevin spent long hours in the office, returning to his apartment well after supper time when he would fall into bed for a few hours of much needed rest. He spent his weekends at the shelter and settled into a pattern of work and ministry that left him very little time for thinking about Lydia. The times she did come to mind, he was gradually able to start praying for her without any of the bitterness that he'd felt before he came to India.

⚬⚬⚬

Lydia hugged Rachel tightly then turned to look at her bags. She let out a deep breath. "I think I'm set."

Rachel grinned and hooked her arm through Lydia's. "I know you are. And I'm glad that I'm leaving tomorrow. You're one of the few things that made this place bearable. Now," she looked sternly at Lydia, "promise me that we'll keep in touch. You have my email address and phone number, right?"

Lydia patted her pocket. "Right here. And you've got mine?"

Rachel nodded and grabbed one of the bags. "Let's get these out to reception. Did you get your perfume back?"

Lydia angled her neck at Rachel who sniffed appreciatively. "Very nice." She waited as Lydia gathered up the rest of her things. "Have you decided what you're going to say to Kevin?"

"I don't even know if he's back in town yet. It's only the middle of August and I think they said his assignment could last into September." She lifted a shoulder. "For right now, I think I'm going to focus on finding a new job and getting my life back in order."

"Fair enough. Keep me posted though, ok?"

Lydia laughed as they pushed through the front doors to wait at the pickup area for her mom and dad. "I will."

She saw her parent's car turn into the circle and waved to catch their attention. "That's them."

She hugged Rachel again and waved to the nurse standing at the doorway keeping an eye on everything.

Paul put the car in park and got out to open the trunk. He came around the car and took the bags from Lydia. "You look great, honey. Ready?" He shut the trunk with a click.

"Definitely." She slid into the back seat. "Bye, Rachel."

"Bye. Take care." Rachel waved while Lydia shut the door and fastened her seat belt. Lydia waved through the window as the car circled back out of the driveway, headed toward home.

હ્ય

The drive home with her parents was relaxed and more normal than Lydia could remember since before she started dating Brad. They caught her up on all the news, including Kevin's extension of his time in India for another three weeks. They had kept up the rent on her apartment for her, and had been in to clean it just before leaving to pick her up. They'd also gotten her phone numbers changed and unlisted so that her dealer couldn't contact her. It was something they recommended at rehab and Lydia agreed it was wise. She didn't know how to thank them. They insisted that having her home and healthy was all they needed. After a dinner of pizza, they made sure she was going to be all right alone and hesitantly left.

Lydia locked the door behind them and flopped onto her couch. Privacy had never been so sweet. She had all the rooms to herself. What should she do first? Watch a little TV? No. A long bath with a good book and no one expecting her to be anywhere.

∞

Lydia slowly settled into a routine. After getting up around seven, she'd go to the gym in the basement of her building and use their equipment for about an hour, focusing on rebuilding the strength in her leg. She didn't need the cane as much anymore and hoped to be completely rid of it soon. Then she'd shower and make breakfast. While she ate, she spent time looking online for job postings that sounded interesting. She'd fill out applications or email her resume until about noon when she'd meet her parents for lunch, either at their house or at a restaurant near the church. In the afternoon, she'd either devote more time to the job search or helping her mother with errands. She'd joined a support group that met three nights a week after supper. The other nights found her puttering around her apartment. Even on group nights, she was rarely in bed later than 9:30.

Three weeks of this found her growing restless. There had already been a number of times when she'd had half of her dealer's number punched in, the siren song of drug induced numbness echoing in her ears. So far something or someone had intervened before she truly relapsed. Was she really that weak? That pathetic?

At lunch with her dad, she frowned and poked at the sandwich she'd ordered.

"What's wrong, kiddo?" Her dad looked at the sandwich then at Lydia.

Lydia sighed and shrugged. "I don't know." She poked the sandwich again. "I guess I thought I'd have at least some interviews by now. I mean, I left the old firm with glowing references and an assurance that my," she made air quotes, "personal problems would be left out of any conversations."

She dipped a French fry into the puddle of ketchup on her plate and started drawing circles on top of the bread.

Her dad watched her fidget for a minute. "Something will come up. Have you been praying about it?"

Lydia shook her head.

"Why not?" Paul took a big bite of his sandwich and made a quiet mmm in the back of his throat.

Lydia picked up half of her sandwich and nibbled at it. Setting it back down with a plop she stared over her dad's shoulder at the busy counter and mumbled, "I just don't think I deserve any more help from God, I guess."

Paul's face filled with concern. "Oh Baby." He reached across the table and squeezed her hand. "Of course you deserve His help. I get where you're coming from. I really do. Maybe I don't have the same sins in my past that you do, but there's sin there. And guilt can be beneficial if it keeps us from falling back into the same trap. But it's gone too far if it keeps you from God's love."

Lydia's lips twitched as she watched her dad. "I see a sermon forming."

Paul shrugged sheepishly. "Maybe so, but it doesn't make it less true. And honey, if you need to hear it, think how many other people need to hear it too."

She nodded.

"Why don't we pray about it now?"

Lydia raised a shoulder. Her dad patted her hand and bowed his head. She followed suit. Why couldn't she pray in private with the ease her father displayed when he prayed in the middle of a noisy, crowded restaurant?

"Amen." Paul squeezed Lydia's hand once more before returning to his lunch with gusto. "Now," he spoke around a mouthful, "promise me you'll add prayer to your job hunt? And hey, while you're praying, you could add us to your list. The renters downstairs are moving out, with very little notice...and while we don't depend on that income, it's really nice to have."

"I'll try."

"What is it that wrinkled green thing in Star Wars always said? There is no try?"

"Yoda, Dad." She snorted. "Wrinkled green thing? Really?"

"You know movie trivia was never my forte." He eyed her. "Have you given any thought to volunteering?"

"Volunteering doesn't pay the bills, Dad."

"No, I know. But it would get you out of the house in the meantime. You'd still probably have plenty of time to look for work, but I've always found helping others helps me, too."

Lydia narrowed her eyes. "And you happen to know just the place that's looking for volunteers?"

"What makes you say that?"

Lydia simply looked at him, eyebrows raised.

"Ok, ok. I *might* have had a phone call from one of the local ministries we support mentioning how understaffed they are right now."

Lydia held out her hand. Paul chuckled and set down his sandwich. He wiped his fingers on a napkin and patted his shirt pocket then his hip pocket. He dipped his fingers into the hip pocket and pulled out his wallet and a small pile of folded notes. Looking through the folded pieces of paper he frowned, tucking a few of them in his shirt pocket. Finally he waved a piece of paper in the air. "Knew I had it here somewhere."

"They've got these really neat things now called smart phones…"

"Don't even start." Paul shook his head and stuffed the rest of his paper back into his pocket. "I've already got elders pushing a BlackBerry at me every time I turn around. I looked at the thing, I did. But honestly, I couldn't even figure out how to make a call on it. I'll stick to paper and a cell phone that can actually be used as a telephone, thank you."

With a smile, Lydia unfolded the paper. The color drained from her cheeks and she swallowed hard before clearing her throat. "Um. I'm not opposed to volunteering somewhere, it's a good idea. But I don't think this is the place for me."

Paul drew his eyebrows together. "Why not, Lydia? The Georgetown Pregnancy Care Center does great work. There are so many college students who end up pregnant, or thinking that they might be. The counselors get a chance to share information about abstinence, or provide resources for making a decision about carrying the baby to term and then either choosing to parent or place the baby for adoption. And throughout all of it, they get to show these girls, well, women, God's love." He frowned. "You've been in enough of my Sanctity of Human Life Sunday services to know how important, and overlooked, this work is."

Her throat was as dry as the Sahara. She downed nearly half of her water, mind racing. Was there any explanation she could offer—anything other than the truth?

"I," she paused, frowned, "I don't know that I'm ready for something that...intense."

"I suppose I can see that. Though their counselor training course would give you all the tools you need. Still, they might need volunteers to do things other than counsel. At least call and find out, ok?"

Feeling trapped, Lydia nodded. She tucked the paper into her purse. She could always 'lose' it on the way to the car.

"Great. Now," he leaned back and set his napkin on his plate, "where have you been applying?"

Lydia pushed her plate toward the middle of the table and grimaced. "Probably easier, at this point, to tell you where I haven't applied. I haven't been sticking completely to PR. I do have a business degree so I thought a complete change might be good for me. Of course, no one seems to think I have what it takes on either front right now."

"Give it some time, Baby. There's something out there for you, we just need to find it." He glanced at his watch and smiled apologetically. "Unfortunately, I need to run and pick up your mother. She was disappointed she couldn't make lunch today, but it's the glamorous life of the pastor's wife."

He winked and Lydia laughed, pushing her chair back.

"Give her a hug from me."

"Will do." He slung his arm over her shoulder and they walked companionably out to the parking lot. He kissed her cheek and got into his car. "Let me know what they say at Georgetown, ok?"

"Sure. Bye Dad." She crossed the lot to her car and got behind the wheel, dropping her purse into the passenger seat. She pulled the paper with the phone number out and crumpled it up, dropping it onto the ground. She sat for several minutes arguing with herself, then, with a sigh, leaned over and retrieved the crumpled note, stuffing it back into her purse. Muttering, she headed back to her apartment.

23

Kevin closed his laptop and rubbed his eyes. He leaned back in his chair and swiveled his neck in circles. A glance at his watch showed that it was nearing midnight. He stood, pacing the small living room of the apartment. Even after being in India for over a month he couldn't quite bring himself to call it home. It was fine to come for a short time, but he could never relocate here permanently. Even if that was what the bosses back home were pushing for.

He opened the refrigerator and stared at its nearly empty shelves. He took a bottle of juice and sloshed it back and forth to mix it before drinking out of the bottle. Wiping a hand across his mouth, he nudged the door shut with his foot and carried the juice over to what passed for the balcony. He slid open the door and put half of each foot out on the concrete protrusion. That was as far as he could go unless he wanted to dive over the metal railing. He stood, looking out over the city and drank his juice as the hot, moist air blew past him. When the bottle was empty, he stepped back and pulled the door shut.

Kevin tossed the empty bottle and cheered as it clattered into the trash can across the room. Tucking his hands in the pockets of his jeans he took inventory of the past week. Things at the office were finally shaping up. The new management personnel were meshing well with the few on the old team that remained under the new rules he'd imposed. Several of the other staff were actually making the changes he'd mandated if they wanted to keep their jobs. Others had left, some politely, others less so. One man had caused such a ruckus they'd nearly needed police intervention. Thankfully it hadn't gotten to that point.

He looked out the patio door again, leaving it closed. Kevin had let the office know that he should be able to come back in another week. They'd insisted he stay in Mumbai for at least another two to be sure everything was going to stay fixed after he left. Charlie was already talking about some of the perks of living here permanently. Kevin had cut to the chase, letting him know that wasn't in the cards. Had he managed to torpedo his career by doing so?

"And why do I care, really?" He muttered, letting his forehead rest against the glass. "It's not like I have all that much waiting for me at home." He sighed, thinking of his house. The first time he'd walked through it with the realtor, he'd had a vision of Lydia and their children playing in the back yard. Not that that was likely. Not anymore."

If nothing else, his time in India had convinced him that God hadn't abandoned him. Kevin smiled slightly; it was good to have that sense of peace back, even if he was completely unsure what would happen when he returned home. He also knew that God was, in fact, calling him to add more active ministry to his life. Just not in India. Even Marvin and Tina had expressed their feeling that foreign service was not Kevin's calling, despite how disappointed that made them. They had offered him a part time staff position one weekend, and withdrawn it the next, making it clear that God had directly intervened. Frankly, Kevin had been trying to figure out the best way to turn it down.

Pushing away from the door he headed into the bedroom. He needed to sleep, somehow. This was his last weekend helping at the shelter. A Youth for Christ speaker was visiting and tomorrow he was running the projector and handling any other technical needs. He wasn't sure exactly what a post abortion seminar was, but since he was the most at ease with the projector, he'd agreed to come and help. Besides, everything else technical had been whipped into shape on his previous visits, so there wasn't much else for him to do. Still, he wanted to go back one more time to thank Marvin, Tina, and the families they helped for all they'd done for him while he'd been there.

Kevin was bleary eyed when the alarm went off. He grumbled to himself about insomnia and over thinking as he showered and dressed. He looked longingly at his coffee pot but there wasn't enough time. He prayed they would have coffee ready when he arrived.

It was early enough that the taxi ride was relatively devoid of traffic. Striding into the main room at the shelter, he heard the joyful gurgling of a coffee pot. He headed over to the pot and searched for the mugs. Laughing, Tina put a large mug in his hand and went back to the kitchen to get another for herself.

"No time for coffee yet today?"

Kevin shook his head and sipped carefully, closing his eyes as the restorative flavor washed over his taste buds. He knew it was psychological, but he felt more awake after that first sip. "I'm going to miss this." He raised his coffee mug. "Coffee in the States doesn't compare."

"You just need to find the right person to brew it for you. Coffee always tastes better when it's been brewed by someone who loves you. Now," she sipped from her own mug, "why don't I show you the set up we have and you can make sure it's all plugged in correctly. Marvin insisted that he was perfectly capable of hooking everything up. So it's probably good you're early."

"I heard that." Marvin poked his head around the doorframe and shook his head at his wife. "Now I have to come along so I can see your face when Kevin says it's all perfect." He clapped Kevin's shoulder. "You'll see. I've been watching you."

Kevin grinned and walked around the table holding a small projector hooked up to a laptop. He followed the cables and pursed his lips. "Let's give it a try, shall we?"

He flipped open the laptop and turned on the projector, letting both warm up.

Marvin gave a whoop when the computer screen was clearly projected in front of their makeshift baptistery. "See?"

"I stand corrected." Tina smiled at Kevin. "Thank you for teaching him how to use the equipment we've had collecting dust in our closet for...five years, is it?"

"Fine, fine. You made your point. Let's let Kevin get situated here. The attendees should be showing up before too much longer."

Kevin sat and opened the folder labeled 'seminar' on the laptop's desktop. Sure enough, it had a power point presentation. He opened it and checked that it was displaying properly on the screen. "I think we're set."

Another woman hurried into the sanctuary looking a little frazzled. She stopped when she saw the slide up on the screen and sighed, clearly relieved. "Oh good. Someone who knows what they're doing. I'm hopeless with that thing. Some days I can get it to go, other days, well, if I didn't know better, I'd say the Apostle Paul had a laptop and that was the thorn in his side."

"They're not all that bad, although this one might be a tad, well, elderly."

"Ancient is the word you're looking for. Missionaries always get the hand me downs. Most days I'm just thankful that I have any type of computer at all. Anyway, I'm Belinda. I don't suppose you've seen Harry rattling around anywhere?"

"Sorry, no. I'm Kevin McGregor. I help out on the weekends while I'm in town."

"Oh. Not staff?"

"No. In town for business and figured this was a better way to spend my weekends than over working. Though I did manage to do some sightseeing. It's India after all."

"I've got a list of places we need to hit while we're scooting around India doing post abortion work for the next several months. Of course, I always have a list and we don't always get to it. But then, since God didn't call me to sightsee, it's hard to be resentful."

"There you are." An incredibly tall man ducked through the doorway and glanced at the screen. "Oh great, I see we've got someone who actually knows what they're doing this time." He looked at Kevin and extended a hand. "I'm Harry, Belinda's other half."

"Kevin. Nice to meet you."

"I'm very tall, I'm told." Harry laughed, winking. "Usually find it's better to mention it and get it over with."

Kevin chuckled.

"It's actually a blessing most of the time. Except in most forms of transportation. Then it gets a bit annoying. Of course, God would call me to travel around.

No one ever said He didn't have a good sense of humor." He stuck his hands in his pockets and glanced down at his wife. "So, we set?"

Belinda nodded and glanced at her watch. "We are. People should be arriving any time now." She turned to Kevin. "Switch slides when I nod, if you would?"

"Sure thing." Kevin sipped at his coffee again and settled back in his chair as Belinda and Harry wandered toward the front of the room, chatting about the plans for the seminar. Watching them together, a familiar pang tugged at his heart. How nice it must be to be a part of a couple that was clearly brought together by God. For the first time in a while, his thoughts strayed to Lydia. How was she doing? She should be out of rehab by now…had it helped her? How was she adjusting to normal life?

Women, and a few men, started to file into the sanctuary, finding seats alone or in small groups. Belinda and Harry took the time to greet each one individually and exchange a few words and a genuine smile. When no one had come in for five minutes or so, Belinda and Harry exchanged a glance and Belinda moved to the front of the room.

With a big smile she gestured to the screen behind her. "Good morning. Welcome to our post abortion seminar. Thank you so much for coming, and thank you to the shelter for giving us space and resources to meet with you today. I know that this is not a topic that's easy to talk openly about. But it's my prayer that as the day progresses, each of you will feel the love and forgiveness of God revealed to you and the peace that acceptance of his forgiveness will bring. Let's start with prayer."

Before the seminar started, Kevin had been annoyed that he hadn't thought to bring a book to read to keep him occupied between slides. As the morning progressed, however, he found himself fascinated by the information being presented. At home, he'd always been careful to choose pro-life political candidates, but that was about as far as his consideration of abortion had gone. Well, that and filling a baby bottle with loose change to donate during the local Pregnancy Care Center's fundraising drives. As Kevin learned about the destruction that an abortion can cause in the lives of the women and men, his heart grew heavy. He needed to find a way to become more involved, do something to help.

When the day was over and everyone had finally left, Kevin approached Belinda as she sat, looking exhausted, at the front of the church.

"That was incredible."

"Thanks, but I just present the material, you know?"

"Still, there's so much I didn't know. Why isn't this something that's more prominent in the U.S.?"

"Oh it's available. The materials I use are all written by the director of a PRC." At his furrowed brow, she amended, "Pregnancy Resource Center. They're the folks who do most of the post abortion work in the U.S. Though there are some pastors and Christian counselors who also recognize an abortion as a damaging experience that needs to be grieved and processed." She shrugged.

"We're doing what we can to get the word out, but the trend is to portray abortion as a simple thing, a removal of some tissue. Most don't even want to admit it's a child. Why would they admit that killing that child can cause psychological and spiritual harm?"

"So the PRCs do this kind of work?"

"Most of them, yes. When you get home, call your local Center and ask. Most that I know always need volunteers, especially men."

Kevin nodded thoughtfully. "I think I will. Thanks."

Belinda smiled and pushed herself from the seat. "Let us know if there's anything we can do to help you get connected."

Kevin paused on the doorstep. He was rumpled from the flight and every bit of his body yearned for sleep, but rather than driving home, he had ended up parking in front of Matt and Laura's house. With a self-deprecating snort he leaned in and pushed the doorbell. He heard it echo through the house and the muffled sound of Laura hollering down the stairs at Matt. The porch light turned on and Matt poked his head around the door, grinning and opening it wider when he saw Kevin.

"Hey man." Matt narrowed his eyes. "Did you come straight from the airport?"

"My car apparently wanted to end up here." He paused and crouched, holding out his arms to Jennie who was peeking around Matt's knees. "Besides, I needed a refill on hugs from my best girl here."

Jennie squealed and threw herself into his arms, jabbering rapidly about her stuffed animal pals and other various topics. Kevin tried to follow her but soon gave up. Gosh it was good to be back with his friends.

"Matt, Honey, who is it?" Laura called as she lugged an overflowing laundry basket down the stairs. Peeking over the top she squealed and dropped it, sending clothes flying. "Kevin. Don't stand there, come in." She grabbed him and gave him a hug, to the delighted squeal of Jennie who was sandwiched between them. "Did you just get in?"

Kevin laughed and set a wriggling Jennie back on the floor. "Suitcases are still in the car. I think I had enough alone time in India and needed to see a friendly face or two."

Matt closed the door. "Let's get you something to drink. Are you hungry? There's a game on, come and flop."

Laura smiled indulgently and began collecting the spilled laundry. "Let me get a load started and I'll bring out some iced tea and manly snacks. You go sit."

Matt crouched and began loading laundry into the basket. "I'll get this, you get the food and then come take a break with us." He glanced at her roundly pregnant belly. "Surely you need to sit for a bit."

Laura rubbed a hand over her stomach. "All right, just leave the basket in the hall."

Matt finished tossing laundry into the basket and slid it out of the way before heading toward the living room.

Kevin toed off his shoes, leaving them by the door and followed after Matt. "What kind of game?"

"Really?" Matt grimaced and plopped onto the sofa, propping his feet on the coffee table.

Kevin glanced at the TV and sat, stretching his legs out in front of him and wiggling his toes. He leaned his head back, stretching his neck. What was that commercial, currently on mute, was trying to sell? Maybe the truck?

"Yes, really. I've been in India and not really gotten into cricket. Knowing you, and the fact that it's the middle of September, it could be football, baseball, or hockey."

"I see you've lost your team loyalty. How could you not know it's rival game day?"

Kevin raised his eyebrows. "That's tonight? I thought it was tomorrow."

"When did you think that?"

"When I was getting on the plane...yesterday." Kevin laughed and rubbed his eyes. "Ok, so I'm more tired than I thought. Next time you travel for over 24 hours straight, remind me to quiz you on game times."

Matt chuckled and unmuted the TV as the game came back on. Kevin deciphered the game info at the top of the screen. It was nearing the end of the first quarter and their college was up by a touchdown.

"How'd we miss the extra point?"

Matt groaned. "They tried the world's stupidest play."

"They're still trying to run that thing?"

"I don't understand how two different coaches continue to think that that play, which has never worked in the past, what?" He looked over at Kevin. "Ten years at least, right?"

Kevin nodded.

"Please no." Laura came in with a tray holding three big tumblers of iced tea, a pink sippy cup, a big bowl of chips and two smaller bowls of dip. She nudged Matt's feet out of the way and set the tray down. Lowering herself onto to the couch next to her husband she leaned forward to take one of the glasses. "Please do not get him started about" she made air quotes and lowered her voice to an ominous rumble, "the play."

Kevin laughed, dipped a chip, and popped it into his mouth before grabbing a glass. "He goes on about it a lot, does he?"

"Only every game. On the other hand, I do kind of see his point."

"Thank you." Matt grabbed a handful of chips and smiled at his wife. "But, in deference to the love of my life, I will simply remind us all that the definition of insanity is doing the same thing over and over and expecting different results."

Laura mouthed the words along with him behind her husband's back as he spoke.

Kevin quickly tried to cover his laugh with a cough.

"Don't think I don't know what you just did."

Laura grinned and sipped her tea, swallowing quickly to cheer a pass completion with a fifty yard gain.

At the next commercial, Matt muted the TV again and Laura set down her empty glass. "Anything about your trip that you didn't already share in an email?"

"Not really. They really tried to get me to relocate but it's not the right position for me. In so many different ways."

"Selfishly, I'm quite glad of that. It'd be quite a trip if we wanted to drop in." Laura shifted so she could prop her feet on the coffee table.

"Still concerned that there'll be repercussions at the office because you turned them down?" Matt grabbed a handful of chips and sorted through them, handing all the curled ones to Laura.

Kevin shrugged. "I don't know. On the one hand, I've done great things for them and I think they're all smart enough to recognize and appreciate that. On the other hand? I didn't fall in line like they thought I would."

Matt nodded and Laura looked concerned.

Seeing Laura, Kevin smiled. "I'm really not worried. Even in today's environment I have some fairly marketable skills. It might mean I end up having to go into the office every day like a normal person, but I don't think I'll have a hard time finding something else if that's what ends up happening."

"You're sure?"

"Yeah. And hey, if nothing else, I know someone who owns his own business and I'm sure he'd take on an apprentice." He winked at Laura as the blood drained from Matt's face.

Matt sputtered and Kevin started laughing, rubbing his arm after a punch from Matt.

"Don't play with me like that, man. You couldn't even shave your head with clippers in college."

"Yeah yeah. Never going to live that down, am I?"

"Not if I have anything to say about it, no. Though," Matt glanced at Kevin, "we could use a better website if you have some spare consulting time. We can set up an appointment to talk that over when the boss here," he inclined his head at Laura, "has figured out the kind of look she's going for. We've had a few bids, but either we have no idea how hard this is to do, or people out there think businesses with websites all rake in the gold."

Kevin pointed at the TV as the game came back on and Matt hit the mute button to turn the sound back up. "Let me know when and we'll talk about it. I can probably work out some kind of friendship discount."

Laura laughed and stood, waggling her empty cup. "Anyone else need a refill?"

Kevin held out his glass, as did Matt.

"Do we have any of those little smoked sausages?" Matt looked hopefully at Laura.

"I'll check." Laura padded toward the kitchen, stopping to chat with Jennie who was playing at the edge of the room. She'd made a little barricade of stuffed animals and pillows that blocked the hall. As her mom moved on, Jennie carefully rearranged so there was a small lane through the middle.

When the game finished, Kevin dragged himself back out to his car, waving off their offers of the couch and breakfast. Now that he'd decompressed, he wanted a long, hot shower and a night in his own bed.

CﬀﬂƆ

For the next several weeks it took all of Kevin's energy to keep his head above water at work. While he'd been out of town, the other projects he worked on had either gone unmanaged or, worse in his mind, been completely mis-managed by temporary replacements. Any worries he'd had about backlash from his refusal to transfer disappeared as he dove into straightening things out. Everyone commented in one way or another on how good it was to have him back.

When he wasn't working on the weekends, he split his time between Matt and Laura, his parents, and the Browns, though he'd yet to actually get a chance to talk to Lydia. She never managed to make any get-togethers that he attended. At church she seemed to be going out of her way to avoid him. He knew that he was probably going to need to make the first move if they were ever going to reclaim any portion of their previous friendship. But how, exactly, was he supposed to go about that?

In the meantime, Kevin had been in touch with the Georgetown PCC to see if they had anything that he could help with on a volunteer basis. They needed some technical work done around the office and with their website. The director was pleased that he'd called, though he hadn't yet made time to see what needed to be done. They were going to be having a seminar all day on the second Saturday of November, and Kevin planned to try and align his schedule to go in then.

CRBO

"Kevin McGregor." He answered the phone absently and continued typing the email to his team leads with instructions for revising the midpoint review report that was coming due.

"Oh. Sorry."

"Lydia?" Kevin hit send on the email and pushed back from his desk, swiveling to look out the window at the colorful leaves on the trees in his neighbor's back yard.

"Yeah…I actually hit the wrong number."

"Oh. All right well, I'll let you go." He spun back toward his desk, lowering the handset to find the off button, then frowned, quickly returning it to his ear. "Hey, Lydia, you still there?"

"Just caught me."

"I wanted to say that I'm glad you're doing better and, well, I miss being friends with you." He paused and cleared his throat. "Which is not in any way meant to be pressuring or anything like that, I just thought maybe…oh never mind. Have a good day, ok?"

He lowered the phone again and hit the end button before he could say anything else.

"Stupid, stupid, stupid." Kevin smacked himself in the forehead with each word and turned back to his computer, still grumbling at himself. When the phone rang again, he let it go to voice mail.

CRBD

Lydia frowned at the phone as she heard Kevin's recorded greeting begin and sighed, hitting end. Glancing at the clock on the DVD player, she leaned back on the couch and tried to figure out what to do with the rest of her day. She should call the former coworker she'd been trying to call when she'd accidentally dialed Kevin, but now, hearing his voice…she shook her head and buried her face in her hands. In the back of her mind, a little voice whispered that what would make things a little smoother right now was a glass of wine. Lydia groaned and pushed herself off the couch and went to the kitchen. Filling a glass with ice water she stood at the sink and forced herself to sip it slowly.

Her phone rang. "Hello?"

"Lydia. It's Rachel."

"Hey, great timing. You don't have cameras in my apartment, do you?" Lydia laughed and hoisted herself onto the kitchen counter.

"I'm not telling either way." Rachel's voice was sly. "So, what's going on?"

"Oh, nothing much. Just a classic case of subconscious phone dialing."

"This sounds intriguing. Spill."

"I got an email yesterday from an old coworker about a possible position with a firm she used to work at. One of her former coworkers had sent her a note wondering if she knew anyone looking, she thought of me, blah blah."

"Sure, nothing beats the 'who you know' job search network."

"Exactly." Lydia grinned and closed her eyes to send up a quick prayer of thanks for Rachel. "So anyway, I scrolled through my contacts on my cell, and rather than dialing Georgia McNichols…"

"You dialed Kevin McGregor." Rachel burst into hysterical laughter.

"Yes, though I don't think either of us found it nearly as hilarious as you did."

Rachel coughed a few times trying to cover the last remnants of her mirth. Finally back under control, she cleared her throat. "I imagine. Sorry. But you have to admit…"

"No, I really don't. At least not until maybe forty or fifty years have elapsed."

Rachel snickered. "So. How'd that go?"

"Unparalleled disaster is, I believe, the term that most accurately represents the situation. Imagine, if you will, me."

"Ok. Let me get a clear picture, what are you wearing?"

Lydia glanced down at her purple plaid pajama pants and fraying dark green long sleeved college t-shirt. "You remember my pajama pants?"

"The purple ones? I thought we agreed you'd burn those. They're tragic."

"Yeah, but they're super comfortable. Anyway, I was making a phone call."

"Uh-uh. Tell me you aren't wearing the green shirt."

"Ok. I'm not wearing the green shirt."

"You are, aren't you."

Lydia hunched her shoulders defensively. "It's comfortable. And I repeat again, phone call."

Rachel groaned. "Ok. So, slovenly dressed you dials the always, at least according to you, impeccably dressed Kevin."

"Gee, thanks for that perspective. That makes me feel a ton better."

"Sorry. Go on."

Lydia cleared her throat and took another sip of water. "He was clearly working from home. He answered with his professional 'I'm working here' voice. And then, of course, I froze and stammered out an 'Oh' and an apology rather than having the sense to disconnect. Then I sat there on the line through what felt like hours of awkward silence. And of course he recognized my voice."

"Of course. Poor baby. What happened next?"

"I blurted out that I misdialed." Lydia pulled the phone away from her ear in expectation of the explosion from her friend. She wasn't disappointed.

"What? Smooth, Lydia. Real smooth."

"I was flustered, ok? I was expecting warm and friendly Georgia, one of the few coworkers who still has a positive word to say about me. I got Kevin."

"All right...I can see that. Go on."

"Well, when confronted with that ever-so-graceful commentary, he said, essentially, 'Oh, I'll let you go then.' Honestly, it was almost like I was a telemarketer. With a phone transmittable plague." Lydia swung her legs, tapping her heels lightly against the cupboards. "So I'm getting ready to hang up and he gets back on the line and tells me that he misses me. Then he backpedals all over it and hangs up. Because apparently I'm now a terrifying entity...I get it. I was pretty horrible to him before rehab. And, well, other than the whole making amends email...I've been pretty good about avoiding him since he got back. He has to have noticed."

"Why are you avoiding him? I thought he was your best friend?"

"He was. Is. Was." Lydia sighed. "But I know I let him down. And even worse, I broke his heart. And part of me is pretty sure I did it just to see if I could. It's not a pretty thing to realize about yourself. Plus...there's no way I could ever deserve him now."

"Hmmm...then what?"

"Then I desperately wanted a drink, so I was practicing savoring some water, you remember, to try and stave off a craving? And then you called. Which is a better tonic than anything else I can think of." She smiled and finished off the water, setting the glass in the sink beside her. "So. Now that you know about my most recent humiliation, what actually prompted your call?"

"A couple of things, actually. First, I called to see what your job situation was looking like, but since you're going to be calling a former coworker when we're done, I can answer that one myself. Second, I got an email from a friend who lives sort of near you about a post-abortion workshop in two weeks. It's on a Saturday and I thought maybe it would be something you'd be interested in."

"Where is it?"

Rachel shuffled some papers around. "Hang on a minute, I printed it out so I could be sure and have it nearby when I called and then, of course, I immediately lost it in the pile of random things I've printed out for various reasons."

"It's tough to be you, isn't it?"

"You have no idea. Aha, here we go. Georgetown PCC? Heard of it?"

Lydia groaned. "Well, so much for that."

"So much for what? I'm confused."

"So much for my avoidance problems. My dad gave me their number a few weeks ago with the suggestion that volunteering while I was looking for a job might help me fill my time and this was such a great ministry and so on and so forth."

Rachel was quiet for several heartbeats. "He doesn't know yet."

"No...I don't even know how to bring it up. What do I say? Hey, Mom and Dad, I know I just finished putting you through heck and destroying your image of me and that we're on really tenuous ground now as we try to rebuild our relationship. And hey, I'm glad you've forgiven me, but while you're at it, I also murdered your grandchild, so could you add that to the list?" Her voice took on a hint of panicked hysteria.

"Ok, ok. Deep breath. Look, you know eventually you're going to have to tell them in order to leave it in the past, right?"

"Do you really think I have to?"

"Oh Honey, I know you do. And I won't kid you, it's going to be hard and more than likely it's going to hurt all of you. But in the long run, you're going to need to get it out there so it doesn't eat you up from the inside. Go to the seminar."

"All right. I'll call and see if they still have room."

"They will. Promise me you'll go."

"Fine…Sometimes you're worse than my mom."

"That's because we both care about you."

"Yeah yeah. I appreciate it though. I do. Mostly."

"I know you do. And since your dad gave you the number already, I'm not going to insult you by imagining that you threw it out with no intention of calling them and assume you still have it."

"In fact, I do."

Rachel waited on the other end of the line.

"Ok, fine. I tried to dump it on the ground as I got in my car but couldn't do it. Happy?"

Rachel laughed. "There's hope for you yet. Call them."

"I will, I will. Was there a third thing or is that enough harassment for the day? Because, I don't mean to be rude, but apparently I have phone calls I need to go make."

"Man I miss you. I don't think I've laughed this much since our last phone call. But no, that's pretty much it. I had also wanted to check and see if things were going better with Kevin, but since you've got the whole avoidance bit down to a science, apparently, I can figure that one out of on my own."

"I'm guessing you think I should pretend that nothing's changed?"

"No, that's not at all what I think you should do. What I think you should do is really pray about what your relationship with him is supposed to be. If you'd really listened to yourself during group, I suspect you'd already have pieced together that you're in love with him."

"What? Kevin?" Lydia huffed out a breath. "Look, you're clearly delusional and also possibly hard of hearing. He was my best friend, also delusional, mind you with his whole 'God told me we should be together' shtick, and now he's pretty much made it plain that he's happy to be rid of me."

"Recently?"

"Weelll, no. But his visit in the hospital was pretty final."

"Lydia."

"Ok, he might have said some things today that could be interpreted that there's a possibility for us to be friends again…but I just don't know."

"Pray about it. And then listen to the answer. And then, if we still need to, we're going to talk about the whole not deserving him thing you mentioned."

"Yes, oh wise one."

"Smart aleck."

"I miss you too. Any chance of a visit?"

"Probably not for a little while, I'm still piecing things back together myself." Lydia heard papers being stacked in the background. "It's always easier to fix your friend's life than your own."

"Anything I can do?"

"Yeah. You could pray for me, too."

"That I can do, now that I'm actually praying again. That's probably the best thing to come out of all this mess."

"Don't I know it. Now, you hang up, then call Georgia and the PCC. Let me know how the seminar went, ok?"

"Yes ma'am." Lydia made a sloppy salute but figured it didn't matter since Rachel would never see it. "Thanks for calling."

"Anytime. Bye now."

Lydia looked at the phone and pushed herself off the counter, setting the kitchen handset back in its cradle. She went to the living room and scooped her cell phone off the coffee table. This time she looked up Georgia's number in her contacts but grabbed the land line handset from the end table and carefully dialed. As the chorus of beeps pulsed in her ear, she bit her lip and waited for Georgia to answer.

Hanging up after the short but friendly conversation with Georgia, Lydia's cell phone chirped indicating a new email. She read it quickly to make sure it had all the information Georgia had relayed and smiled. The job sounded promising. She was definitely qualified, and, an even better bonus, it seemed like something she'd enjoy doing. Satisfied, she made a mental note to fill out the application and email that and her resume over tonight. Narrowing her eyes, Lydia looked back and forth between the phone and her laptop. It wouldn't take too long to get that done now, but it probably would take long enough that the PCC would be closed when she called.

"Tempting. But, of course, I promised. Stupid." She made a face at the phone and dialed the number off the smoothed out paper her dad had given her. As it rang, she chanted, "Don't answer, don't answer" under her breath.

"Georgetown PCC, how may I help you?" A very chipper, young sounding woman answered on the third ring.

"Hi. I was calling about the seminar next Saturday?"

"Oh great, hang on one second while I transfer you to Maureen Murray, our Executive Director." There was a click and then silence for a few seconds before the phone was once again answered.

"This is Maureen."

"Hi. I was calling about the seminar next Saturday."

"Did you have any questions about it, or did you want to go ahead and register?"

Lydia cleared her throat. "I think I have the basic details, time and place, so just to register?"

"Sure. Let me get your name so we can have a packet ready for you."

"Oh, sure, sorry. My name is Lydia. Lydia Brown."

"Great, thanks, Lydia. I'm not sure if you know, but we have small breakout sessions throughout the day for more intimate discussion. We try to group attendees together by experience. Would you like to be in the information purposes only group, or in the group for women who have personally had an abortion?"

Lydia smiled slightly at the phrasing and took a deep breath, her stomach clenching as always when she said the words. "I've had an abortion."

"All right. We'll group you accordingly." There was no judgment in Maureen's tone. "Now, we try to start right at 9:00, so if you can be here by 8:45 at the latest, it makes things run more smoothly. The seminar is free. We do offer a catered lunch for five dollars, or you're welcome to bring one."

"What's the catered option?"

"We have a selection of sandwiches and cookies brought in from a local deli."

"I'll go with that."

"Great, I'll make sure you're on that list. Bring a check or cash to registration. Do you have any questions?"

"No, I don't think so." Lydia worried a hangnail on her thumb.

"Then we'll see you in two weeks."

"Right. Bye." Lydia pressed end and dropped the phone on the couch next to her, frowning at the loose skin on her thumb. She bit off the hangnail and sighed before grabbing her cell phone and quickly texting Rachel.

"Done and done. Happy?"

The reply was almost immediate. "Very. Go eat a cookie."

Lydia laughed and shook her head as she dropped the cell next to the other phone at her side. She arranged herself cross-legged on the couch, flipped on the TV and found a real estate show for background noise, then tugged her laptop into her lap and hunkered down to tweak her resume and killer cover letter.

When she was finished, she strode into the kitchen and ate not one, but two cookies.

25

Kevin waited two weeks to tell Matt about the accidental phone call from Lydia. When he related the story over dinner, Matt nearly doubled over with laughter.

"Thanks, Matt. I knew I could count on you for support."

"Honestly, Shakespeare had nothing on you two. Talk about star crossed."

"Star crossed implies that feelings are shared. As in mutual."

Matt clapped Kevin's shoulder. "You never know, Kev. You never know."

"In this case? I'm pretty sure I know. I thought that I had distanced myself from it. First with the whole situation this summer and then in India when I thought I'd made peace with it. But hearing her voice?" He made a disgusted face. "It was pathetic. It's all still there."

"I get it."

"I know you do. But this time? I said my piece, though I still question the sanity of that moment."

"Insanity or Holy Spirit?"

Kevin pursed his lips. "I'll have to think about that. It certainly wasn't a conscious decision. Either way, I've finally been able to let it go."

"That's great, Kev."

"It really is. I can say with certainty that it's completely in God's hands and I can also say with certainty that I trust Him to make the situation what He wants it to be. And while I definitely have an outcome that I want, I know that no matter how things finally end up, I'm going to be able to be content."

Matt grinned. "Now, tell me about this thing you're doing tomorrow? Some kind of seminar?"

"I don't think I'm actually going to be at the seminar. It's the Georgetown PCC." At Matt's furrowed brow, he amended, "Pregnancy Care Center? They help women, and men, who are dealing with an unexpected pregnancy. Basically they provide alternatives to abortion like adoption or parenting. You should look at their website just to see how dreadful it is. I haven't gotten my hands on it yet. But at least the basic information is there. Anyway, they also do post-abortion counseling. The one day seminar is, from what I gather, kind of an intro and then they recommend an 8-week Bible study that focuses on accepting God's healing and forgiveness. I ran the projector for a similar seminar in India. It's a powerful day."

"So, you're not attending, you're helping?"

"Yeah, but not even with the seminar itself." Kevin grunted. "To my knowledge, a man who has never been with a woman cannot be responsible for her having had an abortion."

Matt rolled his eyes and gestured for him to go on.

"I called a few weeks ago about helping out somehow. The folks who came to do the seminar in India really impressed me and I felt like this was a ministry I needed to be a part of. The director…Maureen…something, I have it written down at home, she was pretty excited about the idea of someone with technical skills being a volunteer. I guess they get equipment donated, or purchased for them, and their expertise doesn't really run to making it all work efficiently. That and their website." Kevin shuddered. "Like I mentioned, it needs some serious work. So, since they'll be open tomorrow anyway, Maureen asked me to come by and get together with the staff member who's been trying to keep things going and who is, from what I gather, responsible for the website. Then we can see what steps need to be taken."

"That makes more sense…I'll have to talk to Laura and see if she can think of any way that the salon could help." Matt drummed his fingers on his glass. "We've been toying with opening a training school as part of the salon. Maybe that could factor in somewhere? I'll talk to the brains of the outfit. She'll have better ideas anyway."

"You two are always coming up with fascinating business plans. A school?"

Matt nodded and launched into a description of their thoughts and plans to date, his enthusiasm for the project clearly showing. Kevin smiled to himself as he listened. If anyone could make a success of something so ambitious, it would be Matt and Laura.

26

Lydia rode the escalator up from the Metro station and looked around, getting her bearings. She headed across the street, ducking into one of the ubiquitous coffee shops that resided on nearly every corner downtown. Letting the hot latte keep her fingers warm in the November morning chill, she briskly walked three blocks to the Georgetown PCC, enjoying the scent of fall.

Since she'd seriously considered driving, she noted that there were still a few street parking spots nearby. But with all the traffic zipping by, they'd fill up quickly. She glanced up to verify the address with the one in her email. Finding the right door, she ducked into an open, brightly lit lobby and glanced around. It felt a little like a doctor's office with the chairs lining the wall and the half-wall reception area, but the décor was warm and inviting, rather than sterile. She noticed piles of magazines and brochures placed around the room as she craned her head to see if anyone was behind the desk.

"Hello?" Lydia checked her watch and frowned. She heard quiet chattering down the hall and a petite, fairy-like woman in her mid-fifties appeared.

"Sorry. We're all in the back having coffee." She glanced at the cup in Lydia's hand and grinned. "Though you look set on that score. Still, we can offer you fresh donuts." She gestured for Lydia to follow her, propping open the door to the area behind the desk, revealing a sign directing people to the conference. "This always gets closed and I never remember to put a sign on both sides. I'm Maureen, by the way." She stuck out her hand.

"Lydia."

"Pleasure to meet you. Let's get you signed in and then I'll show you where the donuts are. Sam, this is Lydia. She should be on the list."

A graying, pudgy man looked down at a piece of paper in front of him, nodded and made a check mark. Looking up again, he smiled at Lydia and extended a purple folder and nametag. "Welcome, Lydia. They have donuts in there, I'm told, though I've also been told I'm not allowed to verify that for myself."

Maureen laughed and swatted his shoulder. "I'll save you one, Honey, I promise. The conference room is through here. You'd think I never fed my husband the way he's been going on about the donuts all morning. Make yourself comfortable, we'll be starting before too much longer."

She strode off, stopping here and there to greet the women and, Lydia was surprised to note, a few men who mingled awkwardly in small groups.

With a sigh, Lydia dropped a plain donut on a plate and grabbed a napkin. She didn't really want it, but she didn't feel like she should forgo them after all the fuss. Tables were arranged in a big U. Where should she sit? The far leg had no purses or folders set down yet, so she made her way that direction, skirting around clumps of people. She put down her folder, donut and coffee and started to slip out of her coat when a familiar voice drifted down the hallway.

"Pleasure to meet you in person, finally, Maureen."

Lydia flinched. What was Kevin doing here? And more importantly, how could she keep him from seeing her? At least she'd come on the Metro so her car wasn't parked out front. Looking around, she spotted the restroom and hurried over to it. She gave an apologetic smile to a woman who was also heading in that direction as she opened the door and slipped in, locking it behind her. Closing her eyes, she leaned against the door and tried to think up a plan.

Muffled voices came through the door. She recognized Maureen and Kevin, then a third voice she didn't know. She pressed her ear to the door and strained to make out words.

"...glad I could get down here to start on the computers today while you're open. I appreciate you coming in, Janice."

The voice Lydia didn't recognize answered. "It's not a problem. Why don't we head upstairs and I'll show you the offices, that's where all the desktops are, or most of them anyway. We can look at the computer in the reception area later if we need to. But they'll be starting the post abortion conference soon and I'd as soon stay out of the way. It can be a sensitive time for people, so we try to minimize the number of non-participants hanging around."

Kevin's reply was inaudible. Had they left the room? How was she supposed to know if the coast was clear? She jumped a little at the tap on the door.

"Oh, um, just a second." Lydia flushed the toilet and washed her hands. She gave the woman waiting another apologetic smile and went back to her seat.

CRBO

Kevin took in the sparse office area upstairs. "Looks like you spent your decorating budget downstairs."

"We haven't gotten to the upstairs yet. We moved to this location just over a year ago and we've been inundated with clients. That was, of course, completely the point of moving here, but it's cut down on the time we have for things like getting the offices prettied up. I suspect that's part of the issue with the computers. I really haven't had the time to dedicate to them."

"Which one did you want me to start with?"

Janice indicated the machine on her desk. "Theoretically this is the server. The idea was to have them networked so we could use some scheduling software, share documents, that sort of thing without having to make copies all the time. So far no one can see anything on anyone else's box."

"All right, well, I'll start with that and see what I can do. Router?"

Janice pointed.

"Great. Did you want to stay and watch or did you have stuff to do? I'm fine with either."

"Would you mind if I left you? I actually have a pretty busy day planned. Normally I'm not in on Saturdays, but it's hard to say no to Maureen. Still, it'd be a big help if I could get going."

"Not at all. As long as no one minds me being up here alone."

"I'll check with Maureen, but if I don't come back up, you'll know it's ok. Here's my cell," she grabbed a business card and scribbled a number on it, "if you run into passwords or whatever that I can maybe help you with, feel free to call." She held up a finger and slid out a drawer. "Speaking of passwords, this notebook has them all written down. I know it's not secure, but we were having a crazy time keeping things straight."

Kevin laughed and took the notebook and the business card. "I'll put it back where it was when I'm finished. If I do anything major, I'll send you an email with any instructions you need."

"Sounds perfect. Thanks so much."

Kevin watched her leave then scooted in at the desk and powered up the machine. Looking around, he grabbed a blank piece of paper from the printer and started making a list of important items, like the fact that if a machine was meant to be the server, it really needed to be left on.

CR80

Kevin got the network up and running, though it took him quite a bit longer than expected. Whoever had tried to set it up before had left a big mess to untangle. He shook his head and made another set of notes. When the computers upstairs could all see one another and access the printer, he installed the software that had been left out for him. It worked fine and was a nice, if simple, shared calendar and contacts program. He wrote down the name so he could familiarize himself with it. It was more likely than not that he'd be getting a few calls when they actually started using it. His stomach rumbled loudly. He glanced at his watch and chuckled, no wonder he was hungry, it was coming up on one o'clock.

Pushing back from the computer, Kevin leaned back and stretched, groaning slightly as his back and neck popped. He stood, twisted at the waist in both directions to stretch a bit more before collecting his notes, the software, keys and cell phone. He glanced around the room to check that he had everything and turned out the lights. He locked the door at the top and pulled it shut behind him before he bounded down the stairs.

The seminar was still going on in the conference room. He set down his notes and various other materials by the reception desk and went down the hall as quietly as he could. He poked his head through the door and caught Maureen's eye, grateful she wasn't the one currently presenting. She slipped out of her seat and joined him in the hall.

"I'm finished upstairs, but thought I'd run out for a quick bite before taking care of the reception machine if you're going to be here a while longer?"

Maureen glanced at her watch and nodded. "We've got another two hours, or thereabout but if you want a roast beef sandwich or chicken Caesar salad, we've got extras."

"A sandwich would be great. Do you have a paper cup I could get some water in?"

"There's sodas, too, or bottled water."

"Water, please."

Kevin retreated to the reception area. He'd just settled at the desk when Maureen returned with bottle of water, sandwich, bag of chips, and a couple of cookies.

"This is wonderful, thanks. Can I give you some cash to cover it?"

"I feel like we ought to be paying you for all your help. But if you want to contribute, we charge the participants five dollars."

Kevin pulled his wallet from the front pocket of his jeans and found a ten. "Keep the change. I'm guessing someone in there probably conveniently 'forgot' their wallet."

Maureen laughed and slipped the money into her pocket. She rested her hand lightly on his shoulder. "Thanks for getting things put right for us, I think everyone will be doing a happy dance on Tuesday when the computers are actually functional."

"I'll do what I can to make that the case."

Maureen returned to the conference room and Kevin worked on the sandwich while waiting for the reception computer to boot. He was more than half finished by the time the machine was ready for use. He made a note to spend some time on another day looking to see if there was anything he could do to speed it up for them.

Tthis computer was slightly less messed up than the machines upstairs. Possibly because it was so slow no one bothered to turn it on very often. Kevin scratched off the note about speeding it up and spent about forty-five minutes doing it. He was able to get it at least to the point of usefulness, but it needed to be the first machine on a replacement list. Some donations weren't worth accepting.

Once he finally had the reception machine able to see the rest of the network he checked his watch. It was nearly three in the afternoon. He wanted to be on the road by a quarter after three at the latest to avoid the bulk of the Saturday evening traffic. He installed the software, drumming his fingers on the desk as he waited.

Music drifted down the hall and Kevin listened, trying to identify the song. He slipped down the hall and peeked around the doorframe. The lights had been dimmed to highlight the beauty of flickering candles at the foot of a small table-top cross. He watched for a few minutes as the participants stood and went forward to light one or more candles. Some returned immediately to their seats, others stood or knelt for several minutes with tears streaming down their cheeks. Kevin offered a prayer for their healing, remembering the power of the memorial service he'd witnessed in India.

His breath caught in his throat when he recognized the blonde hair and gait of the next woman who rose and went to the altar. He watched, unable to turn away, as she knelt and lit a candle and bowed her head, her shoulders shaking with silent sobs. As she started to rise several minutes later, Kevin flattened himself on the outside of the doorway then hurried back to the reception area. His blood slowly began to bubble beneath the surface of his skin as he exited the program and shut down the computer. He collected his notes, left a short thank you and promises of an email on a sticky note for Maureen and strode from the office, barely managing to avoid slamming the door.

Once in his car, Kevin pulled recklessly into traffic, making several lane changes to a chorus of blaring horns as he wove through the streets at speeds well over the limit. He made it home in record time and took great pleasure in slamming both the car and the front door. He looked around his house. How was everything still the same as it was this morning? How was it possible that the bottom had just fallen out of his world? Again. He grabbed the vase he'd bought for Lydia at the London airport. Thinking of her sent his blood pressure surging and he heaved it across the room. A small jolt surged through him as the vase gouged a hole in the wall and shattered to the floor in shards.

The explosion of china left him finally able to take a breath and he slid down the door, knees drawn to his chest. Kevin leaned his head forward and rested his forehead on his knees.

"Oh, God." The groan was all the prayer he could muster as he sat there, reliving the shock of recognition as Lydia knelt by that small, flickering candle.

27

Lydia was relieved to see the reception area was empty as she poked her head around the door when the seminar was over. She'd been trying to figure out how to slip past Kevin ever since she overheard that he was going to be working on the computers. She flinched as someone touched her shoulder and turned.

"Lydia?"

Lydia nodded at Claire, the woman who'd helped Maureen with the bulk of the presentation. "Hi."

"Thanks for coming today. Maureen wanted to be sure you got a flyer about our upcoming eight week post abortion Bible study."

"Is it in the folder?"

"Actually, no. We didn't end up getting the calendar set before we stuffed the folders. They were over by the food during lunch, but we noticed not many of them got picked up. We'll be sure to get them stuffed in the folders next time. Do you have time for me to run and grab one for you?"

Lydia nodded and folded her coat over her arm as Claire hurried back down the hall. She emerged a minute later brandishing two brightly colored flyers. "The pink one is the eight week study. This one," she switched to the lime green one, "is about our volunteer counselor training. Maureen thought you might want that one as well?"

"I think she's been talking to my dad. He's been trying to get me to volunteer while I'm job hunting."

"Oh? What type of work are you looking for?"

"I have an MBA, though I've been working primarily in PR for the last several years. I've been exploring both of those options. At this point, I just want something that's going to make it possible to pay my rent every month."

"Hmm." Claire narrowed her eyes. "Wait here one more minute, would you?" She trotted back down the hall without waiting for an answer. Several minutes later she and Maureen appeared.

"Your father didn't mention you were job hunting."

"I guess he didn't trust me to actually call about volunteering."

Maureen's eyes twinkled. "He might have indicated you seemed hesitant. I suspect that might have something to do with today's conference?"

"He doesn't...no one, family I mean, knows."

"Oh. I see. Well, that would have to change. And the eight week study and volunteer training would both be required before you could start, but, we actually have an opening that might be what you need."

Lydia blinked, confused.

Claire finished rooting around in one of the desk drawers and handed Lydia a small packet of papers stapled at the top corner. Maureen glanced at them before offering them to Lydia. "Take some time to read over the job description and more detailed information about our mission and statement of purpose. Pray about it and, if you're interested, we can set up a time to talk further. It's possible that you could start before completing the various training and Bible studies." Maureen pursed her lips again, drumming her fingers on her thigh. "We'd have to talk about it with the Board. Still, you might be who we've been praying for."

Lydia glanced at the paper just long enough to see the title Director of Marketing, Statistics and Development before tucking it, with the other two brightly colored flyers, into her folder. "Ok, um, thanks."

"It was nice to meet you, Lydia. Thanks for coming." Maureen waved as Lydia turned and nodded.

"Thanks. You too." Lydia made her way to the door before things got any more bizarre.

The house phone rang. Kevin ignored it, listening for the answering machine. When it picked up, the caller disconnected. A few seconds later his cell started buzzing. He sighed and dug into his pocket. Leaning his head back against the door he answered, his voice weary. "Hello?"

"Hi Kevin...hey, are you ok?"

"Hey Allison. Yeah, I'm fine." He glanced down at his watch. He'd been sitting in the entry hall alternating between fuming and moping for a little over an hour. "What's up?"

Kevin pushed himself to his feet and went to investigate how badly he'd damaged the living room wall.

Allison took a deep breath and let it out slowly. "Ok, here's the thing."

"Nothing good ever starts that way, Al."

"No, this is. Or might be. At least, I think it *could* be. Maybe?"

"Is this how you win cases in court? Cause I'm thinking I should switch careers if that's all it takes." Kevin tucked the phone between his ear and shoulder and frowned at the big dent in the drywall. A few layers of spackle would probably fix it, no need for an actual drywall patch. He glanced down at the ceramic shards and headed to the kitchen to find his broom and dustpan.

"Everyone's a comedian tonight. Ok," she took another deep breath, "let's try this again." She cleared her throat. "I suspect you remember our rather disastrous date?"

Kevin headed back toward the mess with the broom and dustpan in tow. "Uh, yeah. Not a highlight of the last few months, sadly."

"True. Well…would you be willing to try it again?"

"What? Allison. You can't possibly think that's a good idea."

"Well, no. Not to date you. But to *look* like I'm dating you, absolutely."

"Aha. The plot thickens. What's his name?"

"Do I really have to go over all the details with you?"

"Yeah. If you want me to be complicit in an attempt to make another man jealous in order to get him to date you, I need details. Look," Kevin glanced at his watch again, "why don't you show up at my house in about an hour with Chinese food, and those details, and we'll see what we see?"

"Am I getting reimbursed for the Chinese?" Allison sounded skeptical.

"Nuh-uh. Cost of doing business."

"Fine." She sounded disgruntled. "Why can't you make this easy for me?"

"Did you forget who you called?"

"I can't believe I ever wasted time pining over you."

Kevin snorted.

"All right, all right. But if I'm buying, you get what I bring."

"Fair enough. But get extra hot mustard. See you in an hour." He clicked off the phone and tucked it back into his pocket before stooping to deal with the shattered china. After several passes with the broom, he got out the vacuum. When it stopped making clinking noises, he rubbed the whole area with a damp paper towel. Satisfied that no one was going to cut themselves, he put the cleaning equipment away and dug the spackle out of his tool box. He'd finished applying the first, rather heavy, coat when the doorbell rang.

He snapped the lid of the spackle shut and carried the spatula with him to get the door. Allison edged past him with a big bag of white cartons. She stopped in the foyer and looked around. "Kitchen?"

Kevin shut the door and pointed, following behind her. He went to the sink and washed up the spatula and his hands then got out two plates and some forks. "Smells good."

Allison lined the containers up along the island. "It actually does. When you said Chinese, I nearly argued with you," she barreled on past his fake gasp of surprise, "but then I started thinking about this place," she tapped the logo on the bag, "and decided I could get behind that idea."

Kevin hopped onto one of the stools and passed Allison a plate. She glanced at the kitchen table then shrugged and joined him on the stool next to his.

"So?" Kevin made a bed of white rice on his plate then went through the line of boxes, sniffing each one before grinning and piling some of each onto his plate.

"Can I say that it really is too bad it would never work between us? You have excellent taste in Chinese."

"Wow, Kevin. You sure know how to make a girl feel special." She followed his example, loading her plate with food. When their plates were set Kevin grabbed her hand and blessed the food. She tugged her hand free and echoed the amen.

"Not to be repetitive, but…inquiring minds want to know."

"Ok. There's this guy at work, Phillip. Physically very attractive, but…even better than that, he heads up the weekly Bible study at lunch on Wednesdays."

"So far so good. Now," he forked up a bite, "why is it that you can't ask him out? Or make it clear to him that you'd like him to ask you out?"

"He's divorced."

Kevin looked at Allison expectantly. When she didn't say any more he raised an eyebrow. "And?"

"Apparently he's of the opinion that once you're divorced you can't be a Christian and remarry."

"Ooh. That's trickier. Who left whom?" Kevin got up and went to the fridge, pulling out a soda. He waggled it at Allison, who nodded. Grabbing a second soda, he returned to his seat.

"She left him, after, apparently, running him through the wringer with multiple affairs. The only tiny blessing is that they'd not gotten around to having kids yet."

"All right. Now, what makes you think the jealousy angle is going to work on him?"

"I don't even know that it will. But I don't really know what else to try."

"Not to turn the tables, but, have you been praying about it?"

"Probably not as much as I should have."

"Ok, here's the deal. You and I both pray about this for a week, starting tonight. If he hasn't made a move and we're both convinced that there's nothing wrong with arranging a situation where he sees you out with another guy, we'll give it a shot. Then we'll hope he miraculously realizes you're the woman God has for him."

"Deal."

They ate in companionable silence for several minutes before Kevin spoke. "It doesn't bother you?"

"What doesn't bother me?"

"The whole divorced thing? I mean, if he was married, he's not..." Kevin paused, clearing his throat and blushing slightly.

Allison laughed. "A virgin?" She poked Kevin in the ribs with her elbow. "You are the most easily flustered man I've ever met." She sobered, sighing and setting down her fork. "Seriously though? I guess maybe it does a little. I mean, here I've been saving myself for my future husband for all these years, against incredible odds. You know how easy that isn't in today's world. So yeah, at first when I started to notice him as more than a coworker and more than a friend, it did bother me." She took a long drink of soda. "But while I might not have a sexual past, I do have a past. I've done stupid things, sinful things. They still have echoing repercussions in some areas of my life, so it's not like I'm perfect, you know?"

Kevin nodded slowly, spinning his soda on the countertop.

"Is this about Lydia?"

He nodded again.

Allison bumped his shoulder with hers. "It's probably not exactly the same, I mean, Phil was married not just hooking up, but," she puffed out her cheeks and let the air explode from her lips, "that's one aspect I have been praying about, and finding that at the end of the day, I'm able to see the past as just that. Past."

Kevin looked at her empty plate. "Finished?"

She nodded and he gathered the plates and silverware and carried them over to the sink. He turned and leaned against the lip of the sink. "Thanks."

Allison grinned and combined the leftovers into as few containers as possible, stacking the empty ones inside one another and carrying them to the trash. "You want to keep the remnants?"

"Nah. You paid, you can have them."

Laughing, she tucked the boxes back into the sack she'd brought dinner in and took them to the foyer, hanging them and her purse over the doorknob. She came back into the kitchen in her sock feet. "All right now, we've had dinner. I think an action flick is in order. Isn't that how good friends bond on a Saturday night?"

Kevin grinned, putting the last of the dishes into the dishwasher. "Either that or football, but I could really go for the movie I think after today."

She followed him into the living room. Kevin saw her notice the dent in the wall but, though her eyebrows shot up, she didn't say anything. "Ok, I have all the film standards you'd expect or," he checked the time, "we could roll the dice on the SyFy original movie. It's bound to be cheesetastic."

After a brief discussion, they decided on the science fiction made for TV picture, Allison on the couch, Kevin in the arm chair next to it. Companionably, they settled in for a few hours of mindless monster movie.

28

When he woke up Sunday morning, Kevin stared at the ceiling for several minutes. He should get up, go to church. He really should. The evening with Allison had provided a good break for him and he'd managed to put his new knowledge about Lydia aside for the time being. But as soon as Allison left, it had all come rushing back and left him feeling angry and betrayed.

"I got over the drug use and forgave that. I even, finally, got past, well, mostly got past, the sex. But an abortion, too? Really, God? How can you expect me to get past this?"

Though he'd hoped for one, no answer was immediately forthcoming. Grumbling, he pulled himself out of bed and threw on workout clothes. He'd skip church and head out for a long bike ride along the Potomac instead.

CRISO

Kevin propped his bike against a tree and flopped onto the grassy bank of the river. Mount Vernon, George Washington's home, was a little farther down the road. There probably weren't that many tourists out at this time of year, but he hadn't wanted to risk a crowd. Miles of full out pedaling hadn't managed to lessen his anger and he knew that fury was written on his face.

With a sigh, he leaned back on his elbows and stared at the river. What was he supposed to do now? Even in India he'd been sure that God would bring him and Lydia together. Though he'd struggled to accept the things she'd done, seeing God work miraculously in the lives of the women and children in India had helped him realize that no sin was worse than any other. Ultimately that had helped him forgive the sex and drugs. But surely taking the life of an innocent wasn't the same to God. Was it? Even if it was…he wasn't God. Where did the ability to forgive something like that come from for an average man?

His cell phone rang. Glancing at the caller ID, Kevin snarled and sent Lydia straight to voicemail. A few minutes later it signaled a new text message.

Where are you? Was hoping to talk you into lunch. Call me.

"Fat chance." Kevin debated ignoring the message, but his mother's insistence on courtesy was too ingrained. He hit reply.

Needed down time today.

He snapped the phone back into its holster and stood, stretching. Remounting his bike, he began pedaling furiously back toward his car, hoping the exertion would finally wear away his anger and underlying hurt.

☙❧

Lydia frowned at the terse message. It wasn't like Kevin to provide so little information. Should she text him again? No. She had to have some pride, didn't she? Shoulders slumped, she pushed through the last of the church crowd in the foyer and made her way out to her car, resigned to lunch on her own.

"Lydia, wait."

She turned to see Laura running after her.

"Phew." Laura rubbed her growing belly and worked to catch her breath. "I always say I'm going to keep exercising while I'm pregnant. Then I never do. Do you have lunch plans?"

"No. I was just trying to decide what I had at home to throw together."

Laura hooked her arm through Lydia's. "Come out with me instead. My parents have Jennie for the day and Matt is heading off to hang out with Kevin. I need adult conversation."

Oh sure, he needed downtime. Why didn't he just say he was meeting Matt? Lydia pushed those thoughts to the back of her mind for later. "Sounds like a plan. What are you hungry for?"

೦೪ಬಿ೦

Kevin got home, sweaty and exhausted but still fuming, and found Matt sitting on his front step.

"What are you doing here?"

"Playing Angry Birds. Good to see you, too, man." Matt shut down his game and stood. "Missed you at church."

Kevin gave a noncommittal grunt and pushed past him to get to the door.

"Hmm." Matt narrowed his eyes. "You going to tell me what's bothering you or do I have to beat it out of you?"

"This isn't high school, Matt. Don't you think I would've called if I wanted to talk about it? Why don't you go back to your perfect life and leave me alone?" He pushed the door open, stepped through, and tried to shut it.

Matt stuck his foot in the rapidly closing space. "Kevin."

He glowered at his friend for several minutes and considered shutting the door on his foot. Finally he relented. "Whatever."

Kevin spun and strode into the kitchen, leaving the door ajar. Matt followed, carefully closing the door behind him.

"So?"

Kevin stood in the door of the refrigerator, letting the cool air wash over him. When he was nearly chilled he grabbed a bottle of water, twisted off the cap, and chugged down nearly half of it. "What?"

Matt frowned and leaned against the doorframe. "You know… if you didn't want to talk about it you could have made up an excuse about church and I'd've gone. So…I'll just hang out here for a while, keep you company. Laura's off on a girl's errand this afternoon anyway."

Kevin simply shook his head and finished the water. He tossed the bottle into the trash and leaned back against the sink.

"Hmm. Small talk." Matt crossed the room and straddled one of the kitchen chairs and drummed his fingers on the chair back. "Oh, I know. How was the computer work at the pregnancy place yesterday?"

Kevin scowled at his friend and grumbled, "You want to know how it was? It was the most screwed up thing I think I've ever encountered in my life. If people are going to have computers they ought to figure out how to use them, otherwise they ought to give people who do know what they're doing a break and leave them alone."

Matt quirked a brow. "That's quite a tirade."

Kevin stared at Matt and felt the wall of rage he'd built in his heart start to crack. Pushing away from the sink, he grabbed another chair from the table and sat. "She was there, Matt."

Matt looked at him quizzically. Slowly understanding worked its way across his face. "Lydia was at the Center? Why...oh. They were doing that abortion seminar."

Kevin nodded.

"She was helping out?"

Kevin closed his eyes and shook his head.

Matt winced. "Oh man...Did you ask her about it?"

"No. I don't actually think she saw me. And once I realized it was her, I left as fast as I could. I'm so angry, Matt."

"Understandable. But...don't you think you need to talk to her about it?"

"I don't plan to talk to her ever again. So no."

"Kevin..."

"Do you really think that if you'd found out something like this about Laura that you'd've wanted anything to do with her? Be serious, man. Especially when you consider everything else." He dropped his head to the back of the chair.

"I can't honestly say. Though Laura and I didn't exactly get off to a perfect start...so I get being angry." At Kevin's skeptical look Matt shrugged. "I do. But..." he looked at his friend and tentatively finished the thought, "…what about the assurances you've had from God?"

Kevin scoffed. "Everyone else apparently gets to choose to sin whenever they want and not deal with any negative repercussions. So now it's my turn. I'm not doing it." He looked up and crossed his arms. "There's such a thing as too much, and this has crossed that line and kept running."

Matt frowned but said nothing.

"I mean it, Matt. I'm done with her. I'm done. I don't have it in me to forgive anything else."

29

By Wednesday, Lydia was starting to get annoyed. Kevin hadn't returned any of her calls or texts since the terse message on Sunday. It was time, she decided, to beard the lion in his den and see what was going on. She drove to his house to see if he was working from home. And she wasn't leaving until she had an answer.

She rang the bell and waited. After a few minutes she heard the clatter of feet on stairs and the door opened. "Hey."

Kevin scowled and started to close the door. "Go away, Lydia. I'm working."

"Uh-uh." She pushed on the door. "This isn't like you. If you're done being friends with me then I think I deserve to know why."

"You do?" He poked his head back out. "You think you deserve that courtesy? When, exactly, did you extend that courtesy to the rest of us this last year?"

Lydia winced. "That's not fair, Kevin."

"Fair? You want to talk about fair now? That's rich." He moved to close the door. "Go away, Lydia."

"Wait."

Kevin sighed and raised his eyebrows through a crack in the door.

Lydia took a deep breath. "Look. I know I've been avoiding you…and I'm not proud of it. But I was worried it would be awkward after the whole hospital thing and…" She frowned and forced her fingers to unclasp from one another. "I wanted to say that I'm sorry…in person. And to thank you for being a good enough friend to tell me the truth even though I didn't want to hear it. I…rehab was a good thing."

He gave a curt nod. "Fine."

It was as if an ice pick pierced her heart. "That's it? Fine?"

"Not sure what else you're expecting. You've made it clear for years that you and I weren't going to happen. I've finally realized that you're right. I really have work I need to get back to. Thanks for dropping by." He shut the door with a click and the locks snapped into place.

Lydia stared at the door and fought back tears. That hadn't gone the way she'd hoped. She turned and headed back to her car. Now what?

After driving aimlessly for nearly an hour, Lydia pulled into a parking spot in front of Laura and Matt's salon. She stared at the rows of hair products visible through the plate glass window that spanned the front of the building. Why had she'd ended up here? With a sigh she gathered her purse.

Entering the salon she smiled slightly at the soothing smell of coconut and sandalwood and approached the reception desk.

Matt looked up from the computer and grinned. "Lydia. What brings you here? I didn't see you on the appointment calendar?"

"I was hoping maybe Laura was around?"

"She should be. Why don't you head on back to the office, I'll let her know you're on your way."

"Thanks." She offered a tight smile. As she walked through the salon, her senses were assaulted by chemical smells and the sounds of trimmers, scissors, and conversation. Lydia hurried down the main aisle and knocked on the office door.

"Come in."

She pushed the door open and poked her head in. "Is this a bad time? Cause I can come back, or call…"

Laura looked up from behind a pile of paperwork and shook her head. "Nope, you're doing me a favor. I think if I had to spend another minute with this inventory software I would need to hurt someone." She clicked a few things on the computer and pushed away from the desk. "Come on in and sit." She gestured to a small table shoved in the far corner. "What's up?"

Lydia shut the door behind her and tugged one of the chairs out. She watched as Laura rolled her office chair over and propped her feet up on the spare chair with a sigh. "I just stopped by Kevin's…to see why he hadn't returned any texts or emails. And…" She took a shaky breath and swallowed the lump in her throat. "He made it pretty clear that he's done with me. And I can't figure out why." She blinked furiously. "I mean, I know why. The whole last year. But…why didn't he just make a clean break? Why all the pretense of still being friends…still being in love with me…I was finally beginning to realize how much I…I think I'm in love with him. And now…I don't understand what changed."

A hot tear dripped down her cheek. She swiped at it and sniffled.

"Oh, Lyd. I'm sorry. He didn't say anything?"

Lydia shook her head, sniffling and desperately fighting the flood of tears that threatened.

Laura pursed her lips and studied Lydia. "Give me a minute, k?"

At Lydia's nod, she pushed herself out of the chair and through the office door. After ten minutes she returned carrying a tray that held two tall glasses of iced tea and a plate of cookies.

"All right…here's the deal." Laura set the tray on the table and resumed her seat. She set a glass in front of Lydia and pushed the plate of cookies her way. "You didn't hear this from me…but I think you deserve to know and I've convinced Matt that we should tell you."

Lydia furrowed her brow, confused.

"Kevin saw you on Saturday. He knows."

The blood drained from Lydia's face and she buried her head in her hands, overwhelmed with mortification that not only Kevin, but Laura and Matt now knew too. No longer able to hold back the tears, she sniffled, "No wonder he hates me."

Laura scooted closer and gently rubbed her back. "He doesn't hate you. He wants to, but he doesn't. He's…well, he's angry. And hurt. And confused."

"What do I do now?"

Laura hesitated. "All I can think to do is pray for wisdom."

After spending some time praying with Laura, Lydia drove home. She still wasn't sure what to do, though she agreed with Laura that, for now, there might not be anything she could do. Heart heavy, she turned out of the elevator toward her apartment and groaned at the sight of Brad and Staci wobbling drunkenly toward her.

"Afternoon." Lydia nodded her head and sidestepped the pair, hoping to leave the encounter at that.

Brad grabbed her arm, grinning broadly. "Lydia, Babe." He leaned toward her, making Staci, whose hand he was holding, stagger slightly as he dragged her off center. "Been too long, where have you been hiding?"

Lydia jerked her arm free and smiled thinly. "Not hiding. Busy."

She glanced pointedly at her watch and started to move down the hallway.

"Aw, don't be like that Babe." He moved to grab her arm again.

"Just keep away. And really, doesn't your wife object to you calling another woman Babe?"

"Nah, do you Baby?" At her head shake Brad grinned. "See. Two is grand, but three makes it better."

Lydia shuddered and hurried toward her door, ignoring the mocking laughter that followed after her. Turning the locks behind her, she leaned against the door and stared, unseeing, at her living room. Tears spilled from her eyes as she dropped her purse and keys on the small table by the door. She grabbed the phone and punched in Rachel's number.

"Hey girl."

"Oh Rach…my life is a mess." Lydia stretched out on her couch, cradling the phone.

"What's up?"

"Apparently Kevin saw me at the seminar Saturday and, being smarter than average, put two and two together."

"You hadn't told him?"

Lydia sighed. "I haven't told anyone here…but I guess I'm starting to realize that maybe you're right. I'm going to have to. But Rach…he hates me now…and I…I don't really blame him."

"What do you mean?"

"I didn't deserve him before this whole mess." She wiggled onto her side trying to get more comfortable. "That's one of the reasons I kept him at arm's length. But now?" She closed her eyes. "How stupid can I be, thinking that he could ever love someone like me?"

"So...he's perfect? Never done anything bad?"

"Not like this. Not like me."

Rachel sighed, her annoyance transmitting clearly over the phone line. "Well then, I guess that's it. Let's figure out how to get you signed up for grocery delivery so you never have to leave the house. Maybe you could start collecting cats. Or newspapers. Heck, why not both?"

"I'm serious, Rachel. I don't deserve him. And I was stupid to think I could."

"Listen to yourself. Didn't you hear anything they said in the seminar about forgiveness?"

"Sure...but it's not like I didn't know better. I did...and I sinned anyway."

"True. But Lydia, that doesn't mean you're not forgiven. Did you grieve God with your abortion? Yes. Was it more damaging to your relationship with Him because you knew better and did it anyway? Yes. Does Christ's blood still cover it? Yes."

Lydia sat up and rubbed her hand over her face. "I hear what you're saying...and I want to believe it, but...Kevin..."

"Kevin is going to have to work through this. Try to put yourself in his shoes...imagine the shock he got. The betrayal he must have felt. Give him some time...some space."

"But...what if he decides he can't, or won't, get through this?"

"Then you wait and see who God *does* have for you. He has a plan, and it's a good one. We just don't know what it is yet."

She took a deep breath and let it out slowly. "Ok…that makes sense. Feel like sorting out the rest of my life? You're on a roll."

Rachel laughed. "Sure. Hit me."

"I ran into Brad and Staci in the hallway. He hit on me. In front of her. She thought it was funny."

"Ouch."

"Plus, I'm seriously considering the job that they kind of offered me at the PCC. And that's never going to pay the rent here."

"Back up. They offered you a job?"

"Didn't I tell you about that?"

"Obviously not…spill."

Lydia filled her in on the position as well as the job with the PR firm her former work contact had hooked her up with. "So I'm not really sure what to do. Working at the Center means telling my parents about the abortion and after Kevin's reaction…"

"Stop. Telling your parents isn't optional, and you really need to do it sooner than later. I suspect Kevin's reaction was so strong *because* you didn't tell him. He found out all on his own. I'm not saying he would have reacted with butterflies and rainbows if you'd told him, but he might not feel quite as betrayed."

Lydia closed her eyes, her stomach sinking through the floor, as the truth of Rachel's words struck her.

"I'm going to take the silence as an acknowledgement that I'm right. 'Cause you know I am. As for the rest…pray. I'll pray for you, too."

"Thanks, Rach."

"That's what friends do…and Lydia? Call me when you've told your folks and let me know how it went."

"I'm having dinner with them tonight." She sighed. "Not like my day can get much worse."

"Call me later."

"K. Bye."

❦

On the drive to her parent's house, Lydia pondered what seeing Brad and his wife meant. She had assumed that they would be living in his apartment. It was much more suited to the hipster style he aspired to, and really, it was gorgeous. She couldn't see any woman turning down the chance to move there. She wrinkled her brow, trying to remember, was it paid for by his parents? Maybe that factored in. But if they were going to live in her building, there was no way that she could.

Lydia dropped her forehead to the steering wheel and moaned, muttering, "Just great. One more problem to solve. Like being unemployed isn't challenge enough."

The tap at her window startled her and she let out a surprised chuckle when her dad pulled her door open.

"Your mother is beginning to wonder if you changed your mind about coming in." Paul winked and offered her his hand.

"No. Just trying to collect my thoughts."

"Come inside, share them, and we'll see if we can't collect them together. Your mom had a pot roast in the crock pot all day. If nothing else, it smells like heaven in there."

Lydia's stomach grumbled at the mention of pot roast and she shut the car door, clicking the lock before following her dad inside.

Lydia leaned up to peck her dad's cheek before heading back to the kitchen. She inhaled deeply as she passed through the doorway. "When do I get to learn your secret, Mom?"

Mary laughed and slid an arm around Lydia's shoulder, pressing a kiss to her cheek. "The recipe is a wedding gift, and you know that."

"I'm going to have to drag it out of Dan." At her mother's look she grinned. "I know it's him, not Prissy, who cooks in that family, give me some credit."

Mary handed Lydia a pile of plates and silverware. "Go set the table and call your father. He's been whining about starving to death for about twenty minutes."

When grace had been said and the food passed around, Paul smiled at Lydia and raised his eyebrows. "So, what has you banging your head against your steering wheel today?"

"I wasn't banging it, just resting it there." She took a bite and let out a quiet mmm. "I ran into Brad and his wife in the hallway. I guess I thought that they would live at his place, you know? He's not really a part of my life I want to be reminded of every day."

Mary nodded understandingly and glanced at Paul before asking gently. "Have you had any progress on the job front yet?"

"Didn't I tell you? I'm sure I told you." She glanced at her dad who wore the same blank look her mom did. "I have two possibilities that I'm praying about right now." Lydia described the positions, leaving out how she came to receive the offer at the PCC. They discussed some of the pros and cons of each that she'd been trying to list as part of her decision making process.

"When do they need a decision by?" Mary swirled a potato through the pot roast juice on her plate.

"The Monday after Thanksgiving. It took a little convincing for them to give me the time… the PR job is obviously antsy. I don't know if they have other candidates or they really need the position filled, but honestly, they're being just pushy enough that I'm a little worried."

"How so?" Paul rested his elbows on the table and steepled his fingers, garnering a frown from Mary as he did so.

"At my old firm, the only time we were really anxious about filling a spot was when one of the accounts was about ready to walk for one reason or another, and they wouldn't work with anyone currently on staff." Lydia shrugged. "It could be nothing, but the companies are comparable, so I have to figure the culture is somewhat similar and I really don't think I want to jump into an enormous drama storm. Especially if they're having to hire from outside. That means there's bad blood on both ends of the spectrum. That's never good."

Her parents nodded and her mother rose and started gathering the plates. "Have you seen any salary figures for the other job?"

"It's definitely not in the comparable realm, though I could still make it work with some stricter budgeting." She sighed. "This is why it's so tough. On the one hand, a good salary but a potentially terrible job, at least to start out. On the other hand, a lower salary and a completely unknown job. I mean, I'm fairly sure I could do it all, but the environment is foreign."

Paul sipped the coffee Mary set in front of him. "How did you hear about the PCC job? I would have thought an ad would have been in their most recent newsletter. I don't remember seeing anything about it, do you Mary?"

Mary shook her head.

Lydia took a deep breath and sorted through her options. The choice was fairly clear. One of the things she'd promised herself during rehab was that she was going to stop lying to herself and to her loved ones. And even though she'd basically promised Rachel that she'd do this tonight, she had really hoped to be able to put the conversation off until, well, never. Clearing her throat, she spoke quietly. "I went to their one day post-abortion conference."

Paul nodded, looking slightly confused. Mary's eyes widened and she drew in a quick breath and looked at Paul, devastated. Slowly, comprehension worked its way across Paul's expression and he closed his eyes. "Oh, Lydia."

"I'm so sorry," Lydia's voice was strained with the effort to hold back tears.

Mary reached over and squeezed Paul's hand before standing and wrapping her arms around Lydia. "Baby, why didn't you come to us?"

Unable to hold back her tears any longer, Lydia turned her face into her mother's shoulder and wept.

Lydia lay in bed that night staring out the window at the city lights on the horizon. Her parents had surprised her. They weren't angry. Shocked and disappointed, certainly, but also hurt. Mostly hurt that she hadn't trusted them enough to ask for help, she realized. She sighed and flipped over, trying to settle her thoughts. It felt strange, good, but strange to no longer have that secret hanging over her head, taunting her in the night. She closed her eyes and let her thoughts drift into a prayer for direction about her job and what to do about Kevin.

She woke early the next morning with a sense of peace she hadn't felt in a very long time. Though singing had never been her strong suit, she found herself singing songs she remembered from Sunday school in the shower. Dressed, she made her way to the kitchen and poured a cup of coffee. At some point in the middle of the night she'd realized the answer to her job dilemma.

Glancing at the clock, she decided to give Gloria's friend a call, even though it was early.

"Good morning, this is Sylvia."

Lydia leaned back against the kitchen counter. "Hi Sylvia, this is Lydia Brown."

"Lydia, nice to hear from you, what can I help you with?"

Lydia took a deep breath to steady her nerves. Even knowing this was what God wanted her to do, the unknown was a scary place. "I'm calling to let you know that I've decided to accept another position. I appreciate your patience with me while I've been deliberating, and once I made up my mind I didn't want to make you wait over the holiday."

"I'm sorry to hear that. Is there anything we can do to change your mind?"

"No, I'm sorry."

"All right. Thanks for letting me know. And if it ends up not working out with your other position, keep us in mind, ok? I'd really love to have you on staff."

"Thank you. I will. Have a happy Thanksgiving."

"You too. Good bye." The phone clicked in Lydia's ear and she set the handset down on the counter and slid to the floor, her hands shaking.

"This was the right decision." Lydia muttered to herself, clasping her hands together to still their movement. She pressed a hand to her stomach and groaned at the butterflies doing cartwheels. "Lord, I'm certain this is what you would have me do. Please," she took a calming breath, "give me peace."

A sense of quiet relief washed over her and she leaned back to rest her head against the counter, whispering. "Thank you."

She sat for a few more minutes in the tranquil silence before pushing herself back to her feet. The PCC wouldn't open for another few hours, so she took her lukewarm coffee into the living room and booted up her laptop. She quickly typed up a repeat of her message to Sylvia, turning down the job offer, and emailed it so they'd have an official written record. Then she emailed the completed PCC forms to Maureen expressing her interest in the position and asking what else, if anything, they would need from her. As she hit send, she realized that she had put all her eggs in one basket. She might have misinterpreted their degree of interest in her. The calm from the kitchen stayed with her, though, so she pushed the doubt from her mind and instead set to work organizing her email inbox.

As she sorted the email that she'd let build up over the last year, she unearthed several messages from Kevin during his first trip to India. Reading over them again, she realized what a good friend he had always been to her, even when she was terrible to him. She hovered her mouse over the delete button then frowned. Instead, she created a folder and funneled the messages from Kevin into it. When her inbox was empty, save for the few messages she had yet to respond to, she felt the folder of Kevin's email once again drawing her attention. Before she could talk herself out of it, she grabbed the phone and punched in his number.

"Kevin McGregor."

"Hi Kevin, it's Lydia...don't hang up."

Lydia was encouraged by the fact that she heard nothing. No click. No dial tone. *Progress. I'll take it.*

"I know you're angry with me. Of course I know that, I'd have to be an idiot not to know that after yesterday. And I'm rambling. But here's the thing...I'm sorry I didn't tell you. I was really hoping to never tell anyone and kind of leave the past in the past. I know I can't do that...I told my folks last night. You don't care about that...really I just wanted to say I'm so sorry one more time and that I hope, at some point, you can forgive me. And maybe we can be friends again?" She chewed her lip as the silence on the other end of the line continued. "Ok...well...I'll let you get back to work."

"Lydia."

"Yeah?"

"I'm working on forgiving you. But don't get your hopes up about being friends again. I think that ship has sailed. Thanks for the apology though. Maybe one of these days it'll help."

The phone clicked in her ear. Lydia sighed and set the handset down. *What did I think would happen? I should have waited to call...maybe twenty years would have been long enough?*

After hanging up, Kevin pushed his chair over to stare out the window. *God...what are you doing?* Hearing Lydia's voice, his heart had lifted. Then he remembered the seminar and all that it meant and his blood had begun to boil. In the back of his mind, he knew his attitude was wrong, but he couldn't seem to shake it.

On a whim, he scooted back to his desk and opened his personal email. Scrolling down, he found the slide presentation from the missionaries he met in India and opened it, flipping through quickly to the slide on anger. Pursing his lips, he printed the drawing of weeds and stared at it for several minutes before grabbing a pen. He drew roots on the weeds and began to label them: Lydia, Brad...he hesitated. *Is it ok to be mad at God?* After a brief internal struggle, Kevin decided God could take it and drew a root for Him as well. Finally he drew the last root and added his own name. "Though I'm not sure why I'm so angry at myself. Is it for loving her all these years? Or because even as angry as I am, I still love her so much it hurts?"

Kevin switched off the vacuum. Had he heard the doorbell? He frowned, he hadn't made any plans for the day after Thanksgiving. It was as good a time as any to fix things around the house and do a little cleaning, so he'd set it aside for just that. The bell rang again and he raced down the stairs to the door, smiling when he saw Allison standing there.

"Hey." Kevin propped the door open wider and gestured for her to come in. "What brings you to this neck of the woods?"

Allison smiled and waggled a takeout bag. "Lunch."

Kevin's eyebrows knit together. "Did we make plans and I forgot?"

"No, you're not senile. Yet. I come bearing gifts."

"Hmm. And ulterior motives, I suspect."

"Guilty. But let's eat first, I'm hungry."

Kevin snorted and shut the door. "You're lucky I'm doing some house cleaning today and happy to take any break I can get."

Allison looked up from unloading the boxes of chicken and sides onto the counter. "I thought you had someone who cleaned every week?"

"Every other week." Kevin shrugged. "Doesn't mean I don't need to push the vacuum around every now and then."

"Fair enough. White or dark?"

"I can get it." He took plates down from the cupboard and handed her one. "You know, this actually smells really good. Most people stay away from poultry the day after Thanksgiving."

"Ah, but this is deep fried poultry. That's a completely different animal. Besides, I thought you were on your own this year, so maybe you had meat loaf or something."

"They make very passable Thanksgiving-themed frozen dinners I'll have you know." Kevin loaded his plate and sat at the counter. "So I did manage to have turkey with all the fixings." He crunched into a drumstick. "Mmm. Still, this is good. Thanks."

Allison sat next to him. "I'm kind of surprised you didn't finagle an invite to the Brown's. You know they'd have included you in a heartbeat."

"True...but Lydia would have been there."

She arched a brow. "And?"

Kevin shrugged. "And I'm kind of avoiding her right now."

"Oookay." She shot him a confused glance. "Something you want to talk about?"

"Not really. No."

Allison looked at him for a minute with pursed lips. "Hmm. Then how about we segue into why I come bearing chicken." She huffed out a sigh. "Our office Christmas, oh excuse me, *holiday* party is next weekend. Will you come with me?"

"Is this the 'make Phillip jealous' expedition?"

"Not really. Well, maybe. I don't know. I do know I don't want to go without a date, because I heard he's bringing someone. But at the same time, I really do want to go. Usually they're a lot of fun and it's nice to hang out with people outside the office every now and then. Plus…I hardly ever get a chance to dress up, so I hate to miss one just because I'm too big a coward to ask the person I want to go with."

"Ouch." Kevin clasped a hand to his heart and feigned injury.

"Whatever. We know we're better off as friends anyway. So?"

"Hang on. Let me go get my phone so I can see if I have anything else scheduled." He slid off the stool and disappeared upstairs. He came down a few minutes later scrolling through the calendar on his phone. "You're in luck. Next Saturday is still open and I own my own tux, so I don't have to worry about a last minute rental."

"Of course you own your own tux. Why wouldn't you?"

"Hey. When you're in as many weddings as I seem to end up in, it very quickly becomes clear that you're going to be happier renting a cummerbund and tie than the whole shooting match." He grinned. "I'm just glad there's no 'always the best man, never the groom' saying. Cause that would be me."

"Well, don't rent a cummerbund on my account."

He laughed. "I have a vest and tie that I wear when I go to parties. I wasn't planning on matching it with your wrist corsage." He sobered and looked at her thoughtfully. "You're sure about this? You don't just want to ask him outright? Recent events in my own life have made me, let's say wary, of secrets."

"I don't know. I'm not really comfortable asking a guy out."

"All evidence to the contrary."

"It's really not the same now, is it? Anyway, as I was saying, at this point, I just want someone to go and hang with me so I don't look like the sad girl who can't get a date to the party. And it'd be nice to get your take on Phillip. I'm really not doing this to try and make him jealous, that was me having a stupid idea."

"That makes me feel a little better about it. Email me the details." Kevin dumped his trash and stacked the plate in the sink. "Wanna help clean?"

"Yeah right." Allison laughed, shaking her head. "I've got to get going."

"Bribe and run, eh?"

"You know it. I'll send you the details later tonight." She let herself out and Kevin chuckled, sweeping crumbs off the counter onto her plate. He tidied up the kitchen before returning to the vacuum and his obsessive and contradictory thoughts about Lydia.

C53&D

Lydia stared at her coffee maker, willing it to brew faster. Even without a job, Monday mornings seemed to be challenging. Add moving day to Monday and she really needed coffee. Lots of coffee. She rummaged around in the box at her feet, pulled a mug free of its wrappings, and set it next to the machine. Slowly, the hot, dark liquid dripped into the carafe. Looking around she ignored the pang in her chest. This was for the best.

After another altercation in the hallway on Friday, Lydia had called her parents to see if they'd be willing to let her rent their basement until she could figure something else out. The truth of the matter was that her current place was going to cost too much if she did get the PCC job, and if she didn't, well, it would definitely cost too much. She was surprised at how happy her parents had sounded and wondered for the hundredth time if they'd wanted to invite her but weren't sure how it would be received. Lydia had wasted no time and spent the rest of the weekend packing.

Now, it was pretty much down to the last few dishes. She still had to pack her coffee maker, if it ever decided to go ahead and finish brewing, but that was about it. Then came the task of actually moving everything. She wandered into the living room where she'd consolidated the boxes from her bedroom and closet. Now, at least, those two rooms were clear of everything other than furniture. Her dad was renting a truck and would be there, with a few friends, to start the move before too much longer. With a sigh, Lydia sank to the arm of the couch. It felt like a step backward in so many ways. Moving back home. Being unemployed. The whole situation with Kevin. She shook her head and closed her eyes, sending up a quick prayer for peace.

The coffee maker beeped from the kitchen and she pushed herself off the couch, anticipating the first taste. She poured a cup and sipped the piping hot liquid. She could feel her muscles relax. Everything would be ok.

At the knock on her door, Lydia took her coffee and went back into the living room. She smiled when she saw her dad and three of the elders from the church through the peep hole and opened the door.

"Morning, Dad." Lydia leaned up to peck his cheek and waved to the others. "Hi. Thanks for your help. Come on in. I have coffee ready, if anyone wants some?"

They all shook their heads and Paul led them through the apartment, planning their packing strategy. Staying out of the way was probably the best way to help. She returned to the kitchen for another cup of coffee.

Several minutes later, her dad came into the kitchen and leaned against the counter. "We've got our plan settled, so we're going to get started. I think it's probably easier if you want to take your suitcases and head over to the house. That way you're not here to micromanage." He winked.

"Or worry about what you're breaking." She nodded and rinsed out her mug and the coffee machine. "I'll take these with me, since they're too hot to pack right now. You sure you can handle it without my help?"

"Absolutely. You go on home and start figuring out where you want things to go. Leave me your keys so we can lock up when all is said and done."

Lydia fished the keys out of her pocket and handed them to her dad. "Thanks, Dad. I really appreciate this."

Paul tucked the keys into his own pocket and threw an arm over her shoulders, giving them a squeeze. "It's my pleasure."

Lydia collected her mug and the coffee maker and stopped to grab her purse from the hook by the door. She turned and surveyed her apartment one last time and with a bittersweet sigh headed down the hallway to the elevator.

⚜

Later that evening, Lydia stood in the middle of a pile of boxes in her parent's basement. It had been a long day of moving things around, and even though her dad and his friends had handled all the heavy lifting, the packing and now unpacking was still a chore. The basement was a good size, only slightly smaller than her previous apartment. It had its own entrance and kitchen and the rent was much more within her realm. Especially since the landlords weren't likely to be quite as fussy about being on time.

She flopped onto the couch that she'd positioned as a divider between the kitchen and the living area and turned the TV on for some background noise. Flipping channels idly, she considered what else needed to be done next. The thought was broken by her cell phone ringing.

"Hello?" Lydia glanced at her watch. It was just after seven, even if it felt much later.

"Lydia? This is Maureen, from the Georgetown PCC."

Lydia sat up and clicked the mute button on the TV. "Hi, Maureen. How are you this evening?"

"Great, thanks. I'm sorry to call so late, but we don't close 'til seven on Mondays and there never seemed to be a minute to catch my breath until now. I'm sure you know how days like that go."

Lydia looked at her jumbled surroundings. "I do, definitely. It's not a problem."

Maureen cleared her throat. "I was so glad to receive your application packet the other day. I wanted to take the extra time to run it past my Board before calling you. Generally speaking, I have the final say in who's hired, but since your position is probably going to interact with the Board more than others, I wanted to at least extend them the courtesy of taking a look before making the final decision. That said, they all agreed that you appear to be a perfect fit. We're all anxious to have you on board. So…if you're sure this is what you want to do, we'd like to set a start date."

Lydia let out a breath she hadn't realized she'd been holding. "That's fantastic. Um." She chewed on her lower lip. "I actually moved today, so I'd kind of like the rest of this week to get things settled again. Could I start on Monday next week?"

"That's perfect. It gives me time to get your training materials together and so forth as well. The staff meets for prayer and devotions at 8:30. I'm usually in by 8. If you want to plan on being here between 8 and 8:15 I'll give you a quick orientation before staff meeting."

"Perfect. I'll see you then. Thanks, Maureen."

"Looking forward to having you on board. See you Monday."

Lydia pressed end on her phone and let out a whoop of delight. She hopped off the couch and took the stairs to the main part of the house two at a time. At the top of the stairs she paused, unsure of how to handle going into her parent's domain. She tapped on the door and pushed it open, poking her head around the corner. "Mom? Dad?"

"In the den, Honey. Come on up." Her mother called.

Lydia leaned in the doorway and smiled seeing her parents curled up on the couch watching TV together, her mom resting her head in the crook of her dad's arm, his hand resting on her hip. They looked over at her and her father spoke. "Getting settled in?"

"Slowly but surely. I should have it livable before too long."

"Do you need something?"

"No, I wanted to come and let you know I just got off the phone with Maureen." She took in their polite, but blank, gazes. "From the PCC downtown? I got the job."

Both of her parents grinned and her mother wriggled up from the couch, crossed the room and gave her a tight hug. "Congratulations, Honey. That's wonderful."

Paul smiled at her from the couch. "Agreed. When will you start?"

"Next Monday. I figured I could use a week to get settled. Maureen seemed fine with that."

"That's a fantastic answer to prayer, sweetheart. We couldn't be more thrilled. Do you want to join us?"

"No, but thanks. I should get back to unpacking. I'm going to try to stay out of your pockets."

Her parents laughed and her mother reminded her, "You're welcome up here anytime."

"I know. Thanks." Lydia disappeared back into the basement, pulling the door closed behind her. Maybe she ought to suggest putting a latch on both sides. That way they could lock it when it would be inconvenient for her to pop in and she could as well. Not that she intended to do a ton of entertaining, but she seemed to recall a poem from high school that said something about strong fences making good neighbors.

Back downstairs, she grabbed her phone, intending to text Kevin. With a frustrated sigh she dropped the phone back on the counter. What was wrong with her? He'd made himself clear. She went into the bedroom. She'd start in here—it was always good to have a room to retreat to. As she unpacked clothes and put them away, she smiled wistfully at the image of her parents snuggling on the couch. She wanted that for herself. She'd been looking for that kind of love with Brad and had been so desperate to try and create it that she'd thrown out everything she believed.

Her thoughts drifted back to Kevin and the incredible friend he'd been to her since high school. And how had she repaid him? She frowned and decided the only word that really fit accurately was horrible. She sat on the edge of her bed and dropped her head into her hands. Was there anything she could do to make amends? Now that she was finally ready, she continued to pray she hadn't completely missed her chance. Even though he'd made it pretty clear that she had.

Lydia gave herself a mental shake and reminded herself to pray about it, rather than worry. She put the last of her clothes away and set to work flattening the boxes before leaning them against the wall in the kitchen. She returned to her bedroom and smiled as she looked around.

"Just needs a few things hung on the wall. Which," she glanced at her watch and winced, "I will not do at nearly midnight." Seeing the time made her yawn. She plugged her phone into the charger, checked the lock

on the outside door, and turned off lights before heading
to bed.

33

Kevin's week started off terribly and went downhill from there. He spent all of Monday and most of Tuesday putting out fires at work caused by a programmer who'd been hired while he was in India. It turned out the man was very good at interviewing but not so good at actually doing anything he'd said he could do. They nearly missed a deadline, and Kevin was not pleased with the manager who hadn't been paying enough attention to see that coming. Though they got the delivery made, the client was already sending emails asking for fixes so that the product aligned with the contract.

Wednesday morning, Kevin headed into his home office and looked at his personal cell phone for the first time that week. There were four texts from Allison about the party on Saturday. He frowned as the absence of texts from Lydia made his heart sink, even though he knew there was no reason for her to have texted him. *Not after how I've been acting. Justified. But why do I miss her so much?*

"I need to get through Saturday with Allison before I can focus on Lydia…whatever that ends up meaning." Thinking of Allison, he scrolled through her texts and shook his head at her palpable nerves. He shot her a quick confirmation of the details and what he hoped was a soothing reminder that it was going to be ok. He set the phone down and powered up his laptop.

When no further texts from Allison came, Kevin turned his full attention back to his work email, grimacing at the long conversation between the incompetent programmer and the client. *Who had connected those two?* He shuddered as he opened the first email.

⚭

Saturday, Kevin spent most of his day doing little things around the house in between managing hitches at work that kept cropping up. He was still in his work clothes when he realized it was six. He'd better hurry if he was going to pick Allison up on time.

A quick run through the shower and the fastest donning of his tux in recorded history, and Kevin was out the door. At least traffic was light. He managed to be only a few minutes late. She opened the door as soon as he knocked.

"Wow." Kevin took in the flattering black cocktail dress. "Don't you clean up nice?"

"I could say the same." She nodded her approval. "Very nice. And the silver-tone vest is a very nice touch. I have to admit to being worried you were going to show up with a random cummerbund."

Kevin laughed. "Not when the joke would, ultimately, be on me."

The drive to the hotel where the party was being held was short. They walked into the ballroom and Allison paused to look around. Tugging on Kevin's elbow, she nodded to the far side of the room. "Let's go over there, I think I see Phil and some others I know."

"Whatever you say, I'm just the arm candy." Kevin grinned and dodged her quick elbow jab to his ribs.

Allison raised a hand in greeting as they made their way across the room. Phil smiled slightly and waved back, as did a few other guys. Kevin surreptitiously looked around for their dates, but failed to see any women in the area.

"Hey Phil." Allison beamed at him and waited for Kevin to join the little circle. "This is my friend Kevin." She tilted her head. "Where's your date?"

Phil shrugged and cleared his throat. "I was going to bring my sister, but she ended up needing to work a double. So, I came by myself. Turns out most of us are solo as well. Except for Jerry who did decide to go ahead and bring his wife." He said the last with a tinge of dry sarcasm that made Kevin and Allison chuckle.

"What does your sister do?" Kevin asked.

"She's a nurse over at the Children's Hospital. Not sure why they ended up short staffed tonight, but really it's kind of par for the course as far as me using her for any kind of plus one." Phil wrinkled his forehead. "I think next time I won't even bother asking."

Kevin nodded in agreement. "My sister got married and moved away so she could stop being my date. At least in your situation you still get to see each other."

"I'm sure that her husband's job had nothing to do with the moving away part." Allison gave him a lopsided grin.

Glancing around, Kevin spotted the punch table. "Anyone want some punch?"

"Sure, thanks." Allison smiled. Phil shook his head.

"Be right back." Kevin sauntered toward the refreshments.

CBEO

Allison stood awkwardly. Why hadn't she worn a dress with pockets? Then she'd have something to do with her hands. Phil broke the silence.

"So, how do you know Kevin?"

"He went to my church in high school." She paused and chewed on her lower lip before adding, "We're just friends, have been since college."

Phil raised a brow.

"It's true. He's been in love with another girl pretty much since I met him. I suspect that things might actually work out between them sometime soon. At least I hope so." She smiled. "He deserves to be happy."

Phil hummed in his throat. "How does one determine that someone deserves to be happy?"

"I don't know. I guess maybe, at some level, I think everyone deserves that. I know the whole problem of evil gets in the way, but," she fluttered her hands in exasperation, "I also don't think that God wants us to mope around being miserable just because life is hard."

"And would you say that's what I'm doing?"

"No." Allison frowned. "That's not what I said, or what I meant."

Phil chuckled. "Got you."

"You've got a mean streak, you know that?" Allison laughed and looked up as Kevin returned, handing her a glass of punch.

"They've got hors d'oeuvres over there as well, if anyone's getting hungry."

Allison shook her head, as did Phil. Kevin stuck his hands in his pockets and glanced between the other two before shooting Allison an 'everything ok' glance.

She smiled, nodding slightly. "Looks like it's filling up a little more, maybe we should do the rounds to make sure I say hello to everyone important."

Kevin extended his hand to Phil. "Nice to finally meet you, Phil. I hear your name a lot."

Allison shot him a look that promised retribution as she stalked off. Phil shook Kevin's hand looking bewildered.

When they were across the room, Allison hissed at Kevin. "Why did you say that?"

"The man is clueless, Al. Maybe now he'll realize that you're not just a friendly coworker."

Allison winced. "I don't want to look like I'm throwing myself at him."

"You don't. Please, don't worry. I gave him a little nudge that guys understand. I believe my work for the evening is complete."

Allison rolled her eyes and glanced at her watch. "Well, we have to stay here at least another hour, so now you have to entertain me."

Kevin stuffed his hands in his pockets. "All right, here's something to chew on: at what point is it ok to decide you don't have to keep forgiving someone?"

"You don't believe in the light topics, do you?" Allison huffed out a breath. "I think, honestly, the answer to that is never. You have to forgive, because Christ forgave you. After that, though, I think you can decide whether or not to let a person back into your life." She glanced at him and narrowed her eyes. "Why do I feel like we're talking about Lydia again?"

"Because you know me." He ran a hand through his hair. "I found out something a few weeks ago. It kind of feels like the last straw. And still," he shook his head, clearly disgusted with himself, "I can't honestly tell you I don't still love her. So much of me wants to forgive her, but there's this other part of me that wonders what horrible thing she's going to throw at me next. I don't know how much more I'm supposed to take."

Allison was quiet for several moments. "Two things come to mind. First, 'Love bears all things.'" Noting the expression on his face one side of her mouth twitched up. "You won't like the second any better, 'Love covers a multitude of sins.' If you love her, and I've never doubted that you do, I think it's pretty clear what needs to happen."

Kevin sighed, his shoulders slumping. "Not really what I was hoping to hear."

"No one ever said life was going to be easy." She patted his shoulder. "Now. Since your attempts at entertaining have failed miserably, I'm taking over. Let's go see what the buffet has to offer."

34

Lydia woke early Monday morning and spent some extra time in prayer, something she was glad to be able to do again. It was her first day at the PCC. Was this really the right decision? She pressed a hand to her stomach to quell the churning. It was absolutely the right thing. Even if the unknown was scary. Still, it was hard to put it completely out of her mind. She'd taken the time to speak to each of her siblings and tell them the whole story about her last year's breakdown. They had been angry, hurt, and disappointed, but each of them had, over the course of the week, found a way to forgive her. *Unlike Kevin.* She pushed the thought and the brief flare of anger at his attitude away. She understood his reaction. But if he really wasn't going to forgive her, then he probably wasn't the right man for her. No matter how much she missed his presence in her life.

Lydia dressed in a black pant suit, pairing it with a cheerful red turtle neck. Casually professional. Hopefully it struck the right note. She wasn't really sure what, if any, dress code they had. And it was just as bad to be over dressed as under. Having decided to use the Metro rather than deal with traffic and parking, she tossed the heels she wanted to wear in the office into her bag and slipped on more comfortable flats for the commute. After double checking that she had all she thought she'd need, she headed out. Hopefully she'd left enough time to be on the early side of when she was expected.

Maureen greeted her at the door to the PCC with a smile. "Right on time...actually a little early. Come on in and I'll give you the tour."

Lydia followed, looking around more carefully than she had when she had come for the seminar.

"The downstairs is primarily used for client interactions. We have the reception area here; the volunteer counselors take turns working reception. Or, on days when we're short staffed, one of us from upstairs will come down, most often our Client Services Director; you met her at the conference. Back here are four counseling rooms. We use them for everything from the initial appointment to follow up appointments and education about parenting, marriage, financial management, adoption," she wiggled her fingers, "you name it. When you've finished training, you'll have all the details and more about the resources we offer." She continued down the hall.

Lydia followed. If she could remember even half of the information Maureen was spouting, she'd be thrilled.

"This is the conference room; you remember it, of course. There's a kitchen behind it and the bathroom there." Maureen indicated the door to the room Lydia had used as a hideout.

"And that's everything on the first level?"

Maureen headed toward the stairs. "Yes. Let's go up and get a look at the nerve center." She unlocked the door at the top of the stairs and flipped some light switches. "I hadn't made it up here yet this morning." She smiled and turned to the right. "Over here is my office. I share it with the Client Services Director since it's so large. It seemed wasteful to have that much room allotted to one person. The door is usually open unless we're in a meeting with parents. I often counsel parents of younger clients up here. It feels homier."

Lydia peeked in the office, taking in the two desks, each with stacked files and books. The small meeting area looked inviting with three plump chairs and a stuffed bookcase.

"Now, over here," Maureen went back down the hallway, stopping half way, "is the break room slash staff room slash kitchen for the upstairs." She gestured for Lydia to look in.

There was a small refrigerator, a conference table littered with books and shelves along one wall that held neatly labeled binders. A copy machine was wedged into the back corner by a small sink and microwave.

"This is where we meet for prayer every morning at 8:30." She checked her watch and continued down the hall. "Down here are our last two rooms. The first is the office you'll be sharing. I think you'll find it's not too cozy," Maureen grinned, "and by cozy I mean crowded. The other ladies you work with are delightful and I have no doubt you'll get along just fine. Your desk is the clean one by the window. And over here," she crossed the hallway as Lydia looked in the office, "is our storage room. We keep donated baby items, maternity clothes, formula, diapers, that kind of thing in here."

She pushed open a door to reveal plastic shelving units all neatly stacked and labeled.

"Wow. You get a lot of donations."

"We do, it's wonderful. We have guidelines for how our clients earn the goods. It's all education based, we want to make sure that they're learning and growing as parents, not just coming for handouts." She tugged the door shut. "Generally speaking you probably won't have much need to go in there, unless you decide you want to start counseling on top of your other workload."

Lydia swallowed and shook her head.

Maureen laughed. "We'll see if that changes as you get your feet thoroughly wet in the ministry. Now," she checked the time again, "we've got about ten minutes until staff meeting and I need to make a few calls. So why don't you go ahead and get settled at your desk. I put some binders in your left hand drawer. They have a more detailed look at what you'll be doing. I also put the HR paperwork on your desk. Get that filled out and back to me at some point this week so I can make sure you start getting paid." She smiled again and headed back to her office.

Lydia sat at her desk and slid open the drawer. She pulled out the two thick binders and set them on top of the desk. She bounced in the chair, adjusting a few of the levers to make it more comfortable and stashed her purse in the bottom drawer of her desk. After swapping her flats for the heels she'd brought, she glanced over the HR paperwork. She could probably get a good start on it before the prayer time.

୧୫

For a first day it hadn't been all that bad. Lydia dropped her bag on the floor by the door as she locked it behind her and kicked off her shoes. She looked around the basement apartment, remembering the setup from childhood. She and her siblings had used it for a hangout, before her parents had converted it into an income suite.

"Who says you can't go home again?" She muttered to herself and padded over to the kitchen to forage for a snack. She had some reading she wanted to get done, even though she'd been assured there would be ample time for her to do it during work hours. Somehow it didn't seem right to her not to try and get up to speed as quickly as she could.

Her phone beeped with a text. She smiled when she saw it was from Rachel asking about her day. She started to text back then shrugged and instead poked the call button as she snagged a soda from the fridge and headed toward the bedroom to change into her pajamas.

"Hey."

"Hey yourself. I was going to text back but figured I was home, so might as well call."

"Works for me. I only texted because I wasn't sure if you'd be home yet. Since you said you were taking the metro, I didn't want you to have to try and talk on the train."

Lydia laughed as she carefully hung her work clothes in the closet and slipped into her nearly threadbare, but oh-so-comfortable, pajamas. "Fair enough. But to answer your question, it went pretty well. Definitely lots to learn."

"Well, that's good right?"

"Yeah. Just a little intimidating. I've been doing PR for so long, I wonder if I'm going to be able to make the switch."

Rachel scoffed. "You'll be great. Let's hear the details."

Lydia flopped onto her bed and propped her feet on the headboard, staring up at the ceiling fan. She described her tour, the staff meeting, and the other orientation activities they'd taken her through during the day, including the start of the volunteer training class.

"Sounds busy. They're going to keep you on your toes."

"More than likely. But it's really good to be at work again. And I feel like this is absolutely where I'm meant to be...I don't think I've ever really felt that way about a job before."

"It's a good feeling."

They chatted a few more minutes before hanging up. Lydia dropped the phone on the bed beside her and frowned at the fan. Chatting with Rachel was nice—it was good to have solid female friends in her life again. But she really wanted to talk over her day with Kevin...she'd gotten so used to having him there as her sounding board, his absence ached like a missing limb. Resigned, she went to the kitchen and pulled a microwave meal out of the freezer. While it cooked, she tried to push her confusion about Kevin to the back of her mind. She dug the binders out of her backpack and set a place at the small table for a little dinnertime reading.

By the end of the week, Lydia felt fairly comfortable with her new job and looked forward to going to work each morning. The two women who shared her office were warm and welcoming and had been quick to include her in lunch excursions and conversation. Everyone seemed personable and friendly and Lydia found herself comparing it to the corporate atmosphere at her previous job. She wondered how she'd survived as long as she had without realizing how cold and unfriendly it was.

Even as much as she'd enjoyed her first week, she was glad it was the weekend. After so much time off, the routine of working was draining. Plus, she was looking forward to a laid back dinner at Matt and Laura's house. They'd gotten together somewhat more frequently since she'd been home from rehab, but with Kevin seemingly out of her life for good, Lydia was hoping that they might be willing to fill some of the void. *Of course, they're friends with Kevin, too…hopefully that won't be a problem for them.* She sighed. *What if he starts dating someone? Oh man.* She grabbed her purse and headed for the door, refusing to follow that line of thinking any further.

Despite Friday traffic, Lydia made it to Matt and Laura's house fairly quickly. She'd picked up ice cream on the way and offered it to Matt as she slid out of her coat.

"Ice cream in December?" Matt looked puzzled.

"Ice cream is always a good idea." Lydia looked at Laura. "How does he not know this?"

Laura laughed. "Come on into the living room. Since Matt's cooking tonight, it's our turn to just sit." She ran a hand over her very pregnant belly. "Which is about all I can manage these days anyway."

Lydia sat on the sofa and looked around at the homey room. "I love how comfortable it is here. Thanks for having me over tonight."

Laura sank into the couch next to her. "Thanks for coming. Since Jennie's off visiting my parents for the night Matt's thought it was the perfect time to line up some Guinea pigs for a recipe he found online so…you might want to wait until after we eat to thank me. I can't make any promises."

"I'm sure it'll be great. And if not," she shrugged, "we have ice cream."

"True. Very true."

The sound of two male voices drifted in from the kitchen. Lydia slanted her eyes at Laura. "Is there someone else here?"

Laura looked around, not meeting Lydia's eyes. "You know what, let me go see how much longer it's going to be until dinner. Can I get you a soda? Tea?"

"Laura." Lydia put a restraining hand on her friend's arm. "What's going on?"

As if on cue, Matt poked his head into the room and grinned. "Dinner is served."

Laura looked relieved and levered herself up from the couch. Lydia watched the process then stood, giving Laura one more suspicious glance before preceding her into the dining room.

Lydia took one step into the room and froze. Matt stood behind the chair at the head of the table. Kevin stood with an expression of panic on his face behind the chair to his left. Laura positioned herself in the doorway, blocking the exit.

Lydia turned to Laura, fighting the tears that burned in her eyes. How could they do this to her? Reaching forward, Laura gently rested her hand on Lydia's shoulder. She raised her eyebrows at Matt. He cleared his throat.

"Here's the thing." He looked between Kevin and Lydia. "It's tough for married people not to talk to each other. And, well…we love both of you and hate to see you hurting like this. So…"

"So we decided to see if we couldn't at least get you to talk to each other again." Laura nudged Lydia toward a chair. "It doesn't have to be more than that. You don't even have to be friends again. But this," she fluttered her hands in the air, "whatever it is has got to stop. You're both miserable and you're on your way to making everyone who knows you miserable as well. Now, let's sit down and eat."

Matt and Laura each took their seat. Kevin and Lydia stood across from each other unmoving. After several seconds of unbroken silence, Lydia choked back a sob and turned on her heel, hurrying from the room.

෴

Kevin knocked on Lydia's car window. She jumped and dropped the key she'd been fumbling to put into the ignition. "Lydia. Wait."

She looked at him through the window. "This wasn't my idea. You made your position clear and I've been trying to respect that."

He sighed, looking deflated. "Could you at least roll down the window?"

She bent down, patting around the floorboard until she found the key. Turning it toward her, the interior lights and her radio came on. She punched the music off and lowered the window, raising her eyebrows at Kevin.

"Thanks." He stooped and set his elbows on the window, resting his forehead against the top of the car door. "I'm sorry."

Lydia arched a brow.

He closed his eyes. "Don't feel like you have to make this easy or anything." He opened his eyes and looked deeply into hers. "I've been a jerk. I'm sorry…and I really hope you can forgive me. I…" He looked away, swallowing the lump in his throat. "Seeing you at the PCC was such a shock. Especially when I pieced together why you were there. I'm not proud of how I reacted." He pressed his lips together. "I helped with a conference like that on my last weekend in India and I came away with such a heart for women who'd had an abortion…I really felt like God made it clear to me that I needed to work in that ministry somehow. Seeing you there, I realized that God had been preparing my heart and all I could think to do was run away." Kevin searched her face for some sign that his words were getting through. "I thought He was trying to make me into another Hosea…but really, I was just turning myself into another Jonah. Running away from God because it was uncomfortable." He reached out tentatively and touched her shoulder. "Please forgive me."

Lydia nodded slowly and cleared her throat. Tears shimmered in her eyes. "I do. I…I haven't really been able to blame you, even though it hurt." She looked down at her tightly clasped hands. "I realize that you can't possibly still love me." A tear dropped onto her hands and she looked up to meet his gaze, regret visible in her eyes. "But I would like it if we could figure out how to be friends again. I've missed you. More than I thought possible."

Kevin brushed a tear from her cheek. "Think our dinner's still hot?"

Lydia swiped at the tears that continued to slide down her face. "Let's go find out."

CR80

Lydia poked her head around the basement door and spotted her mom sitting at the kitchen island with a cup of hot tea. "Hey Mom."

"Hi, Baby. How was your dinner?"

Lydia sighed and hitched herself onto the chair next to her mom. "You mean ambush?"

Mary frowned and stood. "Let me get you a cup and you can explain."

Lydia propped her elbows on the island and rested her chin in her hands. "Matt and Laura teamed up to get me and Kevin back on speaking terms."

Mary hummed low in her throat and handed Lydia her tea. "How did that go?"

"It was rough…but I think maybe we're on a path that can lead back to friendship. Maybe not the same friendship we used to have, but it's better than nothing." Lydia looked down and blew into the steaming liquid.

Mary sipped her tea and watched her daughter for a minute. "Would you really want it to be exactly the same friendship?"

"No. But I think the chance for what I do want is long gone."

"Oh Baby." Mary slipped an arm around her daughter's shoulders.

Lydia leaned her head on her mom's arm. "Really, Mom, why would I think that it could possibly work out now? I had my chance and was too stupid to take it."

"You don't know that."

"Yes I do. Who could possibly want me now, Mom?"

"Why don't we wait and see what happens?"

Lydia sniffled and leaned back. "I'll make myself go back to when he was just a friend and deal with it. At least he's not completely out of my life anymore."

"Can you do that?"

Lydia shook her head miserably. "No. But I can at least put a good face on it and try." She slid off the chair and kissed her mom on the cheek. "Night, Mom."

35

Lydia poured herself into her work over the next week. The PCC would be closing for two weeks starting on the Friday before Christmas. She was going to be up to speed when they got back from the break. Kevin texted and called a few times, but it was easy enough to convince herself that she was too busy and would get back with him later. Though later never seemed to come.

Sunday at church, she deliberately sat in the back row, even though she saw Kevin closer in with a spot clearly saved next to him. Lydia spent the entire service alternating between praying for God to remove her feelings for him and chastising herself for having them in the first place. At the close of the service, she didn't move fast enough and the family sitting next to her, newcomers to the church, engaged her in conversation about Sunday school classes and how to get to various locations in the building. Once she got them sorted out, she turned and ran straight into Kevin.

"Slip in late, did we?"

"No, just trying for a change in perspective."

Kevin frowned and extended his hand for her Bible. "Can I get that for you?"

"Sure. Thanks. Sorry about not returning your calls this week, work has been busy. I'm trying to get on top of things, you know?"

"I understand completely. We've been pretty busy too. But it's been nice to know that I can text or call again. I'd missed that."

"Me too."

"So." He paused and cleared his throat. "Are you free on Saturday, Christmas Eve? I was thinking maybe we could have dinner and go to the Lessons and Carols service together. Then maybe get some dessert?"

"I'd like that. And, as a bonus, it's better than my current offer to come to all the Christmas Eve services to help Dad." Lydia's heart leapt in her chest but she tried not to read anything into the invitation. *We do this every year…he's just getting our friendship back on track.*

Kevin chuckled. "Glad to provide a better option for you. I'll pick you up at seven thirty, ok?"

"Perfect."

⊰⊱

Kevin pushed through the doors of Matt's salon and wrinkled his nose at the distinctly floral smells that assaulted him. He smiled at the receptionist as he made his way to the back office area.

"Knock knock?" Kevin poked his head through the door, ignoring the large PRIVATE sign.

Matt looked up. "Hey man, come on in." He pushed away from the computer, turning back to quickly save the spreadsheet he was working on.

Kevin shut the door behind him and stuffed his hands in his pockets as he looked around.

"So. What brings you here on a Wednesday afternoon at," Matt glanced at his watch, "2 p.m., when you should clearly still be hard at work?"

Kevin grinned and rocked forward on his toes before tugging a small black velvet box out of his pocket and offering it to Matt.

"I don't know what to say, Kev, but, well, perhaps I should reintroduce you to my wife, Laura?"

Kevin laughed. "Idiot. It's finished. I just picked it up at the jeweler's. I thought, seeing as you're a man who's had a positive reaction to one of these things, that I might get your opinion while there was still time to change my plan."

Matt smirked and gestured for Kevin to sit before taking the box and popping it open. He let out a low whistle at the large oval emerald in the center and the swirl of diamonds surrounding it. He pulled his gaze away from the sparkling gems and took in the setting itself, raising his brows. "Vintage?"

"Semi. It's sort of Deco-inspired, a lot like what my grandmother had the emerald originally set in, but we had to finagle it some to incorporate the diamonds."

Matt handed back the box. "There's no possible way for her to say no to that. Nicely done."

Kevin stuffed the box back into his pocket. "Thanks. Though I have to admit I'm unaccountably nervous about this whole thing."

Matt snorted out a laugh and slapped Kevin on the back. "That's as it should be. If you weren't, there'd be something wrong with you."

"Strangely, that actually makes me feel better."

Matt chuckled. "Now, unless you've decided you'd also like a haircut in preparation for the big night, I should get back to my spreadsheet before Laura gets in here and cracks her whip over my head."

"I wouldn't want that to happen. I'm meeting Paul for dinner tonight to make sure it's ok." Kevin stood and eased out the door. "Would you pray for that…and for Saturday?"

"You know we will."

36

Paul was already seated when Kevin made it to the pancake house. He raised a hand in greeting when he saw Kevin enter and gestured him over.

"Evening, Kevin. I got here early, so I started on the coffee already. But there should be plenty left."

"Thanks." Kevin poured a cup for himself from the gold toned carafe. He held the mug between his hands and stared at the dark liquid.

"So." Paul sipped his drink. "What brings us here this evening? Not that I ever need a reason to have pancakes, but you look like you've got something on your mind."

Kevin nodded, clearing his throat. "I actually didn't need to talk to you as a pastor, um." He cleared his throat again before taking a sip of the hot coffee. "I wanted to talk to you about Lydia."

"Oh?"

Kevin set the coffee down, wrapping his fingers tightly around the mug. "You know our history, right?"

Paul nodded, watching Kevin intently.

"Right. Of course you do." Kevin shook his head. "I'm not sure why I'm struggling with this so much. I'm in love with Lydia. I have been for years. And even with all that's gone on in the last year, I still love her. In some ways, seeing her work through things and come out victorious has made me love her more. When I was in India this last time, I prayed night and day for God to release me from loving her and bring me someone who deserved me." He managed a wan smile. "Instead, He continued to show me Lydia, and reveal to me how little I deserve her." He paused to sip his coffee. "Then there was the whole issue with the PCC. The abortion." He swallowed. "I haven't actually said it out loud. But that rocked me…and I'm not proud of how I acted…but God keeps reminding me that His grace is sufficient and that His strength is made perfect in weakness." He sighed and stared into his coffee for a minute before looking up to hold Paul's gaze. "We're going to dinner and then Lessons and Carols together on Saturday. And…I want to ask her to be my wife. But I'd like to know that it's all right with you before I do."

Paul blinked, stunned into momentary silence. "Are you asking my permission to marry Lydia?"

"Yes sir."

Paul grinned. "I can't speak for Lydia, but Mary and I would like nothing better. You're not worried that you're skipping the courtship aspect of your relationship?"

"We've been friends for so long, even when we weren't friends, if you know what I mean? Dating, courting, is so you can get to know a person. I know her. She knows me. I don't really see the point, though if that's what she says she wants before she'll answer me, then we'll do that. But…I've gotten a little tired of dithering where she's concerned. And part of me wonders if I'd been more up front years ago if I might have been able to help her avoid some of her problems."

"Son, Kevin, don't go down that path." Paul shook his head to emphasize his words. "Lydia is the only one responsible for her choices. Besides, it may be that the old Lydia, the one untouched by fire, would never have been in a position to understand the gift that God is offering her in you."

Kevin smiled. "Thanks."

"Mary's going to be over the moon. I'm pretty close myself, and I'm not given to great displays of emotion you know." Paul winked.

"Right. That's why some small groups still have pools on how many Sundays you're going to leave the pulpit in tears."

Paul snorted. "I thought I weeded all those pools out. I'll have to take a closer look. Now that that's out of the way, what do you say to some waffles, my treat?"

Kevin laughed. "Sounds good."

Kevin knocked on the door to Lydia's apartment and resisted the urge to pat the ring box in his blazer. Butterflies were doing the Nutcracker suite in his stomach as he waited for her to answer the door.

"Right on time." Lydia grinned as she opened the door. "Come on in. I am, as you would imagine, running a tad late." She held her index finger and thumb a small space apart. "Have a seat, I won't be long." She darted back down the hall.

Kevin looked around, admiring the homey touches she'd made to the once sterile basement apartment.

Lydia hurried back out wearing a long, red and green plaid skirt topped with a cream sweater. Her hair was pulled up into a knot at the base of neck, revealing dangling teardrop shaped crystals at her ears. "Ready."

"You look lovely. Don't forget your coat, and maybe a scarf, it's getting chilly out."

She grabbed her black wool coat off the coat rack and checked that the pocket held her scarf and gloves then collected her purse from the kitchen table.

"All set?"

Lydia nodded and smiled as Kevin held the door for her, tugging it shut and checking to see that it had locked. "So, is it all one big surprise, or are you going to tell me where we're eating?"

Kevin laughed as he opened the car door. "It's a surprise."

Lydia rolled her eyes as she settled into the seat and fastened her seatbelt.

It wasn't a long drive. Lydia grinned as Kevin parked in front of a small family owned restaurant they'd frequented as high school students. Large groups of kids had gathered there before football games and the place held pleasant memories for both of them.

"I haven't been here in ages."

"I try to get over here every couple of months. It's as good as ever though, and we can count on being finished with plenty of time to make the 9:30 service."

The restaurant was practically deserted. They had a lovely meal and casual, light hearted conversation as they ate. When she tried to convince him to share a slice of their famous seven layer cake, Kevin reminded Lydia that they'd have dessert after the service. He suppressed a grin as he thought of the small seven layer cake he'd had specially made. It was tucked in a basket, along with some homemade hot chocolate, for later.

They arrived at church forty minutes early. Even with that much time, the sanctuary was crowded. Kevin and Lydia found seats and settled in, chatting with each other and the friends who squeezed in around them as the service began.

At the end of the service, the lights in the sanctuary were dimmed as everyone lit their candles. Kevin slipped his hand into Lydia's as the opening strains of Silent Night began. She squeezed his hand briefly before twining her fingers through his and smiling up at him.

They kept their hands linked as they filed slowly out of the sanctuary, singing in the candle light with the rest of the congregation. They blew out their candles and dropped them in the containers by the doors and exited the building in reverent silence. Back in the car, Kevin looked at Lydia and smiled. "Ready for dessert?"

Lydia nodded.

"Your dad always does a wonderful job on Christmas Eve. Not," he amended, "that he doesn't do a wonderful job the rest of the year."

Lydia laughed. "I know what you mean. It's his second favorite service of the year, and it shows."

"Easter?"

"That's his absolute favorite." She glanced out the window. "Where are we going for dessert?"

Kevin grinned mischievously as they circled onto the highway leading into DC. "That's another surprise."

"Will I be home in time for Christmas? It's nearly eleven."

"You'll have to wait and see." Kevin wound his way through traffic. He carefully made his way through the always busy streets of downtown DC. "Look at that. Couldn't have planned it better."

He grinned at Lydia as he pulled into a parking spot on the street near the Jefferson Memorial.

He dashed around to get her door, then opened the trunk and pulled out a picnic basket. Checking to see that the car was locked, he offered her his elbow. "Shall we?"

Lydia buttoned her coat before slipping her arm through his. They walked the short distance to the memorial, enjoying the crisp air and the lights sparkling in the reflecting pool. Kevin led her around to the steps that looked over the silvery reflecting pond and set down the basket. He spread a plaid blanket over the steps. "If mademoiselle would care to sit?"

Laughing, Lydia sat, wrapping her arms around her knees. "Gosh, this is gorgeous." She watched her breath crystallize on the air. "If also cold."

She glanced at Kevin, watching him take a thermos from the basket.

"Hot chocolate?"

"Definitely." She wrapped her hands around the cup he gave her letting out a contented sigh when he sat next to her and slid an arm around her shoulders, drawing her close. "This is perfect."

Kevin smiled and sipped his hot chocolate, casually checking his watch. As the hands ticked nearer to midnight, he set the cup down and twisted so he could look into Lydia's eyes. He took her cup and set it aside, taking her hands in his.

"Lydia." He took a deep breath. "I've loved you for so long it's hard to remember a time when I didn't. I didn't always handle it perfectly," he smiled wryly, "but I hope I can at least get some points for sincerity and a little leeway for youth." He watched Lydia's confused smile and continued. "This past year has been hard. I've been angry and hurt and confused, but the one thing I've realized is that even through all that, I couldn't stop loving you. If anything, seeing you come out of this victorious has made me love you more." He paused and reached into his jacket for the ring box, slipping onto one knee. "Marry me, Lydia."

He opened the box and offered it to her, smiling at her surprised gasp.

Lydia reached hesitantly for the box, her gaze flickering between him and the ring. Slowly, so slowly that Kevin's heart began to sink at the delay, she grinned, tears filling her eyes. "Oh...of course. Yes!"

She laughed and met his eyes, her love for him shining clearly in her eyes.

Kevin took the ring out of the box and tugged off her left glove before gingerly sliding it onto her finger. Leaning forward, he pressed his lips to hers.

Lydia squeezed his hand, eased back from the kiss and rested her forehead on his. "I should have said this years ago, instead of running from you like I did." She looked steadily into his eyes. "I love you, Kevin McGregor. Merry Christmas."

If you enjoyed *Wisdom to Know* and would like to read Allison's story in book two, *Courage to Change*, you can receive a free download simply by signing up for my newsletter here: http://bit.ly/2g0AGvf

Resources

While this is a work of fiction, the story is one that I've seen aspects of many times in my twenty years working in various capacities at a Pregnancy Care Center. So often it seems that the church fails to recognize that women and men who have been wounded by abortion are filling the pews every week, ashamed and afraid to seek help. It's my prayer that if you or someone you know has been touched by an abortion you will seek out the healing and hope God offers.

The Abortion Recovery International Care Directory can provide referrals to local resources who offer group counseling and Bible studies: www.abortionrecovery.org

Chalfont House Publishing has two individual study guides (one for men and one for women) if you'd prefer to work on your own.

Repairing Her Story: Abortion Stress Recovery for Women
http://www.chalfonthouse.com/WomensPASStudy.html

Repairing His Story: Abortion Stress Recovery for Men
http://www.chalfonthouse.com/MenPASStudy.html

Acknowledgements

I've always loved reading the pages of thanks that authors put at the end of their books and dreamed of one day having my own to write. It would, without question, still be just a dream without the support and encouragement of my husband, my sister, and my parents. Each of you, at one point or another, has believed in me more than I was able to believe in myself, and I am forever grateful. I am particularly grateful to my sister for the tough love approach to encouragement she often provided—while I might have balked at being told to sit down and write and stop wringing my hands about the what ifs, it was what I needed to hear. And do.

Thanks also go to my critique partner, Janice Elder, who reminded me that if people rolled their eyes in real life as often as they did in the first draft of this book, we would all be eternally dizzy. Janice, and my other beta readers, your tweaks and comments have made this a much better story than I would have managed on my own.

Most of all, I'm grateful to God for putting stories in my head and giving me the words to get them out on paper. My sole desire is to be faithful to His calling and write the words I'm given so that they might be used for His glory.

You can always keep up to date with my writing news via my occasional newsletter. There's a sign-up form at my website (www.ElizabethMaddrey.com) and also on my author Facebook page (www.Facebook.com/ElizabethMaddrey).

About the Author

Elizabeth Maddrey began writing stories as soon as she could form the letters properly and has never looked back. Though her practical nature and love of math and organization steered her into computer science for college and graduate school, she has always had one or more stories in progress to occupy her free time. When she isn't writing, Elizabeth is a voracious consumer of books and has mastered the art of reading while undertaking just about any other activity. She is the co-author of *A is for Airstrip: A Missionary's Jungle Adventure*, a children's book based on the work of a Wycliffe missionary, and is a member of ACFW.

Elizabeth lives in the suburbs of Washington D.C. with her husband and their two incredibly active little boys. She invites you to interact with her at her website www.ElizabethMaddrey.com or on Facebook: www.facebook.com/ElizabethMaddrey

Discussion Questions

1.   Lydia justifies sleeping with Brad because they are practically engaged. Are there sins that you or people you know are prone to justifying because you're almost not sinning? Do you think there's a difference to God?

2.   Brad uses their almost-engagement to convince Lydia to have sex. What does the Bible say about premarital sex? What are your thoughts?

3.   Lydia says she should be respected no matter what she wears. What's your reaction to this?

4.   The Bible has several suggestions for women's modesty and adornment. What does the Bible suggest (See Proverbs 31, 1 Peter 3:1-6, 2 Timothy 2:9-10)? What is your reaction to those suggestions?

5.   If you found you were pregnant after ending a relationship, how do you hope you'd respond? How do you hope your friends and family would respond?

6.   Do you think the reality of those responses would be different in the heat of the moment? In what way?

7.   Lydia chooses to have an abortion. What does the Bible say about the unborn (refs)? What are your thoughts?

8.   The elders debate whether Paul should be held for Lydia's behavior even though she's an adult child (reference). What are your thoughts?

9.   After marrying Staci, Brad suggests Lydia join them in a threesome. What does the Bible say about that? What are your thoughts?

10.   Kevin wonders how many times he has to forgive Lydia. How do you interpret this parable? Have you had times in your life where you've been tempted to stop forgiving?

11.   Kevin compares himself to Hosea. Read the story of Hosea. Do you feel Kevin is overreacting?

12.   Matt suggests that he and Laura join Kevin in praying for Lydia. Why is group prayer beneficial?

13.   Lydia notes that her single adult Sunday school class does just enough Bible study to get by. What have been your experiences in Sunday school groups? What do you wish you could change?

14.   What has been an event in your life that made you really angry? Identify the roots of your anger. What does the Bible have to say about anger and how we should deal with it?

15.   Have you ever lost a significant relationship? How did you react? What stages of grief did you go through?

16.   Allison suggested Kevin go to the Christmas party with her to make Phil jealous. What are the moral and ethical issues with this type of behavior?

17.   At the end of the novel, Kevin realizes that rather than being Hosea, he is acting more like Jonah. Have you ever run from God? What were the consequences?

18.   Kevin is Lydia's best friend. Can members of the opposite sex be best friends or will there always be some level of sexual tension in the background?

19.   Lydia feels she doesn't deserve to be loved. If you were counseling Lydia, what would you say to her? How can you affirm your love for the people in your life?

20.   Lydia feels that she's the black sheep of the family when compared to her "perfect" sisters. Have you ever felt that way? How did/do you deal with it?

Made in the USA
Monee, IL
25 October 2023

45222749R00225